THE WEB THEY WOVE

CATHERINE YAFFE

Mark, Daniel & Sadie.
For always having my back.
This book simply wouldn't have
happened without your love and support.

PROLOGUE
JUNE 2002

The heel of her shoe snapped as he dragged her along the stony path. She struggled, trying desperately to free herself from his grasp, reaching up and hitting the hands that yanked her along by her ponytail. Her shoes finally lost their grip and slipped from her feet. She could feel the small, sharp flints from the path slashing at her heels. Her feet tried to gain purchase, but there was little hope. The little black dress she was wearing had risen up around her thighs, exposing her bare legs to the cold night air.

She had resorted to holding onto her scalp with her hands to try to alleviate the pressure as she begged him to let go of her hair, every tug screaming at the roots. She shouted and yelled, trying to make as much noise as possible, hoping to attract attention, but the wind blew the screams back into her mouth, trapping them in her throat.

With a jolt, he released her and forcibly pushed her flat onto her back, the damp, uneven ground soaking into her dress. The stones pushed sharply against the fabric, breaking through and embedding into her flesh as his weight bore down on her.

He shifted, straddled her chest, and slipped a silk scarf around her neck.

'Please, no... Don't...' She gasped as she fought for her life.

He laughed, a cruel, hollow sound, and looked down at her prone body beneath him. Crossing the scarf, he pulled tight on either end. She looked directly into his eyes, silently pleading for him to release her whilst twisting her head from side to side, but this only made breathing harder.

She stopped thrashing and lay still, tears running down the side of her face, diluting the mascara she had so carefully applied earlier in the evening. Multicoloured dots and stars appeared in her peripheral vision, then blackness enveloped her.

SMILING, he watched the rise and fall of her chest as it rose, fell and stopped. He pulled himself upwards and gently wrapped the scarf around his gloved hand. He lifted it to his nose and inhaled, pleased that the faint smell of her perfume still lingered: Estée Lauder Youth Dew. For a moment, he was transported to a different time and place; a place he'd fought hard against, but one that had ultimately consumed him.

He liked it when they fought back. The feisty ones were always the most satisfying. When their bodies were still, screams silenced, and the life leached out of them, he felt at his most powerful.

It had been many years since his last one; she had fought hard too.

Despite the lapsed time, he was pleased to find that he

still felt satisfied. Yes, he thought as he sat back on his haunches. It had been a good experience, a good way to start.

He'd raise the ante next time. Because there would definitely be a next time, of that he was certain.

1

_____

Saturday, 1 June 2002

D I Andrew 'Ziggy' Thornes took a deep breath as he stood behind the armed officers as they prepared to break down the door. Following a countdown, the door crashed open and Ziggy stood to one side while the premises were searched by Armed Response. Pretty soon, five of the gang members were led out in cuffs to the waiting police vans.

The search teams followed them in, and after donning a Tyvek crime scene suit, Ziggy, along with his deputy DS Sadie Bates, took a look around. A violent gang had been plaguing the city of Leeds for weeks now, committing raids on jewellery shops, and Ziggy and his team had been on the case, trying to catch those responsible. The covert team had had the ringleaders under surveillance, and it was finally time to see what their hiding place had to offer.

'Regular treasure trove isn't it?' commented Sadie as they moved from room to room.

'Isn't it just? And we haven't even been upstairs yet.'

The hiding place was a mid-terrace house in Harehills, Leeds. From the outside, you wouldn't know that a violent gang operated from there; washing was hanging on the line, garden bins were lined up neatly against the wall in the tidy back yard and net curtains framed each window. Hidden in every possible space was over one million pounds' worth of jewels that would take forensics days to seize and store.

Once they'd ensured the crime scene had been secured, Ziggy handed over to the crime scene manager and headed back to West Yorkshire Police's Leeds HQ to brief his team.

DS Nick Wilkinson, DC Angela Dove and DS Sadie Bates had worked together for the last five years. During that time, they had developed an almost intuitive way of working that saw them with the highest arrest and conviction rates of the region, and as their senior officer, Ziggy was proud of every one of them. They each had their strengths, and they were utilised to the full.

Sadie was massively ambitious, and Ziggy knew that she wasn't destined to stay in his team forever. She was due to take the next step in her career within the next twelve months and he had done everything he could to support and promote her, even though he'd be sad to see her go. She acted as his deputy on all major cases, and her unfailing enthusiasm spurred everyone along when the going got tough.

Nick was the warhorse of the team; diligent, laid-back and very rarely phased by anything. He'd reached the rank of detective sergeant with ease but was happy to stay there until he retired. Somewhat older than the rest of the team, Nick – or 'Wilko' as he was affectionately referred to – remembered a time when policing had been done using good old fashioned shoe leather rather than fingers on keyboards.

In complete contrast, Angela, the youngest and most recent member of the team, was a whizz with anything technical and was also the most organised of them all. She thrived in her role as office manager and organised anything from the incident room where she played a vital role in co ordinating all the information that an enquiry generated to team birthdays; Angela could turn her quick, analytical brain to any task. She worked speedily and efficiently, though Ziggy often suspected she had a tendency to like things a little too perfect.

His team complemented each other well, and Ziggy was there to bridge all their abilities, having spent time working for Missing Persons, Child Sexual Exploitation and the drugs squad over his twenty-five years in the force. He liked variety, but he had found his feet with the Major Investigations team as detective inspector.

PULLING INTO THE CAR PARK, Ziggy reversed into a parking space and he and Sadie exited the car. The building was new by policing standards. It had been purpose built and was equipped with all the latest technology. The MIT was located on the top floor of the building in a large, open plan office. It was filled with workstations, separated off by low partitions, and when they were in the throes of an investigation, the noise levels were tremendous.

Ziggy's team were located in the far corner, near the windows that looked out on the city of Leeds. His own, rarely used office was situated at the back. He preferred to be out, in amongst everyone else. He enjoyed the buzz and thrived off the energy that an investigation invariably generated.

He did have his foibles, though. As a very visual person,

Ziggy needed to *see* the progress of an investigation. White-boards were fine, but Ziggy also had flip charts around the room where he could work things out on paper. His mind maps were legendary and had proved useful on more than one occasion; tiny details that at the time made no sense were meticulously noted down and left visible for everyone to see, for the dots to be later joined and the resolution of cases achieved.

Making his way to their corner of the floor, Ziggy watched as Angela took down the various images and sheets of paper that had been Blu-Tacked to the walls for the jewellery robbery case. Everything would be filed away as they built the case for presentation to the CPS and, further down the line, in court.

As they walked across the office, Ziggy headed to check his emails and DS Sadie Bates headed for her own desk. 'After that success, lunch on you, right?'

Ziggy laughed. 'Sure, fish and chips all round. Sound good?'

'Hell yeah. Wait until I tell Wilko – he'll be beside himself.'

Ziggy grinned and shook his head as Sadie walked away. He felt his phone vibrate in his trouser pocket and pulled it out to look at the screen; it was the control room.

'DI Thornes,' he answered.

'Sir, a body has been found on Woodhouse Moor, near the university. Scene of crime officers are on their way, and I've been asked to assign you as deputy senior investigating officer by DCS Whitmore.'

Ziggy immediately felt his adrenaline pumping. 'OK, send me the details and we'll head over there now. Who's on the scene already?'

'Uniform, they were alerted by a bunch of kids. They've

set up the cordon and started the log. As I said, SOCOs have also been informed.'

Ziggy ended the call and walked into the incident room. Everyone had packed up their desks and were waiting for Ziggy to join them for lunch.

'Lunch is cancelled, I'm sorry to say. Just in, body found on Woodhouse Moor.'

The whole team stopped chatting and started removing their coats and replacing their bags on the floor.

'What do we know?' asked Sadie, walking forward, raring to go as always.

'Not much, call was from Control.' Ziggy stood, shaking the creases out of his carefully pressed trousers.

Sadie pulled her jacket from the back of her chair. 'Let's head over there. Nick, we'll give you a call once we know more.'

'Sure thing,' said Nick, logging back into his computer.

Angela stood up and walked to the whiteboard, setting it up for the information that would be coming their way.

SADIE DROVE the unmarked pool car through the back streets of Leeds. Ziggy had lived in the city for twenty years and still didn't know all the shortcuts. Sadie was a risky driver at the best of times, and even with the blue light flashing on the dashboard, she honked every car out of her way.

'Calm down, the body isn't going anywhere,' said Ziggy as he gripped the overhead handle.

'Sorry,' she said, clearly not meaning it.

Ten minutes later, Sadie dumped the car at the side of the road, and they made their way over to the edge of the green expanse.

Woodhouse Moor was a large recreation ground right in the heart of the university district, surrounded by a plethora of take away shops. Popular with locals and students, it was notorious for large social gatherings in the summer months, but more nefarious activities when the nights drew in. The weather recently had been typical of the British summer; scorching hot one day, then November-like winds and unusually low temperatures the next. That day, the weather had settled on 'quite pleasant'. Well, it wasn't raining, at least.

Ziggy and Sadie made their way onto the grass and ducked under the outer cordon. They signed the log and followed the designated approach path. The white forensic tent had already been erected, protecting the body from prying eyes. Once they were fully clothed in protective suits, they entered the tent and edged closer until a hand was frantically waved towards them, stopping them in their tracks.

'Careful! And move – you're blocking my light,' cried a woman dressed in a forensics suit without looking at them. Dr Leila Turner, or Lolly as she was more widely known, was somewhat unconventional but the best pathologist that West Yorkshire Police had at their disposal, and it didn't hurt that she'd been best friends with Ziggy since childhood. Not that it improved her manners at all, either way.

'Oops, sorry.' Ziggy stepped over to the right. 'Good to see you, Lolly. Drew the short straw, did you?'

Lolly looked up from her kneeling position. 'I was in the area when the shout came in. Couldn't resist.' She grinned. A quirk of the job; not many people in Ziggy's life would be thrilled to receive a call about a body being discovered.

As Lolly continued with her careful examination process, Ziggy and Sadie took in the scene in front of them.

The body of a young female was laid flat on her back, and for all the world, it looked as though she was sleeping – if you discounted the blueish tinge to her lips. No matter how many times they were confronted with a dead body, the sight never got easier to digest.

'What can you tell us?' asked Ziggy, pulling his face mask away from his lips as he spoke.

'Looks like asphyxiation. See the marks here' – Lolly pointed a nitrile gloved hand towards the throat of the victim where there was considerable bruising around the neck – 'which also fits with the petechial haemorrhaging around the eyes.' Lolly shone her pen torch so they could get a better look.

'How long do you think she's been here?' asked Sadie, itching her head. The nylon suit created a scratching noise that made Ziggy's toes curl.

'Overnight, definitely. Full rigor mortis and distinct lividity to the underside of the body. Plus, there's mottling on her legs, which would fit with the temperature change overnight.' Lolly stood up. 'Take a look at her feet.'

Ziggy and Sadie moved down the body as directed and bent to look at the soles of the feet. They were shredded with tiny stones embedded. Lolly joined them and lifted the left foot in her gloved hand.

'Looking at the heels, it would seem she has been dragged along the path.'

So where are her shoes? Ziggy wondered as he leaned in closer and saw the dried blood on the bottom of the foot and around the Achilles heel. 'Ouch, whilst she was still alive by the looks of it.'

'Yep. And it's the same on the backs of her legs, and I suspect on her back as well.'

Ziggy stood up. 'When will you get to the post-mortem?'

'Later today, just need to finish up here.'

'OK, we'll see you there later.' The officers said their goodbyes and left the tent. Ziggy and Sadie headed to the crime scene manager, who was busy outlining the scene to his team and adjusting the outer cordon. The SOCOs had already started work, on their hands and knees at the far edge of clearing where the body had been found, carefully searching the tarmacked area. A yellow marker had been placed at the side of a black, high-heeled shoe, minus the heel.

'Any ID found?' asked Ziggy. 'Any sign of the heel to that shoe?' He pointed towards it as he spoke.

'No ID, and that's all we've found of her shoes so far. No bag or coat or anything on the victim either. We've just extended the search perimeter based on information from Dr Turner, so we might find a student ID card or bus pass or something.'

'Right, OK.' Ziggy looked around for Sadie, but she had wandered off to speak to the first attending officer. He walked over to join her.

'Have you spoken to the witnesses?' Ziggy asked the young police constable who'd been first on the scene.

'Yes, I've moved them over to the bench just there. A group of skateboarders trying tricks on the handrails came across her. They called it in from their mobiles. I think their average age is around twelve.'

Ziggy took the information on board and glanced at the youths who were chatting on the bench. 'Great, thanks. I'll head over and have a word.'

'I've taken preliminary statements, sir,' the constable said, 'but I don't think they're involved.'

Ziggy raised his hand in acknowledgement as he turned and walked away.

Sadie started the conversation with the skateboarders. 'Now then, lads, we hear you found the body?'

A tall, gangly youth stood up and flipped the skateboard he was holding. 'Yeah, man, I mean, scared the life out of us. Thought it was a dummy at first.'

Another one of the boys jumped in. 'It wasn't us,' he said defensively.

'No one said it was, sunshine. Have you given the police officer your names and addresses?' asked Ziggy.

They all nodded.

'Was she murdered then? Will we have to go to court and that?'

Sadie smiled. 'No, it doesn't quite work like that.'

The lad seemed disappointed; clearly, he had found the whole thing exciting. 'Shame, never been to court.'

His mates pulled his arm and made him sit back down. 'Shut up, Ned, you dickhead.'

Ziggy's instinct told him that they were unlikely to be involved, so he told them to go home and that if any further information was needed, someone would be in touch.

Once he'd made sure the boys had left the park, he turned to Sadie. 'We need to get uniform down here, start a house-to-house. Also, let's see if the CCTV over that parade of shops reveals anything.'

'On it, boss. I'll give Wilko a ring and update him.'

ZIGGY TOOK a few steps away from the scene, as he was known to do, and looked around him. He'd attended a couple of incidents on Woodhouse Moor over the years. For a while it had been the much-disputed territory of two rival gangs, and fights had broken out, often involving stabbings. There was the odd scuffle with drug dealers and the occasional sex worker was arrested, but nothing like they were facing now.

It would be highly unlikely or extremely unlucky to turn up no clues in an area that was as popular and as busy as Woodhouse Moor. Of course, it also ran the risk of being too popular, potentially diluting any real traces of the killer. He watched as SOCOs continued their painstaking search through the grass and undergrowth. But why had the body been dumped so publicly? Was it a pick-up gone wrong? But it didn't appear accidental; it was too precise for that, based on his experience. Had the killer been interrupted?

Looking back from the edge of the green where he now stood, he saw that the location was just off the main road. The location of the body had meant it was just off the usual well-worn path and carefully placed. The killer must have needed a car or some mode of transport to bring her here. Somebody must have seen something, surely?

The killer was either extremely brave or innately stupid to leave a body so exposed. Ziggy hoped it was the latter.

2

The mortuary was located in the bowels of Leeds General Infirmary. Ziggy and Sadie passed through endless winding corridors, all of them dark and gloomy. It always gave Ziggy the creeps. He had no problem viewing the bodies, it was the build-up that set him on edge.

His partner shared his views. 'God, I hate this place,' Sadie said, shivering.

'Yeah, not the most welcoming of places, is it?' Ziggy had attended plenty of post-mortems over the years and had realised that you never became immune to the fact that a life had been extinguished. His own parents had been killed when he was just fourteen and viewing their bodies before the funeral had stayed with him for a long time, filling many of his childhood nights with haunting dreams. It was, in part, why he had wanted to join the police. No one had ever given him the answers as to why and how his parents had died, which had always felt heartless to him. He had wanted answers that even his older siblings hadn't been able to give him. When he was dealing with victims and their families now, he answered as many questions as they asked, as honestly as he could. It was all about respect, ultimately, for the dead and the living.

When they entered the viewing area through the swinging double door, they found Lolly busy recording her notes as she continued working her way around the body. Assistants were taking photographs and bagging trace evidence as she pointed out every graze, bruise and scratch, of which there were many. The victim now lay on her stomach, and Ziggy could see the lividity across her back and legs. That at least would give them some idea of the timeline.

Lolly looked up and clicked her voice recorder off. She removed the face mask she had been wearing and indicated for the two detectives to come in to the lab below.

'The poor girl had a torrid time of it prior to death,' she said sadly as the officers joined her. 'There are numerous bruises all over her body.'

All three looked down as the mortuary assistants gently turned the girl over onto her back. They stood in respectful silence for a moment until Lolly broke it as she started to share her findings. Or lack thereof.

'Estimated age between twenty and twenty-five. I would also estimate that she had been placed where she was found up to twelve hours before the body was called in, so the early hours of Saturday the first of June. She had been restrained at some point – you can see marks around her wrists and ankles.'

Ziggy glanced at the delicate hands of the victim, which were encased in protective polythene bags. Lolly pre-empted his question. 'Nothing significant recovered from under the finger nails unfortunately.'

'Any other DNA recovered?' Sadie spoke up.

'Not as yet. We've combed the hair and recovered some debris, but I predict that's from the deposition site. We'll send it off to Forensics, of course. The only thing of note is a piece of silk we found caught behind one of the earrings she was wearing.' Lolly reached over to the evidence table and retrieved a clear evidence bag. 'Again, we'll send it off for analysis to see if it yields anything.' She passed it across to Ziggy, who peered through the plastic bag.

'No scarf or similar that might match found at the scene?' asked Ziggy.

'Not as yet, but as per instructions, SOCO extended the search area to cover all the undergrowth so maybe chase up with them?'

Ziggy nodded and folded his arms as Lolly continued. 'Cause of death confirmed as strangulation. There are no signs of sexual assault.'

'Any identification? Where are we with that?' asked Ziggy.

'Obviously we've taken fingerprints and dental imprints. Just waiting for results, so I'll let you know as soon as I hear anything.'

'That's great Lolly, thank you. We've enough to be going on with, I think, but ID is critical if we're to catch who did this.' He again looked at the victim and felt a stab of grief. Another silence fell over the room.

'Right, let's head back for the briefing. At least we can give the team something, and Lolly, if you would let us know as soon as you have an ID that would be great,' said Ziggy as he took one last look at the body. 'Poor girl, no one deserves that.'

· · ·

Arriving back in the incident room, Angela and Nick had been busy retrieving as much information as they could from the local area and entering it into the HOLMES computer system. Ziggy and Sadie stood at the front of the room going over the post-mortem notes, waiting for the others to file in. They had managed to add a few more temporary PCs to the team, to be the feet on the ground.

As everyone filed in and took up various seats, Sadie arranged her notes ready to host the briefing. It was an aspect of the job that she enjoyed. Everyone would be buzzing with adrenaline, eager to solve the case as quickly and efficiently as they could.

Ziggy had taken his customary spot, perched on the edge of the closest desk, and smiled his encouragement. Since she joined the team, he'd been eager for Sadie to lead briefings where appropriate, saying it would be an opportunity for her to gain confidence and further enhanced her hopes of promotion. However, she still got nervous just before the start.

Taking a deep breath, Sadie consulted her notes and shared the discoveries that had been made at the post-mortem.

'A piece of fabric, possibly silk, was retrieved from behind an earring. It's been sent off for analysis, so fingers crossed it throws something up. It could have come from our victim – perhaps she had been wearing a scarf when attacked. Whilst we're waiting for ID and forensics, we'll need to rely on the door-to-door enquiries and CCTV.' She turned to Nick. 'How far have you got with that?'

Nick coughed. 'Not very, to be honest, but now we have a timeline, namely overnight on the Friday to the victim being found on the Saturday, it will make it easier to search. I'll stay on top of it, but could I get some uniforms to help out?'

'OK, can't see it being a problem.' She looked at Ziggy for confirmation, who in turn nodded his agreement. Turning back to the officers seated in front of her, she continued. 'The theory so far – and it is very early days – is that the victim was restrained for an amount of time before being taken to the deposition site on Woodhouse Moor and placed away from the path where she was later found. That in itself seems a bit off, she was clearly visible. Was the killer disturbed, perhaps? We've spoken with the group of youths that called it in, but we believe they aren't involved. This required careful planning and deposition. Uniform have already been to their homes and taken further statements, but ultimately we've ruled them out.'

Sadie glanced at her pad. 'Angela, any luck with the door-to-door?'

Angela blushed, as she was prone to do when being placed in the spotlight and turned her notebook over. 'Erm, nothing that helps, I'm afraid. A few people heard cars passing, but no one saw anything.' She looked up at Sadie and shrugged. 'Sorry, can't add any more than that.'

Sadie felt like she was flogging a dead horse. 'Right, well let's chase up the forensics and see if we can get an ID. Anything to add, boss?'

Ziggy stood up. 'Some initial thoughts from me, and feel free to jump in, anyone. As Sadie has said, our victim was restrained somewhere before being placed on Woodhouse Moor. Where was she held? Are there any outbuildings in the park grounds? Are all the houses occupied, any that are neglected or abandoned nearby? Have they been searched? We've got another crime scene out there, so we need to find it.' Ziggy was scribbling his thoughts down on the flip chart as he spoke, creating various 'bubbles' with arrows leading from one point to the next. 'Why was she left next to the path? It's an obvious place, and the killer must have known she would be found quickly. Why? As DS Bates has said, was he interrupted? And how did he transport the body?' He looked around at the faces before him. Although all these angles would be covered off, if they hadn't been already, sharing his thoughts was an important part of how the boss liked to work an investigation; asking questions when they were all in the room together. Often it triggered another avenue or gave someone a chance to voice their opinions.

'I'm assuming no mobile phone was found at the scene?' asked one of the seconded uniforms.

'Nope. The area is still being searched, but nothing so far.'

He waited for further questions, but it seemed the team were all on the same page. It was past 6 p.m. on a Saturday evening, and there wasn't much more they could do without an ID, so everyone was dismissed and told to be back in early for a Sunday briefing.

Everyone took the opportunity to leave and head home to their families. They knew that once the victim had been identified it would trigger an avalanche of work, and possibly long hours of overtime.

As the room emptied, Sadie stayed behind with Nick, Angela and the boss, who were all looking over the notes on the whiteboard and flip chart.

'Not much to go on is there?' commented Nick.

'Not really. I'm just confused how something like this could happen and no one see or hear anything? The body was placed in plain sight,' said Sadie.

Pulling his jacket from the back of a chair, Ziggy shrugged his arms into it. 'There's nothing more we can do now. Head home,' he instructed. 'Hopefully we'll get more info overnight and make inroads tomorrow.'

As the others made their way to the door, Sadie stood in front of the boards, dressed in her coat. Maybe she'd give it another half an hour. It wasn't like she had anyone other than her parents to head home to.

No sooner had Ziggy walked through his front door when his mobile went off. It was Lolly.

'Your timing is very poor, Lolly. I've just got home,' he said.

'Ha, at least you've *been* home. Got an ID for you.'

'Fantastic, go on.' Ziggy was all ears.

'Her name is Susannah Leibniz.'

'Nationality?'

'British, I think, why?'

'Leibniz. It sounds a bit Eastern European, German maybe. How did you find her?'

'She was arrested in 2000 for shoplifting.'

Ziggy's mind was already working overtime. Two years ago, and nothing prior or since, so she didn't have much of a record. 'Do we have next-of-kin details?'

'I've sent everything over to Sadie, who is still in the office by the way.'

'Was that a dig?'

'No, not at all part-timer.'

'Bugger off.' He laughed and ended the call. He immediately made another call to Sadie, who sounded as though she was in her car.

'Hey Sadie, heading home, are you?' he asked, confused. Lolly had said she was still in the office, but as a boss he was glad; he and Sadie had had chats about work-life balance before.

'No, I'm on my way to yours. I've got Susannah's last known address.'

Ahh, there's the Sadie we know and love. Always the eager one.

'Great, see you soon.' Ziggy ended the call, re-locked the door and waited outside. He lived fairly close to the station, and with Sadie's driving, he knew she'd be there imminently.

Sure enough, ten minutes later and they were heading towards Cross Gates, a suburb of East Leeds.

'It's that house on the left.' Sadie gestured out of the car window as she pulled up outside a semi-detached house in a small cul-de-sac. The front had a neat and well-kept garden, and there was an old, grey Ford Fiesta parked on the drive. Despite the living room curtains being closed, they could see the flickering of the TV through the gaps in the fabric.

'Ready?' asked Ziggy. Notifying family members was any detective's least favourite task, and no matter how many he delivered, they never got any easier.

Sadie took a deep breath. 'As I'll ever be.'

They exited the car, Sadie taking a note of the car registration number and walked up the path.

Ziggy knocked lightly on the front door. They heard footsteps approaching from inside the house, and a blurred figure appeared through the etched glass panel. An elderly lady opened the door fractionally, leaving the chain across.

'Yes?'

'Mrs Leibniz?'

She raised her eyebrows and looked at Ziggy questionably. 'It's the police, Mrs Leibniz, I'm DI Andrew Thornes and this is my colleague DS Sadie Bates. We're looking for the relatives of Susannah Leibniz?' he said gently, showing both of their IDs through the small gap.

'Susannah? Oh goodness me. You had better come in.' Came the heavily accented reply. The door opened fully to reveal the elderly, frail looking lady and a gentleman of a similar age stood behind her. They were clearly in their seventies, and not in the best of health. The woman was slightly hunched over, and the man was clutching a walking stick. They both seemed out of breath, as though the trip to the door had taken a great deal of their energy.

Ziggy introduced themselves again, and they were invited inside.

Slowly making their way into the living room, it was like stepping back in time. Red-and-white gingham table cloths covered the coffee table, with lace doilies for place mats. Artificial flower displays were gathering dust on and around the fireplace, and on a sideboard at the back of the room there were family photos and lots of trinkets.

Ziggy looked at the couple and saw their ashen faces.

This is going to be hard on them.

'How can we help, officers?' asked the man nervously. As he spoke, Ziggy detected a strong German accent.

'Do you know a Susannah Leibniz?'

The old couple looked at each other. It was the man who spoke again. 'Yes, Susannah is our granddaughter. She's the oldest of our grandchildren belonging to our son Marech, but she is in Germany with her father. She stays with us whilst she's studying.' He tilted his head questioningly whilst Sadie and Ziggy looked at each other.

'Shall we sit down?' asked Ziggy. The couple looked understandably shaken, and they wanted them seated before they went any further. Once they had all settled, as agreed, Ziggy delivered the news that would tear their lives apart.

'I'm really sorry to have to inform you,' he began, 'but the body of a young woman matching Susannah's description was found last night. We believe it to be Susannah.'

Mrs Leibniz took a sharp intake of breath and buried her face in her hands. Her husband shuffled closer to her to offer some comfort, even though it was obvious his own grief was overwhelming. For a moment, nothing happened. There was no sound from the couple, and Ziggy shifted in his chair. Then a quiet sobbing emanated from Mrs Leibniz. It was an outpouring full of anguish and despair. Sadie reached across the coffee table for the box of tissues and passed them to Mr Leibniz. Even in the depths of his own grief, he politely thanked her and pulled a couple out for his wife.

After a few minutes of passing on their condolences, Sadie and Ziggy left the room to give the couple some privacy for their grief and found their way to the kitchen. They returned to the living room with a tray of tea things.

Grandpa looked at them through red-rimmed eyes. 'Are you sure it's Susannah? How do you know? It can't be her. We left her at the airport…'

Grandma had wiped her eyes and sat nodding in agreement. 'Yes, that's right, it might not be Susie?'

This was a common occurrence in Ziggy's experience. The glimmer of hope that they were wrong. 'We found the body of a female yesterday and following tests it would seem that it is Susannah.'

'But I don't understand? How do you know it's our Susie, how can you be so sure?' asked Grandma, looking searchingly at Ziggy's face.

'We ran DNA samples against those in our database and

Susannah came up as a match. I truly am sorry. I can see she meant a lot to both of you.'

Sadie continued gently. 'Why did you think she had gone to Germany, Mrs Leibniz?'

'We bought her ticket and took her to the airport.'

'And did you hear from her after she landed?'

'No, but we didn't expect to. Where they live in Germany, it's a very small village, very remote with no signal. She sometimes phones from the airport, but often gets caught up in being home again and instead she would call when she was in the town next.'

'Can you tell me when you last saw Susannah?' Sadie addressed the question to them both.

They looked at each other for a few minutes, clearly trying to work out why they were being asked and where the conversation was going.

It was Mr Leibniz that finally spoke whilst scratching his chin. 'It was a month ago. She was going home to visit her mother, who hasn't been well. We're too old to fly now, so we let Susannah go on her own.' He gripped his wife's hand in a reassuring gesture.

'Do you know where she was living before she returned to Germany?' continued Sadie.

'Why yes, she was living here with us,' exclaimed Mrs Leibniz with a note of panic in her voice. 'But... but she's in Germany.' Mrs Leibniz was shaking her head and wrapping the tissues that her husband had given her between her fingers.

Sadie broke the silence, and in a gentle voice she reconfirmed what they knew before adding. 'It would seem that she came back to Leeds at some point.'

Sadie poured everyone a cup of tea, adding sugar

whether they took it or not. After a while, Ziggy cleared his throat.

'I'm really sorry but I have to ask you some questions, and it's better to do it now so that we can find out what happened. Do you feel up to answering some questions?'

Sadie took out her notebook and prepared to take notes

Ziggy shifted in his seat, sitting forward a little to close the gap between himself and Susannah's grandparents. 'Just take your time, but what can you tell me about Susannah?'

Grandpa answered as his wife wiped her tears away. 'She's a lovely girl. Works very hard and is always trying to improve her prospects.'

'What does she do for a living, Mr Leibniz?' asked Ziggy.

'She's a make-up artist, for weddings and that kind of thing. She works two days a week at a salon in town, but she's building her own freelance work.' Mr Leibniz's voice was full of pride. 'She had started a course to learn theatre and stage make-up too. She wanted to move to London, the West End theatres, you know?'

Mrs Leibniz clutched the scrunched-up tissue to her chest. 'She was a very good girl. She took great care of us.' The tears started again, and her husband gently stroked her knee.

'There, there, my love.' He kissed her forehead before turning to Ziggy. 'How did she die, Inspector? I have to know.'

Ziggy coughed a little, knowing that the next piece of news would be the hardest to take in. 'I'm afraid it looks like she was murdered.' He paused and waited for the news to sink in. His heart nearly broke as the elderly couple turned to each other and embraced. He knew from experience that life would never be the same for them.

He left a respectful silence before continuing. 'Is there

anyone that Susannah was close to that she might have stayed with if she wasn't staying here?' Ziggy was wondering why she had returned from Germany, or even if she had ever gone in the first place. Being dropped at the airport didn't necessarily mean boarding a plane.

'I can't think of anyone,' said Mr Leibniz, shaking his head, his arm around his wife's shoulders.

'Did she have any boyfriends, or girlfriends?' asked Sadie.

Mrs Leibniz spoke. 'Not recently. There was a boy, Shaun, I think, some months ago, but he ended the relationship when he met someone else.'

'Any close friends that maybe she worked with?' Ziggy didn't think they were going to get much more information from the distraught couple as their grief began to overwhelm them.

'There was Claire. She worked with Susannah at the salon, but we've never met her. She was someone that Susannah spoke about, but all her spare time was spent studying or working for herself, not much time for socialising.' Mrs Leibniz let out an anguished sound as a wave of grief hit her.

Waiting a few moments for Mrs Leibniz's sobs to subside, Ziggy spoke. 'Just a couple more questions if that's OK, then we'll leave you?'

Mr Leibniz nodded, encouraging him to continue.

'You mentioned that you dropped Susannah at the airport. If she worked freelance, did she have her own car?'

The couple shook their heads. 'No, Inspector, she borrowed mine if she needed to,' Mr Leibniz said. 'I don't get out much and it's a waste to see it sat there.'

'OK. And did Susannah have a mobile phone? Was that how she contacted her clients?'

'Yes, she had a diary as well. I'll get it for you.' Mr Leibniz left his seat and headed into the kitchen.

Deciding that they had as much as they needed for now, Ziggy wound up the conversation as they waited for Mr Leibniz to return. 'If we could just take the name of the salon where Susannah worked, we'll leave you. A family liaison officer will be in touch shortly too. They'll keep you up to date with progress, and if you can think of anything else, you can call me direct.' Ziggy handed over his business card. 'Or you can talk to the FLO.'

Mr Leibniz shuffled in from the kitchen, clutching an A4 diary that he offered to the officers. 'I don't know where her mobile is. Didn't you find it with her?'

'No, she didn't have any ID on her at all,' said Sadie, taking the proffered diary.

'Susannah would always have a bag with her. Are you sure it's Susannah?' Grandma looked up from her seat on the sofa with hope in her eyes.

'I'm sorry, we are certain.' Ziggy knew it would take a while before they accepted the truth. 'We'll be in touch, and once again we are very sorry for your loss.'

Ziggy and Sadie turned to leave, and once they were back in the car, they both sat in silence.

'God, that was awful,' said Sadie, feeling drained.

'I know. Those poor grandparents. The best thing we can do for them now is deliver justice.'

'You're right, but it's just so painful, seeing them receive news like that.' She sighed. 'Do you want to head in now and go through the diary?'

'No. Let's get home and get some sleep. I have a feeling this one is going to be long haul.'

. . .

ZIGGY LET himself in the house and placed his keys on the hook by the door. It had been a very long day, and he doubted he would get much sleep with the investigation whirring round in his mind. He headed into the kitchen, which was still in a state of refurbishment. He opened a beer from the fridge and sat heavily on one of the kitchen stools while he checked his phone for messages.

Two years ago, Ziggy had bought the mid-terrace house after the divorce from his second wife, Rachel. It had been a bargain, but in desperate need of work. At the time, he figured he wouldn't be doing much outside of work hours, so he'd take on the challenge himself. It had two decent-sized bedrooms and a small box room – more than enough for himself and his seven-year-old son, Ben that he shared with Rachel.

His thoughts turned to his son as he read a text from Rachel asking if he was still having Ben the next day. For months, he and his ex had been disagreeing over weekend visits. Rachel knew that the demands of his job meant that he had to work long hours, and that weekends were no exception. Since she'd moved on and now had a new man in her life, she had been more insistent that Ben stayed overnight at Ziggy's and although he'd love to spend more time with his boy, sometimes that just wasn't possible. He was yet to meet the new man, and if he was honest, he wasn't in any great rush to do so. Shaking his head, Ziggy had hoped to take Ben for the day tomorrow – well, today now, as he glanced at the kitchen clock and saw that it was past midnight already. He would call her in the morning and let her know that a case had come up. He'd have to deal with the repercussions later.

3

Sunday, 2 June

R achel rolled over in bed and felt the empty space next to her. She checked the bedside clock; the time read: *00:30*. Gone midnight and Scott still wasn't back. But that wasn't much of a surprise to her. He worked as a DJ, so it often meant that he wouldn't come home until the early hours, sometimes, if at all.

Snuggling back under the duvet, she closed her eyes and attempted to go back to sleep. After ten minutes of fretful tossing and turning, she gave up and headed into the living room. Ben's toys were still all over the floor, so she collected them up and placed them back in the cupboard. Sitting down, she poured herself a glass of wine from the bottle she had opened earlier. This would help her sleep. She swirled the wine around the glass, mulling over a conversation she had had with Scott earlier that day. In a fit of spontaneity, most unlike her, Rachel had asked him to move in properly. He spent most nights here anyway, but this would be official. She hadn't received the response she had been expecting, which had stung a little if she was honest. He had seemed hesitant, reluctant even. She knew it was a big step for both of them, but he had really gelled with Ben, and she couldn't remember a time when she'd been happier. She was certain that Scott felt the same, but now she was questioning whether she'd misread the signs.

Scott had entered her life just at a point where she was ready to meet someone new, and he had swept her off her feet. They had met through work, both working in the hospitality industry. Scott was the complete opposite to Ziggy; outgoing and continually looking for excitement – a far cry from the boring, routine life she had been living. Though Scott was ten years younger than Rachel, it had made no difference to them. A few friends had raised their eyebrows, but she didn't care. She was happy, and Ben was happy. That was all that mattered.

She drained her glass and headed back to bed. Ben was with his dad tomorrow, so at least they would get some time together.

A LITTLE AFTER 8 A.M., Rachel's mobile rang. She reached over to the bedside table and looked at the screen. She had hoped it would be Scott, but it was her ex. She knew what that meant.

'Don't you dare!' she said before Ziggy could even get a word in.

'I'm so sorry. A murder case has come up and I need to be at the station.'

'For God's sake, you can't do this,' she spat through gritted teeth. Not only did it muck up all her plans, but Ben would be absolutely gutted. He had looked forward to seeing his dad all week.

Swinging her legs out of bed, she pulled on her dressing gown and headed for her son's bedroom. 'Here, you can tell him yourself.'

Ben was awake and playing with a video game in bed. He looked up as his mum entered the room.

'It's Dad on the phone for you.' She passed the handset across, keeping it on speaker so she could hear what excuses he came up with this time.

'Hiya, Dad,' said Ben quietly, half his attention still on the games console.

'Morning, buddy, listen. I know I was meant...'

'But you can't make it?'

'I'm so sorry, pal, you understand, don't you?'

'Sure. No worries. Go catch the bad guys.' Without breaking his gaze from the screen, he passed the phone back to his mum.

Rachel turned from Ben's room and moved out of earshot. 'You are unbelievable, Andrew. You know he only acts like he's not bothered for your benefit, don't you? I'll have to spend the day coaxing him out of his room and dealing with his miserable mood.' Rachel was so annoyed. She headed downstairs and started the coffee machine, slamming the cartridge into the dispenser.

'I know, look, I am so sorry. I'll try and get around this afternoon to see him, maybe take him out for pizza.'

'Yeah, course you will. Sweep in after a miserable day like the bloody hero. Well, don't bother.' She ended the call, let out a stream of expletives and threw her phone across the table in frustration.

SCOTT STRETCHED across the bed and ran his hand through his hair. God, he felt rough. He didn't think the after-party would go on that late. Champagne had been flowing freely, and he knew his boss, Jon, would appreciate the money over the counter. He might even give Scott a bonus, finally, as a result. He picked up his phone; one new voicemail. He listened and heard Rachel explain that Ben wouldn't be with his dad after all, so did he fancy doing something with them for the day? He lay back and thought about it. It would be nice to see them both, but he needed to shift this hangover first. And he'd left his jacket in the office at the club, so he'd need to call in there. He groaned and rolled over, but rather than cool sheets he felt warm bare skin next to him. *Shit.*

He had completely forgotten that he'd had a visitor overnight. That was the only thing with living above the club; too convenient for late-night guests. He'd promised himself he wouldn't cheat on Rachel after the last one, but his lack of willpower coupled with temptation proved too much. It was lucky he hadn't been caught before. The previous girl had definitely outstayed her welcome, but he figured she'd finally got the hint. He couldn't even remember the name of this one snoring gently next to him. And he definitely wasn't in the mood for small talk. Trying not to disturb her, he slowly slipped out of bed and headed for a shower.

Scott had worked at Sweet FAs for over a year, and he loved it. A regular night-time slot had always been his goal, though owning the club would be the dream. He'd made an effort to grow pally with Jon, the owner, even though he found him a bit odd and irritating. Jon had big plans for the place, or so he said, so Scott had stuck around. He was certain that he would be made a partner in the near future. It was Scott's idea to introduce seventies and eighties disco nights and they had been a huge success. Last night had been an Ibiza-themed evening, which had gone down a storm. Scott's ultimate ambition was to own one of the big clubs in London, but Sweet FAs suited him for now. He'd know when it was time to move on.

As he stepped into the shower, he thought about his relationship with Rachel. It was going well and had definitely lasted longer than most of his past flings. He had really landed on his feet with her. She was so trusting, not needy like most of the others. He guessed that was down to the age difference; ten years between them, but although he was still twenty-five, he had always acted older than his age.

Reaching for the shampoo, he thought about the little lad too. He quite liked Ben; clumsy as anything but was no trouble really, and so easy to wind up. Scott laughed to himself as he rinsed his hair. He switched the shower off and grabbed a towel. Wrapping it tightly around his waist, he wandered into the bedroom and admired himself in the full-length mirror. He took a lot of time over his appearance. The punters appreciated it, and Rachel definitely did. As had the pretty blonde that was still lounging around in his bed, come to think of it, now his hangover fog had started to lift. With a promise of meeting up later and a quick kiss on the forehead, he marshalled her on her way.

Once he'd said a final farewell to her, his thoughts again returned to Rachel. He grabbed his phone and called her back.

'Hey, honey, how are you?' He hooked the phone under his chin as he ran gel through his hair.

'Hey. I'm good. Well, I'm not actually, but I'll tell you about it later. Are you coming over?'

'Yeah, course. Just need to do a few things and I'll head to yours.'

'Can't wait to see you. I missed you last night,' said Rachel.

'Aww, I missed you too. Be there in a bit.'

She missed him. That was sweet. She'd asked him to move in with her yesterday, but he wasn't sure. He enjoyed having his own time and space, and he wasn't sure he wanted to give up the party lifestyle just yet. Maybe he could have both, he thought as he shrugged his arms into his hoody. Keep the flat, and just move a few of his things over to Rachel's. Did she need to know he'd kept the flat on? It was worth thinking about, he decided, heading for the door of the flat, grabbing the keys to the club and his BMW on the way.

The flat was accessible by a different door and staircase, so he fished the keys for the club out of his pocket and walked through the side gate to the rear. He unlocked the back door and closed it behind him. He was surprised to find lights on when he walked through to the bar. He was certain that the cleaners weren't due until the afternoon. He called out but didn't receive a response. Had someone broken in? Scott looked around for a makeshift weapon. Spotting a fire extinguisher, he unhooked it from its stand and slowly walked forward. He shouted again, and a figure popped up from behind the bar.

'What the fuck!' exclaimed Jon, who had just been emptying the tills.

'Don't "what the fuck" me. What about you? What the hell are you doing?' Scott put the fire extinguisher down and walked over.

'Making sure the tills are empty – was a late finish, so I left them.' Jon stuffed the cloth bags with notes and change.

'You scared the life out of me. How did you get in? The back door was locked.'

'Front door, left the alarm off.'

'Jesus, Jon, you're asking for it, aren't you? Till full and no alarm. What were you thinking?'

'Yeah, yeah, I know.' Jon walked past Scott and headed to the office that was at the back, out of sight from the punters. Scott followed, hoping to just grab his jacket and leave.

'Good crowd last night,' Jon said as he sat down at his desk.

Scott wasn't sure if it was a question, so he stayed silent. Jon hadn't shown his face until late in the evening, which suited Scott just fine. Jon was rarely there recently, and Scott preferred to do things his own way.

'Everyone behave themselves, did they?' asked Jon as he chucked the bags of money into his desk drawer. The man's attitude to his profits was unbelievable.

Scott followed him. 'What does that mean?'

'No drugs or anything?'

Scott shook his head. What kind of question was that? 'No one shared any with me.' He wished he could just leave it there, but he'd never hear the end of it if he walked away now. Thinking of the bigger picture, Scott steeled himself for another lecture. 'Why? What's on your mind?'

'I don't want the club getting a dodgy reputation, that's all.'

'Won't happen on my watch.'

'Yeah, well, you know these themed nights of yours?'

'What about them?'

'Just a bit worried that it's giving off the wrong image?'

'Wrong image? Don't make me laugh, the reputation of this place has gone up a notch or two since I started here!' It was true. When Scott had first started at Sweet FAs, it was well known for its outrageous drag acts, not always done in the best of taste.

Jon was offended. 'It wasn't trashy,' he snapped.

'That's as maybe, but if there's money coming in, what do you care?'

Jon huffed and changed the subject to refurbishments. It was a constant battle of Scott's, trying to get any of the outdated furnishings replaced, but Jon was always reluctant to put his hand in his pocket.

Jon sat back in his leather chair, swinging from side to side. 'True, true. Been thinking a lot about updating the place.'

Hallelujah. 'Great idea,' said Scott, as if it was the first time he'd heard it. He sat back as Jon waffled on, literally repeating everything that Scott had been saying to him for the last three months. When he finally paused for breath, Scott took his chance to jump in. 'Why don't you get it all down on paper and speak to an architect?'

Jon nodded. 'Yes, great idea though...'

'Look, mate, it's never gonna happen if you don't stick your hand in your pocket.'

'True, true. Yeah, I'll have a think.'

The man was literally a broken record.

Scott stood up and pulled his jacket on, calling after him as he hurried out of the back door before Jon could collar him again. 'You do that. Enjoy the rest of your day.'

If Scott had anything to do with it, he bloody deserved to own the place, never mind just making partner.

4

Monday, 3 June

Despite his best intentions, another Sunday had passed by without seeing his son. Ziggy now stood in front of the whiteboard in the incident room. Operation Silk, as the murder inquiry had randomly been named, wasn't progressing as quickly as he would have liked. Ziggy and his team had spent much of the previous day chasing down CCTV leads, and it had proved fruitless. Today they were focusing in on those who knew the victim, Susannah Leibniz. Ziggy was due to speak with her colleagues at the salon later, and there had been a few people in Susannah's diary that they hadn't been able to make contact with, so Wilko and Angela were homing in on those.

'Morning, boss.' Sadie passed a cup of coffee to Ziggy and sat on the edge of her desk. 'Looking pretty bare on there, isn't it?'

'I was just thinking the same.' Ziggy took a sip.

Sadie agreed, just as Wilko and Angela walked through the door.

'Morning, boss, anything overnight?' asked Wilko through a mouthful of bacon butty.

'Nothing. Not a thing.' Frustration was creeping into Ziggy's voice. 'Press release is going out this afternoon, and I have a press briefing with DCS Whitmore tomorrow morning, so that might generate something.' Ziggy dreaded the thought of press conferences. He had a massive dislike of public speaking, and all those cameras pointing at him made him hugely uncomfortable. It showed in his delivery too. No amount of media training could remove all traces of his loathing of the press. They were like a pack of hyenas, eager to gorge on any scraps thrown at them. And there was one journalist in particular who he couldn't stand: Chrystal Mack – Mack the Knife – from the *Yorkshire Post*. A young, go-getting kind of journalist, she'd sell her own grandmother if it meant getting a front-page story. He'd had more than one run-in with her over the years, and she was bound to be there this afternoon.

'How about CCTV, anything from that?' asked Angela as she placed her bag neatly under her desk and rearranged her desk accessories, so they were precisely lined up.

'Nothing as yet but the briefing starts in' – Ziggy looked at the wall clock– 'ten minutes, so let's see if there is anything.'

The team fired up their computers and logged their activities ahead of everyone else filing in. Ziggy ran through his notes with Sadie, making sure they hadn't missed anything and waited for the others.

Once they were all in place, Ziggy was just about to start when the looming form of DCS Steve Whitmore entered the room. Whilst Ziggy towered over most of the team, Whitmore made him look like a midget with his nearly 6ft 9 build. Everyone stood, showing their respect and acknowledged his presence as SIO, albeit a very hands-off one, but he remained at the back of the room like an ominous black cloud.

When they were all once more seated Ziggy began, 'Morning, everyone. As you know, yesterday was spent chasing up everyone who had a place in Susannah's life. There were a few people that we hadn't managed to track down, so DS Wilkinson and DC Dove are following up on those this morning.' He paused and looked across at PC Jones who had been seconded from another team for the duration of the inquiry. Young and ambitious, Ziggy was pleased to have him on board, 'Do you have all the CCTV now?'

PC Jones sat upright. 'We're just waiting for the pub over the road to send us theirs. They had a few tech difficulties yesterday, but the landlord has assured me they have the footage for the times we need.'

'Good stuff. Can you stay on that, please, and update as soon as possible?'

PC Jones nodded, clearly pleased to be singled out for an important task.

Ziggy continued, 'DS Bates and I are going to the salon where Susannah worked. We're still waiting for the forensics results on the debris found in her hair and the silk fabric that Lolly— sorry, Dr Turner found at the post-mortem.'

Ziggy looked around at the small team. He had every faith that they would all give 100 per cent, but he would need more people after the press conference to deal with the enquiries. 'Right, let's get to it team. Back here for four p.m. updates please but call in if there's anything in the meantime.'

Everyone turned to their tasks, and DCS Whitmore stepped forward and approached Ziggy.

'Morning, sir,' said Ziggy as he collected his notes from the desk.

'Morning. How's it going? You don't seem to have much to go on.' Whitmore stood with his hands behind his back, staring at the whiteboard and tapping his foot. To say Ziggy and Whitmore had a fractious relationship would be an understatement. They were complete opposites in character; Whitmore was wildly ambitious with his eye on the top job, whereas Ziggy was quite happy leading his team and delivering results with no aims for climbing the greasy pole.

'Not much right now, sir, but I envisage that will change as we dig further into Susannah's lifestyle.'

'All eyes are on you, Thornes. You need to deliver results on this one.'

No shit, Sherlock.

'Of course, sir. We're all on it. If we could have a few dedicated bods helping out in-house to deal with any incoming calls?' Ziggy already knew the answer.

'Let's see what today brings, shall we?'

Typical. Results on a shoestring, as always. 'Sure. I'm hoping the press conference will help.'

'Yes. About that, obviously I'll issue the prepared statement, but if you could field the media questions?'

Ziggy's heart sank. He had hoped to just be a background figure, but he wasn't about to let Whitmore know how pissed off he was. 'Absolutely, sir.'

Whitmore gave a short nod of his head and turned to leave. 'I'll leave you to it. Keep up the good work and keep me in the loop.'

Sir, yes sir. Ziggy did a mock salute behind Whitmore's

back and turned abruptly when he heard giggling behind him.

'That was close – he could have turned around.' Sadie was leaning against Ziggy's office door.

'You weren't supposed to see that,' said Ziggy, walking round Sadie into his office and sitting down at his desk.

'C'mon, we all do it, even behind your back.' Sadie sat down on the one spare chair in the room.

'You'd better not!' said Ziggy in good humour, but he knew everyone did it at some point. He didn't mind a bit of banter amongst the team. God knows, it was needed at times.

'So, we're heading to the high street then, to chat to Susannah's colleagues?' asked Sadie.

Ziggy nodded, stood up and pulled his jacket on. 'Yep, there's two people that worked closely with her; Claire and her boss, Sheila. They should be there now so we can head off.'

ONCE THEY WERE in the car, with Ziggy at the wheel this time, Sadie shared some thoughts she'd had overnight about their killer.

'It seems to me he knows the area well. I mean, we say *he*, but it could be a female.'

'It could be,' acknowledged Ziggy. 'But it would take some strength to drag a body along that path. I agree the killer's familiar with the area though. He – let's say *he* for now – must have a place where he held her, and the means to restrain her. It's difficult to know how long she was held before he killed her because we haven't yet met anyone who has seen Susannah or spent any time with her recently. I'm hoping the salon will hold some clues.'

They turned left onto the high street, located the salon and parked in the supermarket car park over the road.

'I think we need to build on the timeline we have for Susannah. What hours she worked, that kind of thing. And if she had any over eager clients,' said Ziggy as he closed the car door.

'Absolutely.' Sadie agreed as they crossed the road, dodging traffic as they went.

Sadie pushed the salon door open and was immediately hit with the smell of chemicals. It was busy, even though it was only nine in the morning. A couple of ladies had foil in their hair, and someone was having their nails done at the nail bar. They looked around at the gaudy interior. It was bright, to say the least, with multiple neon pink signs covering the walls and vintage posters advertising old time music halls and theatrical productions were randomly tacked all over. The overall effect was cluttered and confused.

Approaching the front desk, they were greeted with a friendly smile from the receptionist who then made a call. Shortly afterwards a tall, willowy figure approached them, walking quickly through the salon.

'Hello there. I'm Sheila, the salon manager.' Sheila thrust a manicured hand towards them, and flicked her long auburn hair over her shoulder.

'Hi, DI Thornes, and this is my colleague DS Sadie Bates. We rang yesterday?'

'Yes. Of course, you wanted to speak about Susannah?' Sheila had turned and was tottering back on her high heels, before opening a door on the back wall. Ziggy nudged Sadie, who was still taking in the overstimulating interior, assuming that they were to follow her.

They had clearly been shown into the staff break room.

Coats and bags were strewn around, half-eaten porridge was still on the table and the sink was overflowing with dirty pots.

''Scuse the mess – the cleaner hasn't been in yet.' Sheila used her hand to wipe some crumbs away from the table they were seated around.

'Don't worry,' he said, 'It's nothing too formal. We just want to ask a few questions.'

'Ooh, would you like a cuppa?' Sheila jumped up and headed for the kettle.

'Erm, no thanks. We're fine. If we could just talk for a moment?' asked Ziggy.

Sheila returned to the table, took a seat and folded her hands in front of her. 'Yes, of course. Sorry, I'm just a little nervous. It's not every day the police want to talk to you. I do hope nothing bad has happened?'

'I understand,' said Ziggy. 'Can you tell me when you last saw Susannah?'

Sadie started making notes.

'Now let me think. She hasn't been here much recently. She rents her chair for make-up sessions with clients. We have an agreement that she only pays when she has a client, so she's not here all the time. If she doesn't turn up, then we just assume she isn't busy. But as I said, we haven't seen her much in the last few weeks. Why? Has something happened?'

With the media conference the next day, the news would be out eventually, so there was no point hiding the truth.

'I'm sorry to have to tell you this, but Susannah's body was found on Saturday morning,' said Sadie.

'Oh, my days, what a shock.' Sheila looked understand-ably upset. 'Poor Susannah. How did it happen? Was she in an accident or something?'

'I'm afraid we can't say much more than that at the moment but it's important that we establish Susannah's whereabouts in the lead-up to Friday and Saturday of last week.'

'Well, I'm not sure what to say. That's such a shock, and so sad. She was only young and had such big plans.'

'Yes, I know—'

Sheila cut in. 'Oh, her poor grandparents!' Her hand flew to her mouth. 'They must be devastated. They were very close. Have you spoken to them? Of course, you have...'

'Sheila, I can see you're upset but if we could just ask a few more questions?' Ziggy tried to be as gentle as he could.

'Yes, yes, of course, anything I can do but I'm not sure I can tell you that much. You'd be better off speaking to Claire – she was closest to her outside of work, I think.'

'Yes, we'll speak to her in a moment. I believe she's working here today, is that right?' asked Ziggy.

'Yes, yes, shall I go fetch her?' Sheila half hovered out of the chair, as if she couldn't wait to be gone.

'No, it's fine and we'll get around to that.' Ziggy gestured for her to sit back down, getting somewhat exasperated. He wasn't the most patient of people at the best of time. Sadie picked up on it and nudged his leg under the table.

Calming his composure slightly, he tried again. 'Tell me, how long had Susannah rented a chair here?'

'She'd been here for over a year. She kept herself to herself while in the salon. She had her own booking system though – she did the wedding make-up for a couple of our regular customers.' Sheila paused for breath. 'Do you know when the funeral is?'

Ziggy sighed inwardly; they clearly weren't going to get far with Sheila. 'There are quite a few things that need to happen first, but I'm sure you'll be notified.'

Winding the interview up, Sadie asked if Claire was available for a quick chat. Sheila left the room, and Ziggy rolled his eyes as the door closed behind her.

'I can't figure out if she's genuinely upset or just after the gossip.'

'Ziggy! That limited patience of yours will really land you in it one day,' she admonished. Thankfully after working together for five years she was used to him and his ways. He doubted anyone else would pick up on it, but she knew all his little nuances. She was just about to say something else when the staffroom door opened again.

Sheila led a young woman, who must have been Claire, into the room. 'I've told her the news.'

Just great. Ziggy looked at Claire and could see that the poor girl was about to fall apart. 'I'm so sorry for the loss of your friend, Claire.'

Claire took a seat and tears spilled down her perfectly made-up face. 'I can't believe it.'

Sheila reached for the box of tissues that were on the counter and passed them across, taking one and dabbing her own eyes even though there was no evidence of tears.

Ziggy waited until the two women had composed themselves somewhat before he started with his questions. First of all, he needed Sheila to leave the room, convinced she was only after gossip and they'd given her enough for one day.

'Thank you, Sheila, we've got this now.' He looked her directly in the eye, hoping she would take the hint. Thankfully, after much flouncing and platitudes to Claire, she left.

Claire took another handful of tissues and blew her nose. 'What happened?' she asked through her tears. She was visibly shaking too.

'We can't say too much right now, but we'd like to get to

know Susannah a little more.' said Ziggy gently, seeing the girl's distress.

'OK, what do you need to know?' Claire pulled herself upright, clearly trying to hold it together.

'When did you last see Susannah?'

'Thursday last week. It was my day off, and we hadn't had a catch-up in ages, so we went for a walk.'

'Was there a reason you hadn't seen each other for a while?'

'Not really, just life, I guess. I mean, Susie was trying to grow her freelance work. She was networking a lot, breakfast meetings that kind of thing, and she went to a lot of wedding fairs as well. I have a two-year-old, so she keeps me busy. We hadn't fallen out or anything, if that's what you mean.' Claire looked from Ziggy to Sadie questioningly.

'No, that's fine. You're doing great,' replied Sadie, patting Claire's knee reassuringly.

'Where did you go for your walk, Claire?' asked Ziggy.

'Just to Woodhouse Moor. It's a green by the uni and about halfway between our houses, plus it's got a little park so Zoe – that's my daughter – could play on the swings.'

Out of the corner of his eye, Ziggy caught Sadie making a note at the mention of Woodhouse Moor.

'How long did you stay there?' he asked.

'About an hour. Zoe got cranky, so we left and headed home.'

'Did Susannah go home with you?'

'No, she waved us off and headed towards the car park where she had left her car.'

Interesting, thought Ziggy. Had that been the same car parked on the grandparents' driveway?

'Was it a place you often went to?' he probed further.

'Not really. I was a bit surprised, as it can a bit rough, to be honest, but Susie suggested it, so I thought we might as well.'

'What time was it when you met?'

'Erm, must have been about eleven. Yeah, that's right cos we left at just after noon, something like that.'

'And you haven't heard from Susannah since?'

'No, but that's not unusual. Like I said, we're good friends, but we don't, didn't, live in each other's pockets.'

'OK. Claire, did Susannah have any boyfriends?'

Claire took her time to answer. 'Not recently. Well, not that she told me, anyway. There had been a lad, but that ended ages ago. He was cheating on her.' Claire sat back and folded her arms.

'Do you know the boyfriend's name?'

'Erm, it was Shaun, something like that. Fairly certain it began with s. She was dead keen on him, but like I said, she caught him cheating, so it was over weeks ago.'

Sadie made a note of the name.

'How did she seem when you were together? Was she nervous or jumpy, for example?'

Claire paused for a minute. 'She seemed distracted, to be honest, but when I said I needed to take Zoe home, she seemed keen to get away too. I just assumed she had other plans.'

'You said she got into *her* car, did you see if she was driving or what car it was?'

'No, she just headed to the car park, and when I turned to wave, she'd gone, so I assumed it was the one she used for her freelance work. I think it's her grandad's.' Claire wiped her face with the tissue she was clutching. 'I just can't believe it. I know you can't tell me much, but can you at least tell me how she died? Was it an accident?'

Ziggy and Sadie looked at each other. Sadie spoke. 'We believe she was murdered, Claire, I'm so sorry.'

Claire started crying again. 'Oh my God, murdered? I can't believe it. Who would want to hurt Susie?'

'That's what we're trying to find out, love, I really am sorry for your loss.' Sadie felt dreadful. Clearly the two girls had been close.

Leaving Claire a card in case she thought of something, the two detectives stood up. Sadie stayed with her while Ziggy brought Sheila from the salon.

'Oh, you poor dear, come here.' Sheila threw her arms around her employee. 'There, there love. Come on now,' she whispered as Claire sobbed into Sheila's shoulder.

'We'll head off now, but if you can think of anything at all, please just call us directly.' said Sadie, leaving the grieving pair in each other's arms.

Once outside the shop, Ziggy's whole body sagged. 'Well, that was awful,' he said, as they headed for the car.

'I know. Poor Claire – they were obviously close,' Sadie replied.

'Would appear so. Who was chasing up the car details? I'm intrigued as to why Susannah was in her car on Thursday and yet her grandparents hadn't seen her even though the car was parked on their drive. Is it the same car? Something not right there, don't you think?'

'Very true. It was Wilko – I'll give him a call and see what he's got.'

While Sadie made the call, Ziggy's mind replayed the conversation with Claire. Her grief was genuine but was she holding something back? And Sheila's reaction had seemed a bit off though Ziggy had seen plenty of people express loss in different ways.

'Great. Thanks, Nick.' She ended the call and turned to

Ziggy. 'Curiouser and curiouser. The car on the grandparents drive is registered to Mr Leibniz, but Susannah isn't on the insurance.'

'Curiouser, indeed,' said Ziggy. 'I think we need to speak to the grandparents again, don't you?'

5

B iding his time was something he was good at. He'd spent his life waiting for his moment, and now, he was finally on the right path.

He didn't want much, just to be loved and accepted. That wasn't too much to ask, was it?

His mother had loved him. Or at least, that's what he'd thought.

It had all been lies. His whole life had been a lie, and it wasn't until her death that he had discovered the truth. Lying bitch whore.

He felt his temper rise, but he fought to regain control. He couldn't think about her now. He had a job to do. Susannah had just been the start. He'd enjoyed spending time with her, though he was disappointed it had been short-lived.

But yes, Susannah had been a good starting point. Just the right amount of resistance, he felt. He would have liked to have fixed her make-up. No doubt, she would have been annoyed at the mascara on her cheeks and the smudging of her carefully made-up face. He smiled. Next time, he wouldn't make such mistakes. Next time he would be more careful. Next time he'd take his time.

But for now, he had adjustments to make for his next visitor.

6

---

*Z*iggy and Sadie pulled up outside of the Leibnizes' home. Sadie had phoned ahead to let them know they would be calling in.

The door was opened before they had the chance to knock. The elderly couple stood in the hallway, politely welcoming the two detectives with an air of trepidation.

'Sorry to bother you again – I know this is a difficult time for you. How are you holding up?' asked Ziggy, following them into the kitchen.

'Thank you, DI Thornes. Yes, it's been hard processing everything,' said Mrs Leibniz as she busied herself making tea. Ziggy wondered briefly how many times that kettle had been boiled and cups of tea made then abandoned as another wave of grief enveloped them. Mr Leibniz was hovering at the side of her, nervous and unsure what to do with himself.

'Please, call me Ziggy, everyone else does. Shall we sit down?'

The kitchen was tiny, and Sadie had been waiting by the door until there was room for the four of them.

'Yes, good idea,' said Mr Leibniz, grateful for something to do. He held a chair out for Sadie, and she sat down, thanking him.

The tea was brought to the table and Mrs Leibniz poured one for everyone in delicate china cups. Once everyone had a cup, she finally took her seat.

'As I said, we're sorry to bother you again. We just have a couple of further questions for you, if that's OK?'

'Yes, absolutely. Have you made any progress?' asked Mr Leibniz.

'We are making progress, but it is slow. We're really trying to build a picture of Susannah's lifestyle. Mr Leibniz, when we were last here you mentioned that you had driven Susannah to the airport?'

'Yes, that's right.'

'And I notice there's a car parked on the driveway. It's your car, correct?'

'Yes, it is.'

'But you said that Susannah borrowed it for work?'

Mr and Mrs Leibniz looked at each other and clutched hands across the table. Ziggy sensed they were holding something back.

'Mr Leibniz, we need you to tell us the truth. We just want to understand how Susannah reached her clients if she was working freelance? It could lead us to whoever took Susannah's life.'

Mr Leibniz patted his wife's hand and nodded at her. 'It's OK, they need to know.' He turned to Ziggy and Sadie. 'Yes, she would borrow the car. She used to use the bus, but she had so much equipment to carry it became impossible.'

'She wasn't insured, though.' Ziggy's tone presented it as fact rather than a question.

Mr Leibniz hesitated and looked flustered. 'No, I'm

sorry to say she wasn't. She hadn't long since passed her driving test and it was her first car. It was so expensive to add her, she's only 24.' Mr Leibniz looked deeply embarrassed and Ziggy could see he was a proud man.

'That's OK, I understand, and thank you for being truthful with us, but it does lead me to another question.' Ziggy took a breath. 'Susannah was seen heading towards a car last Thursday, which means if it was this car she had to have returned here at some point after you dropped her off at the airport, not only to use the car but also to return it, as the same car is now parked on your driveway. Can you explain that to me?'

Ziggy watched their faces closely as they registered the information with shock and a surprised look.

'No, I'm sorry, that's not true.' Mr Leibniz shook his head as he spoke.

'What do you mean?' asked Sadie. She had kept quiet until now, studying their reactions.

'We already told you. She was supposed to be in Germany. We took her to the airport. The car has been parked on the drive ever since.'

Ziggy would get the team to check ANPR when he returned to the station. If it had left the driveway, there was no way it wouldn't have been picked up somewhere.

'Did Susannah have access to anyone else's car?' asked Ziggy.

'No. Not that we are aware of.' The couple looked at each, as confused as Ziggy and Sadie.

'OK, and you're absolutely certain that you haven't seen Susannah for a month?'

'Yes, absolutely,' asserted Mr Leibniz.

It was time for a change of direction. 'OK, do you think it

would be possible for us to take a look in Susannah's bedroom?'

'Yes, of course.' Mrs Leibniz stood and slowly headed upstairs. Ziggy followed. 'It's that door on the left,' she indicated.

'Thank you. We won't be long.'

Ziggy stood at the open door and looked inside. The bedroom was long and narrow, presumably it had been the box room at some point. The decor was consistent with the rest of the house, dated and tired. The only sign that a woman in her twenties had once occupied the room was the small dressing table in front of the window that was covered in a wide range of skincare products and make-up, including false eyelashes and various coloured lipsticks. Ziggy didn't touch anything; he just pivoted round, taking it all in. There were no pictures on the walls or photographs next to the bed. He opened the old-fashioned wardrobe and saw clothes hanging neatly on the rails. There were two very distinct sections. One side was obviously workwear; neat tunics in various colours, all freshly washed and ironed. On the opposite side, there were much more casual clothes like jeans and T-shirts. No sign of any scarves or anything silk, even after checking Susannah's underwear drawer.

After searching further through bedside drawers and under the bed, Ziggy muttered to himself. 'What was your story, Susannah?' He couldn't help but think there was more to this case than met the eye.

'What was that?' asked Sadie, who had been looking through the various make-up paraphernalia.

'Just wondering what her story was.'

'Feels like we're missing something, doesn't it?'

'But what? It looks like she led a simple life.'

They left the bedroom and headed back downstairs. The elderly couple were sat next to each other on the sofa.

'Did you find anything?' asked Mr Leibniz.

'Nothing out of the ordinary, no. I just want to make you aware that we will be holding a press conference first thing tomorrow morning, so it may be on the local news. We just wanted to prewarn you so you can prepare yourselves.'

'Yes, your colleague had already let us know. Thank you.'

'We're heading back to the office now. Thank you for your hospitality, we'll be in touch as soon as we hear anything more.'

Feeling frustrated, they headed back to the incident room. With any luck, one of the team would have had better luck and give them something to go on, otherwise Whitmore would be all over Ziggy's back.

7

Tuesday, 4 June

Ziggy read through the press release and prepared himself to face the media. Whitmore had collared him the minute he'd walked into the station, reminding him of the need to close the case, like he needed the prompt. He had eventually made it to his desk, waiting for Wilko to return from speaking to a couple of the contacts in Susannah's diary, all the while trying to keep his impending public appearance out of his mind. But, with any luck after the press conference they'd have more leads. So far, despite the fact that Angela had updated the board with the details of the grandparent's car, and PC Jones still on with the CCTV, the flip charts looked strikingly empty.

'Ready, boss?' asked Sadie, popping her head round his office door.

'As I'll ever be. I hope this doesn't take long.' He stood, smoothing his shirt and trousers and straightened the tie that he kept in his desk drawer for emergencies.

'Very smart, sir.'

'Oh, shush you. Are you coming too?'

'Yeah, I want to stand at the back and make faces at you.'

'Ha, good luck with that. You'll have to get past Mack the Knife first.'

They headed into the conference room just as Whitmore was taking his place behind the podium. The room was full, and, sure enough, Chrystal Mack, the *Yorkshire Post* reporter, was front and centre. She winked at Ziggy as he entered the room, and he could hear Sadie chuckling behind him. He ignored both and focused his attention on the podium. He waited to the side until Whitmore had finished and passed over to him.

The room fell silent as Ziggy walked onto the makeshift stage.

'As DCS Whitmore has just said, we are currently investigating the death of a female whose body was found in the Woodhouse Moor area of Leeds on the morning of Saturday the first of June. At this stage of the inquiry we are asking the public to provide us with any information they have specific to the area in question. If anyone does have any information, they should contact West Yorkshire Police. The telephone number is on the bottom of the press release that is now being handed out. I'll now take questions.'

Chrystal Mack's hand shot up and she didn't wait for Ziggy's acknowledgement.

'*Yorkshire Post*, do you have any suspects?'

'As I said, our inquiry is still ongoing.'

'So, does that mean you haven't?'

'Again, this is an ongoing investigation, so it wouldn't be right for me to comment at this time.'

'We'll take that as a no then?'

Ziggy stood staring at the woman in front of him and ignored her question. 'Any other questions?'

Another hand appeared, 'Rob Smith, '*Leeds Weekly News*, should women be scared to go out on their own?'

'Usual safety precautions should be taken.'

Chrystal piped up again. 'Does that mean you're expecting more attacks?'

Oh, here we go. How long before the Yorkshire Ripper gets a mention? 'I would advise anyone, male or female, to exercise the usual caution when walking late at night. If possible, do not walk home on your own if it can be avoided. I'm not suggesting there will be further attacks – we believe this to be an isolated incident, and I sincerely hope your coverage reflects that.' He stared directly at her as he delivered his last sentence. He received a withering look in return.

After a few further pointless questions, he was grateful that Whitmore brought the press conference to the end. Ziggy left the room, deeply annoyed. He hadn't meant to go off-piste with his comments, but it infuriated him that people seemed to think every murder was an episode of *CSI* or somehow related to the tragedy of the infamous eighties case. They were already up against it enough without the media turning it into a complete frenzy and sensationalising every move they made.

DCS Whitmore followed him out of the room. 'Well done, Andrew – you've just given them this evening's headline,' he called after him, voice dripping with sarcasm.

Ziggy stopped and turned around, causing Sadie to almost bump into him. 'Sir, I just don't understand where the people get their ideas from. Not once have we suggested there will be more attacks. It's bullshit.'

'Bullshit or not, you should have stuck to the official line.'

Ziggy knew there was no point arguing. He shrugged his shoulders. 'If you'll excuse me, I have an investigation to cover.'

'Pressure is on now.'

'Thanks, I hadn't noticed,' Ziggy muttered under his breath.

RACHEL PASSED Scott his cup of coffee and sat down on the sofa next to him. Ben had been dropped off at school, so they had the rest of the day to themselves. Scott took a sip of his brew and flicked over the TV channel to the regional news.

'*The body found in Woodhouse Moor over the weekend has been identified as that of 25-year-old Susannah Leibniz...*'

As the photograph of a young woman stared back at him, he almost spilt his coffee. The blood drained from his face and his hands were shaking uncontrollably. He carefully placed his mug on the coffee table and looked at Rachel. She was oblivious to his reaction and calmly sat sipping her drink.

What the fuck?

Next time he looked at the TV, Ziggy's face filled the screen as he fielded questions from local reporters.

'That's your ex, right?' asked Scott, trying to sound casual.

Rachel cringed in response. 'Yep, that's him in all his glory. This must be the reason he couldn't have Ben on Sunday,' said Rachel, tucking her hair behind her ear. 'But, God he'll be hating this – he can't stand the press.'

Scott shifted round in his seat, restlessly. 'Will he be in charge of the investigation?'

'Yeah, it's what he does.'

'Big stuff, like this?' Scott pointed at the screen. The picture had moved back to the studio and onto the next story.

'Don't you listen to anything I tell you? This is why he couldn't have Ben on Sunday.'

'Sunday? Was that when they found her?' He felt sweat breaking out on his forehead and tried to discreetly wipe it away.

'Erm, dunno. I think the reporter said she was found on Saturday morning. Why are you so interested?'

'Oh, no reason.' He picked up his cup, hoping his hand had stopped shaking enough to hold it steady. He took a sip in an attempt to get rid of the cotton mouth he'd developed and ignore the sick feeling in his stomach. He needed a reason to get out of there.

'Listen, I've been thinking about your question, you know about moving in and I think it's a great idea.' *Anything to distract her*. 'So how about you make some space in the bedroom and I'll go get some of my stuff?'

Rachel threw herself at Scott, kissing him deeply. 'That's amazing. I wasn't sure if I'd put my foot in it. I mean, you didn't seem keen last time we spoke about it.'

He laughed, a nervous, light laugh and stood up. 'Yeah, well. It seems like a good idea.'

Rachel thought her heart was going to burst. 'I know it might seem quick to some people but if it feels right, you know?'

Scott kissed her again, keen to get away.

'Wait until I tell Ben, he'll be over the moon,' said Rachel.

Scott was already heading for the door. 'I'll be back in a bit then – make sure there's plenty of room.'

He left the house and got into his car as quickly as he

could. He drove around the corner, out of sight of the house, and parked up again. He screamed and banged his head against the steering wheel. 'What the fuck!' He lifted his head and bashed the steering wheel with the heels of his hands. He needed to think, and fast.

8

Wednesday, 5 June

Ziggy hit refresh again on his computer screen. Still nothing. He'd been waiting on his inbox ever since the press conference, as the forensics were due back on the piece of fabric found on Susannah's body, but there'd been no joy all morning.

Frustrated, he ran his hands through his closely shaved hair, as he was prone to do when stressed. Unsurprisingly, there wasn't much left. He stood up. It wasn't yet lunchtime and Ziggy already felt like he'd done an eighteen-hour shift. He hadn't slept well the night before, worrying over the press conference and running over the evidence so far in his mind. He checked his watch; the team were due to update him again at noon.

He walked into the incident room and took another look at the case boards. Several things were still unanswered in his mind. Why had the body been placed so publicly? Had the killer been disturbed? Or more worryingly, did he *want* to be caught? Ziggy didn't think so. Or hoped not. Because then the dumping of the body would be acting as a signpost, a way for the killer to draw attention to himself, feeding his narcissistic personality. If that was the case, then this wouldn't be the last one, and that thought sent chills down Ziggy's spine.

As he stood in contemplation, he could hear the activity of the room behind him. Sadie was currently coordinating the few leads that had started to filter through from the control room. The press conference had triggered the usual nutters, blaming errant husbands or partners, but somewhere in there, there might just be a tangible lead, so every call had to be thoroughly followed up.

'Anything?' asked Ziggy, moving to stand behind Sadie as she signed off an enquiry form with *No further action required*.

She passed the form back to the telephone handler and turned to Ziggy.

'Usual nutjobs plus a couple of local residents who claim to have heard screams around the time. I've sent uniform to follow up, but we've spoken to these people before, so we'll see. Anything from Forensics?'

'I haven't checked in, oh, at least three minutes. Check your emails, you should be copied in.'

Sadie headed for her workstation, woke up her screen and hit refresh on her inbox. A ping and a slew of new emails landed. 'It's here,' she said, double-clicking to open the attachment. 'Let me print it off.'

Ziggy headed for the printer and stood waiting in anticipation. As it printed, he anxiously grabbed each page as it appeared. It was the fabric analysis. He quickly scan read the document until he reached the summary.

'Based on analysis, yada, yada, yada, it's a natural fibre, silk. Blah, blah, blah. Dates back to early nineteen forties.

Imported Chinese silk.' Ziggy looked up from the report. It
didn't really tell them anything new. He'd hoped for more,
but all was not lost. 'It came from a silk scarf. That's got to be
something, right? Susannah didn't have anything like that in
her bedroom, and her grandparents don't strike me as the
type to splash out on luxury silk scarves.'

'That's quite specific as well, how the hell do they do
that?' Sadie took the report from Ziggy. He was what he
would call a headline person when it came to reports,
whereas Sadie liked to know the finer details. It was why
they made such a good team.

Ziggy headed over to the whiteboard, picked up a dry
wipe marker and was about to make notes when Angela
took the pen from him.

'Here, I'll do that,' she said.

Ziggy gladly handed the pen over, knowing that Angela
was a stickler for neatness and even he agreed his hand-
writing was messy.

They spent the next few minutes making sure everyone
was up to date. Uniform had radioed in to say they had
spoken with the residents around Woodhouse Moor, but
their information was vague to say the least. Ziggy thanked
them – he hadn't really expected anything more; if you
heard a scream in the middle of the night, you were unlikely
to forget it, or suddenly remember after a TV appeal.
Another reason for his dislike of the media; everyone
wanted their fifteen minutes of fame. He knew that was a
cynical view, but he put it down to years of experience.

'Right, let's go grab some lunch and work on the
concrete evidence we do have when we get back.' He was
starving, and in serious need of carbs.

They spent the rest of the day chasing people up,
wading through the incoming enquiries and trying to pull

all the strings together. At 6 p.m. he sent the team home. He was due to take Ben out for tea, so he switched off the office lights when everyone had left and headed to the car park.

SHORTLY AFTER, he pulled up outside Rachel's house. He was a little later than he'd expected thanks to the horrendous traffic on the M1, and he hoped Rachel wouldn't kick off.

As he closed his car door and walked up the path, Ben came running out to greet him. 'Daddy!' he yelled, launching himself into Ziggy's arms.

'Hey, buddy. That's a lovely welcome.'

Ben grabbed Ziggy's arm and dragged him inside the house. Rachel was standing in the kitchen, and her boyfriend – Ziggy couldn't remember his name – was at the side of her. He nodded his head in acknowledgement.

'Late again.' Rachel folded her arms. 'He's been so excited since he got home from school. For a minute there, I thought you were letting him down *again*.'

Ziggy ignored the dig, focusing on Ben instead.

'Where are you taking him?' she asked.

Ziggy shook himself free of Ben's grasp and urged the boy to fasten his laces before looking over at Rachel. 'Just for a pizza, I think. If that's OK with you, buddy?' He directed his question at Ben.

'Yummy, yes, please.' Ben was desperately trying to tie his laces but getting too many fingers involved. Ziggy squatted down to help him. As he knelt down, he noticed a stack of removal boxes in the hallway, just off the kitchen. It was none of his business, but he couldn't stop himself from asking. 'Moving?' he asked, trying to sound casual, hoping the answer was no - he couldn't bear it if she moved Ben away.

Rachel's boyfriend pushed himself away from the worktop and walked over to the table. 'They're mine,' he said.

'Ah, right. Scott, isn't it? I don't think we've properly met.' Ziggy held his hand out.

Scott took it and gave it a solid shake. 'Should I call you Ziggy or Andrew or Inspector?' he asked.

An awkward silence descended as Ziggy tried to work out if Scott was being funny or sarcastic. He also picked up on a nervous tilt to the other man's voice.

'Ziggy is just fine.' He turned to Rachel.

'Sorry, Ziggy, I haven't had a chance to tell you, Scott is moving in.' Rachel spoke, and Ziggy acknowledged her with a nod of the head, relieved she wasn't moving, unsure how he felt about the boyfriend moving in but now wasn't the time for that conversation.

'Right, well I'll have this one back for eight at the latest,' he said, ignoring Scott's look and heading for the door. *What a weird man.*

RACHEL KISSED Ben and waved them off from the doorstep before stepping back into the kitchen.

'Doesn't have a sense of humour your ex, does he?' commented Scott.

'Another reason I'm no longer with him.' She stood on her tiptoes and pecked Scott on the cheek. 'Shall we go out for some food too?' she asked.

'Oh, honey, I'm sorry, I can't. Jon's not around again and I'm needed at the club. Shouldn't be too long, though. Why don't you unpack some boxes whilst I'm out?'

Rachel was gutted. She had hoped that they would unpack together, maybe drink the champagne she'd put in the fridge to celebrate. She was about to tell him so when he walked straight past her and headed for the door.

'What? Don't I even get a kiss?' she asked, folding her arms.

'Of course, you do. Hey, you're not in a mood with me, are you?' He lifted her chin. 'Cos you know I don't do sulky females.' He kissed her on the nose.

'Don't be daft, just wished you'd have said something that's all.' But she was sulking, just a bit.

'I'll make it up to you, promise.'

As he hurried out of the door, Rachel wondered what had come over him.

9

He watched the rerun of the local news for the fifth time, revelling in the coverage. He had been somewhat distracted whilst it played in the background on the previous four occasions.

Finally, he thought, glancing momentarily at the screen, someone was paying attention.

When the reporter had asked if there would be more attacks, he nearly burst out laughing.

'More attacks?' He couldn't resist a low chuckle at the innocence of the question. 'If only they knew.'

He'd seen enough for today, so he stepped away from the window and closed his computer, congratulating himself.

He couldn't believe that he had been so slow to spot his next guest. He didn't believe in coincidences; it was crazy how the universe just seemed to deliver opportunities straight into your hands if only you kept your eyes and heart open to them.

Looking in the mirror, he touched up his make-up.

His mother had loved make-up. He had never seen her without her 'war paint', as she called it. Even if she was popping to the shop or dropping him off at school, she always wore make-

up. That was the sign of a real woman, she had told him, and he believed every word. A woman who took pride in her appearance, cared what the world thought of her. Appearances were everything in his mother's book.

'If you keep yourself looking nice, it goes without saying that you keep a nice home, look after your husband. You set an example for the younger generation.'

But he'd been disappointed in the end, hadn't he? Underneath all that make-up his mother wore, she carried a dark secret.

Lying bitch whore. He felt his pulse rate increase and blood rushed to his face. He breathed deeply.

Having regained his composure, he locked the door behind him and headed out. He didn't want to be late for his meeting.

10

After yet another bedtime story, Ziggy insisted to Ben that he had to leave. They had had such a great night, his son had him in stitches with his made-up jokes that Ziggy dutifully laughed along with. As he headed down the stairs, he said a brief goodbye to Rachel and once in his car, his head had switched to work mode, but his overall mood felt lighter, less weighted down about the investigation albeit only briefly.

He missed Ben terribly and hated letting him down. He'd tried to explain to his son over pizza why he hadn't picked him up on Sunday, but he had seemed cool with it all. He had also tried to quiz him on Scott moving in, which had felt awkward, clumsy so he'd stopped, feeling guilty for putting Ben in that position. He figured it was probably natural. No man wanted someone else to raise their son. As it turned out, Ben didn't seem at all fussed and had simply shrugged his shoulders, more interested in his pizza.

After arriving home, Ziggy grabbed himself a beer and plonked himself down on his battered sofa. Music played softly in the background while he tried to unwind. He looked around the sparse living room. Yes, this room would be his next task, once he'd finished the kitchen renovations. Problem was, by the time he finished work, he was just too knackered to do anything. He felt like he spent his life working, fighting insomnia or feeling guilty for letting people down. He needed to change but didn't have a clue how. He knew he needed to phone Lolly at some point and invite her round for a meal. It was his turn to host, which meant putting up with whichever one of her friends she chose to pair him up with. Since Lolly had met Frankie and was now in a settled relationship, she seemed to think that Ziggy should do the same, despite two divorces by his mid-thirties. Being too tired to call, he dropped her a quick text promising a catch up soon. His reply was a tongue out emoji.

He laughed to himself, took a swig of his beer and as always, his thoughts turned to work. The team were making progress, albeit slowly, but they were further on than they had been this morning. The threat from Whitmore was also hanging over him like the Sword of Damocles'.

The silk scarf was a mystery. Angela had spoken to Susannah's grandparents, who confirmed what the team had suspected; they didn't own and had never owned a vintage silk scarf, confirming Ziggy's gut feeling. Which potentially left one other person: the killer. They hadn't retrieved any DNA evidence from it – the sample was just too small – but at least they had something, a starting point.

It was getting late, and Ziggy had to at least try to get some sleep, so he put his bottle in the bin and headed upstairs, wondering what tomorrow would bring.

.   .   .

Rachel heard Scott arrive home in the early hours. She had calmed down since he'd left but had taken herself off to bed by eleven thirty when he still wasn't home. She had unpacked a couple of his boxes, but there didn't seem to be much in either of them. Just a few clothes, books and toiletries. She waited for him to come upstairs, but half an hour later, he was still rattling around in the kitchen, so she threw on her dressing gown and went downstairs.

'Hey, sorry, did I wake you?' he said, as he sipped from a glass of water.

'No, I was awake anyway.' She yawned and pulled out a kitchen chair. 'Didn't think you'd be so late.'

'Yeah, well, Jon turned up. He had some ideas he wanted my input on. You know what he's like, can't make a decision on his own. Looks like there'll be more money coming my way too.'

'Oh, that's great news. Let's hope you actually see some of it this time.' She yawned again.

Scott stopped what he was doing and turned to face Rachel. 'Was that a dig?'

Rachel looked up at him, surprised at the aggression in his tone. 'No, not at all. He just always seems to be promising you the world and never delivering.'

Scott reached for the open bottle of wine in the fridge. 'You just don't understand how it works. It's not that simple,' he said dismissively.

'I work in hospitality too, remember, Scott – I know how the industry works as well.'

'Yeah, you're a part-time receptionist at the local hotel, hardly the same, is it?'

Rachel took a deep breath, furious. 'Are you joking? I've run events all over the world, I know how it works. And a cheap backstreet dive isn't exactly the height of glamour, is it?'

Scott slammed down the glass he was holding so hard that it smashed against the worktop. 'Now look what you've made me do!'

Rachel had never seen him angry before. 'Be quiet,' she hissed. 'You'll wake Ben.' Completely taken aback by this side of Scott, she found herself shaking. She waited for him to apologise.

Scott still had his back to her, and she could see his shoulders rising and falling as he breathed deeply. 'Go to bed,' he commanded.

Fuming, Rachel stood up. 'What the hell has got into you? Way to ruin our first night living together, Scott. You can sleep on the sofa,' she spat as she pulled her dressing gown tighter around her and stormed upstairs. She heard the front door slam shut and collapsed at the top of the stairs in floods of tears, anger, frustration and the sudden realisation that perhaps she'd made a big mistake.

11

Friday, 7 June

Claire tucked Zoe into bed after reading her a bedtime story. She was tired herself. Working full time at the salon and having a toddler was demanding and hard work, but she wouldn't change it for the world. Her boyfriend, Lee, was so supportive, and though they were both only in their early twenties, they had a solid relationship. He had started a new job that meant he worked from four until ten in the evenings, but it also meant that he could be at home during the day with Zoe. Checking her little girl was safely tucked up, she switched on the night light and headed downstairs.

It was the end of the week, and she was looking forward to having a glass of wine and some quiet time to herself. She was still reeling from the loss of Susannah and talking to the detectives had been stressful. As far as she could work out, she had been the last person to see Susie alive. She let out a gasp as the realisation hit her again, as it had done every time she paused to think since the detectives delivered the horrific news. Could she have done something differently? What if she had invited Susie back to her house? Would she still be alive? She should have asked her why her phone had been constantly pinging with new messages as they strolled. Did they have something to do with it? And thinking about it, Susie *had* seemed on edge. All of this had been driving her crazy, and when she spoke to Lee about it, he'd told her to phone the detectives and let them know. But she was worried she would be in trouble for not saying anything to them at the time, but she had been in so much shock. She'd call them in the morning, that's what she'd do. Even if what she told them was useless, it would hopefully allow her some peace of mind.

She headed into the kitchen and opened the fridge, retrieving the bottle of chardonnay she'd bought from the local off-licence on her way home. As she reached for a glass out of the cupboard, the rear security lights came on and lit up the small back garden. She ignored it. It was probably a cat triggering one of the sensors. She kept meaning to ask Lee if the sensitivity could be adjusted.

Walking into the living room, she went to draw the full-length curtains that covered the French doors, but her eye was caught by something moving in the garden. She peered through the glass to get a closer look. Was it the neighbour's cat again?

Her heart jumped into her throat as, out of the gloom, a figure emerged. This was no cat. It was dressed all in black and was pointing right at her.

She stifled a scream, threw the curtains shut and ran back into the kitchen to grab her mobile phone from the worktop. Reaching for her mobile, heart pounding and panic setting in, she fumbled with the keypad and dropped it on the floor. *Shit.* She knelt down to pick it up and the cool night air chilled her bones. She glanced up. The back door was wide open.

Out of nowhere, a tremendous blow crashed down onto the back of her head.

The last thing she saw was the hooded figure leaning over her.

But she knew that face.

As CLAIRE STRUGGLED to open her eyes, she blinked rapidly. She had no idea where she was. The thumping in her head was debilitating, and although the room was dark, it was still too bright. All she wanted to do was to close her eyes and stop the banging in her skull, but fear kept her awake. She tried to bring her hands to her face, but they were somehow fastened behind her and her feet were bound to the chair that she was trapped in. She jerked violently, hoping to loosen the ties. The rope rubbed angrily against her wrists and ankles, nipping at her skin.

Her next coherent thought was for her Zoe. She feebly called her name. Was she in here with her, wherever here was? She tried to shout again, but her throat was so dry. She needed water. Reaching into the depths of her soul, she summoned the strength to scream, furthering irritating her throat. She started coughing, tears and snot streaming down her face. Where the hell was she? As her sobs turned into choking hiccups, she heard a noise from her left-hand side. She turned her head and saw a hooded figure approaching her.

It took a minute or two for her eyes to adjust. 'Help me,' she croaked. 'Please help me.'

The tall figure walked over and squatted down in front

of her. He raised a plastic cup to her lips, and she gratefully took a sip.

'Where am I?' she asked him tearfully. He was wearing stage make-up, which had been badly applied but she still knew who he was.

'Why are you doing this?'

There was no answer. He stood up and walked away towards the door.

'No, please. Don't leave me here. Where's my daughter?' she begged, terrified that he would leave her and not come back.

The figure turned and raised a black gloved hand, before placing his index finger against his lips in a shushing gesture.

'I know who you are!' she screamed, before collapsing exhausted against her bindings in hysterical sobs.

HE CLIMBED THE STAIRS, *laughing. They always started out like this. He knew that given time she would calm down eventually. There was no rush. No one would find her. He was patient. He would bide his time. He'd had plenty of practice, and ultimately, the rewards were worth it.*

12

Saturday, 8 June

'What's going on?' asked Angela as she re-joined the team after spending the last two hours trawling through CCTV frustratingly with nothing to show as a result. She could think of better ways to spend her Saturday morning.

Sadie was furiously tapping away at her keyboard. 'Briefing in ten minutes. One of Susannah Leibniz's work colleagues, Claire Foster, has been reporting missing.'

Angela stared at Sadie, feeling her stomach take a dive. 'What? No way. When?' she asked, sitting at the workstation next to Sadie and logging into the system.

'Late last night. Boyfriend returned home, and Claire was nowhere to be seen. Little girl was asleep upstairs in her bed.'

'The little one was left on her own? Was she hurt?'

'No, it doesn't seem so, but she was left in bed. That's why the boyfriend called – apparently, she'd never abandon her daughter like that. Ziggy's due in any minute. He's just updating Whitmore.'

As Sadie spoke, Ziggy strode into the office, an urgency to his step.

'Everyone here?' he asked, looking around.

'Think so – Nick is just getting the coffees,' Angela responded.

Ziggy nodded and waited at the front of the room for everyone to pull their seats forward.

'Right, as you may have heard, Claire Foster, colleague of Susannah Leibniz – our first murder victim – has been missing since approximately eleven p.m. yesterday evening. Her boyfriend, Lee Chadwick, returned home late last night and found the back door open and their little girl Zoe upstairs asleep but no sign of Claire. He's said that there was no way she would leave her daughter on her own, and that the back door was usually kept locked.'

There were murmurs around the room as the team digested the information.

Ziggy continued. 'SOCOs are at the house. Missing Persons are dealing with it initially, and it's being treated as high priority due to Claire's connection with our first victim. House-to-house enquiries have started. DC Dove, can you liaise with MisPers, please?'

Angela nodded her acknowledgement; she'd worked with the Missing Persons team previously.

'Nick, Sadie, I need you to speak with the boyfriend. He's currently at the next-door neighbours in Holbeck, here's the address.' Ziggy passed it over to Nick. 'I believe the grand-parents have taken the little girl who, thankfully, slept through everything and is unharmed. Bring the boyfriend to the station if you think it will help.' He paused and looked at the faces of the team. 'I'm know, like me you want Claire found and returned to her family, so we need to move fast on this one. We can't rule out the possibility that the disappearance of Claire isn't unconnected to Susannah.'

IT WASN'T difficult to spot the house shared by Lee Chadwick and Claire Foster. Liveried SOCO vans were parked on the street, and two police cars were on the drive. Nick and Sadie acknowledged the team that were working in the front garden as they headed up the path to next door. Nick knocked and pulled out his ID, ready to show whoever answered. It was opened by a nervous-looking young man. The poor bloke was clearly stressed and hadn't had much sleep.

'Lee Chadwick?' asked Sadie, also showing her ID.

'Yes, are you the police? Come in, come in.' He moved to one side and let the two officer's past, directing them into the living room. Lee's elderly neighbour offered them a cup of tea, which was gratefully accepted.

As they each settled into their seats, Sadie opened her notebook and looked at Lee before asking, 'Lee, we're just here to ask a few questions about Claire's disappearance.'

Lee nodded. 'Yes, yes, of course, that's fine. Anything.'

'Can you just run me through exactly what happened when you got back to the house yesterday evening?'

Lee was wringing his hands anxiously. 'Erm, I got home from the pub at about eleven and let myself in the front door.'

'So, the front door was locked?'

'Yes, I dropped my keys, so I remember it clearly. When I opened the front door, I heard the back door slam shut, which it does if they're open at the same time because of the through-draught. I thought that was odd, as I imagined

Claire would be in bed – she'd had a rough week, what with Susannah and everything.' He looked up at Sadie and glanced across at Nick. 'Oh God, you don't think Claire's disappearance is related to that, do you?' His eyes filled with tears, and he wiped his nose across his sleeve before holding his head in his hands. 'She wouldn't have left the little one on her own. Zoe was her world.'

Sadie sat forward, feeling sorry for the young lad. Although they couldn't rule it out, she didn't want him jumping to conclusions about Claire's disappearance. 'I'm sorry, Lee. I know this is hard, but we really need to understand what happened, and you're our best lead so far.'

Lee sighed heavily and sat up. 'I'm sorry, it's just not like Claire to disappear. I really can't stress that enough.' His eyes bored into them both, reinforcing his words.

'It's OK, Lee, we understand. Let's pick up where you left off. The back door slammed, then what?'

'I headed straight into the kitchen. I saw Claire's mobile phone on the floor and then opened the back door, thinking maybe she'd gone outside for some reason. I shouted her name and walked forward so the outside lights came on but there was no sign of her.'

'Did you see anything in the garden that had been disturbed? Any broken glass, fences, plant pots and such?'

'I didn't really take it in. My next thought was for Zoe, so I ran upstairs and headed into her bedroom. She was fast asleep, thankfully.' He spoke haltingly and rubbed his eyes with the heels of his palms. 'Sorry, I'm just...'

'Lee, there's no need to apologise,' said Nick, who'd been sitting back, watching Lee's body language. 'It's a scary time, we completely understand.'

They all paused and took a sip of their tea. Sadie replaced her cup on the coffee table and adjusted her position. She knew the next line of questioning would trigger more emotional reactions.

'Once you'd checked on Zoe, what did you do then?'

'I rang her parents, they only live down the road but it was quicker to call them. I even wondered if she might have had some kind of breakdown. I don't know, I just couldn't understand it. Her mum and dad said they hadn't seen her and that I should phone the police. Just them saying that made me feel sick. I've never had owt to do with the police before.'

Sadie's heart went out to him. She could see he was heartbroken, and she softened her tone. 'Lee, I'm sure you understand but we need to ask these questions. What was your relationship like with Claire?'

He smiled for the first time; it was weak, but it was there. 'Brilliant. We got together when we were still at school, but we're a team, you know? Zoe was an unexpected but very welcome surprise; we both adore her, and Claire is a great mum. I lost my job a few months ago but Claire picked up extra hours at the salon and did some freelance work to help us out. That's what we do, we work it out. I've just started a new job – mail sorting for Royal Mail. It's boring but good pay and working the late shift means I can be at home with Zoe, so it saves on childcare.'

Sadie was impressed. For someone so young, he had a very sensible head on his shoulders. 'What do you class as the late shift?'

'I work between four in the afternoon until ten in the evening, seven days a week.'

'And where were you last night if you didn't get home until eleven?' asked Nick.

'I went for a pint with some of the lads. It was payday

and Claire wanted an early night, so I said I'd be home about eleven.'

'And your mates, they can vouch for that, can they?'

'Yes, of course. I can give you their numbers.'

'We'll get them off you in a second. Let's just finish off here first,' said Nick. 'Do you or Claire drive or own a car?'

'No. We can both drive, but we're saving up for a cheap run-around for when Zoe starts school.'

'How do you get around then? Bus, is it?'

'Yeah, Claire gets the free bus to the high street, and I either cadge a lift off one of the lads I work with or I bus it too.'

Sadie glanced at Nick, and they silently agreed that they had all the information they needed. Sadie stood up. 'Can you get those contact numbers for us please, Lee?'

'Yeah, they're on my phone.'

He started scrolling through his contacts when Nick cut in. 'You said Claire's phone was on the floor. Did you pick it up?'

'I picked it up once I'd checked on Zoe to see if she had made any calls, but the screen was smashed. I think those guys next door have it. That's another thing, Claire wouldn't go anywhere without her phone.'

'OK, thank you, that's great.' Sadie took a note of the phone numbers for Lee's alibis before concluding the interview. 'Thanks again, Lee. A family liaison officer will be in touch, and they'll keep you in the loop as we progress, but if you think of anything at all, here's my card. Just give me a call, my mobile number is on there too.'

'Thank you, please find her. My little girl needs her mummy.' The man collapsed into himself onto the sofa and began to sob.

Nick and Sadie turned and left, both of them feeling the anguish that appeared to choke Lee's whole body.

Once they were in the car, Sadie said, 'Poor lad. I don't think he's involved, Nick, do you?'

'If he is, then he's the best actor in the world. I've never seen anyone so cut up. He's clearly very much in love with her,' commented Nick, pulling the car out of the street.

'I know, right? So level-headed for such a young couple. I'm not sure I was that mature at that age.'

Nick laughed. 'I imagine that when you were that age, you were a needy PC desperate for promotion.'

Sadie laughed with him. 'True.'

WHEN NICK and Sadie returned from visiting Claire Foster's boyfriend, they were surprised to see DCS Whitmore follow them in onto the Major Investigations floor. It was rare to see him in the station on a weekend, so it wasn't any wonder the two detectives looked at each other questioningly as they held the door for him. Trying to delay his inevitable conversation with his senior officer for as long as possible, Ziggy turned to Nick and Sadie, leaving Angela to finish off updating the new board for Claire Foster. 'How did it go?' he asked.

'Yeah, didn't add much more than we already know,' Nick answered, 'but my feeling, our feeling, is that he isn't involved. Plus, he's got an alibi – was down the pub with his mates. He's given us the names of the people he was with and I contacted them while we were on our way back. They can all vouch for him being at the Coach and Horses between the times in question. One of his friends dropped him off at home but they didn't see anything.'

'Damn. Right, anything else?' asked Ziggy.

'SOCO have Claire's mobile and have handed it over to the techies. Let's see what they can retrieve,' said Sadie.

'Great, thanks. An update on where we are with Susannah. A couple of things came in while you were out. The pub over the road from Woodhouse Moor finally sent their CCTV so Angela has an update on that. We've been looking at the times Susannah went for a walk with Claire on the Thursday, and, of course, to see if anything shows up in the previous twenty-four hours before the body was found.'

'Brill,' said Sadie.

'Yep, exactly. Angela, can you update on CCTV for Susannah?'

'Sure,' the young DC piped up eagerly. 'We've trawled through the times that Susannah and Claire walked through the park. The cameras aren't focused directly on the path they took but you can see them, along with the little girl, arriving and leaving at the times Claire told us.'

'What about the car park?' asked Nick.

'Susannah gets into a dark blue car, not a grey Fiesta. We're trying to sharpen up the image. Tech will let us know when it's done so we can get a better look. Again, not a perfect angle but it's better than nothing.'

'Fantastic, Angela, I know you've put some hours into that, so thank you. Right, let's focus here,' said Ziggy, very aware that Whitmore was still listening in. 'Angela, if you stay on MisPers and CCTV. Let's see if we can get Claire's phone data fast-tracked and let me know if anything comes up? Sadie, can we have a quick catch-up in my office in a minute?'

Sadie nodded, as if acknowledging that he'd have the fun task of speaking to Whitmore first, and went back to her desk with the rest of the team.

Ziggy went towards his office, processing the information they had so far. He really wanted a one-to-one with Sadie to get her gut feelings about where they were at. But first, he had to deal with what Whitmore wanted. No sooner had he sat down than DCS Whitmore was on him.

'Seem to be making inroads,' said the DCS, seating himself opposite Ziggy.

'Would seem so, I think the next break will come from CCTV.'

'And what about the missing girl?'

'Just waiting for SOCOs to finish at the scene and update. We need to get the data from Claire's mobile as soon as, too. That could hold some key info.'

'Yes, I agree,' said Whitmore, nodding as if it had all been his idea.

'I just want an informal catch-up with DS Bates to strategise and make priorities.' He indicated to his office door as Sadie hovered nearby, hoping he'd get the hint.

'Yes, you go ahead,' said Whitmore but made no attempt to leave.

Ziggy sighed. 'Come on in, Sadie.'

Sadie grimaced and shrugged her shoulders behind the DCS's back before moving closer to the desk. She had to stand as Ziggy only had one empty chair in his office and Whitmore made no attempt to move.

Addressing his boss, Ziggy gave it one last try. 'You don't have to stay, sir, if you have other things to be getting on with. It is Saturday, after all. I can update you tomorrow.'

'No. It's fine. This is important.' Whitmore folded his hands across his substantial stomach and nodded for Ziggy to proceed.

Ziggy stood up and turned to the whiteboard behind his desk, closing his eyes and breathing deeply to quash his impatience. He picked up a marker pen and divided the board in two.

'I'd like to start by drawing up the similarities between the cases.' He turned and looked at Sadie, who was leaning awkwardly against Ziggy's desk. 'Take my seat, Sadie, it's fine.'

She did as he suggested and looked at the board again. 'There's the salon for a start. I know Susannah only rented a chair there, but it was her main source of income.'

Ziggy wrote it down and drew an arrow. He then wrote *Sheila* and drew a bubble around her name. *Freelancing – both of them.* Same again.

'What about the elusive Shaun?' questioned Sadie. 'I mean I know it's a bit vague, but we don't have anything from Tech yet, so it has to be a possibility.'

The pair spent the next hour going over everything that they knew so far and by the time they had finished, the board was a cluster of multicoloured bubbles and arrows. They agreed on the priority actions going forward, and Sadie's to-do list had grown exponentially.

Whitmore had been unusually quiet throughout, and now they had finished, Ziggy and Sadie were waiting for him to say something.

'Very good, very good.' Whitmore stood up, filling the cramped space even further. 'No suspects as yet though. I have to say, DI Thornes, I would have expected arrests by now – it's been a week after all.' Ziggy was about to answer but Whitmore waved him away. 'No, no. No need to say anything, I can see you're up against it, but you should know that there is pressure from above.'

'As you say, sir, it's been a week, but our perpetrator is clearly forensically aware so...'

Whitmore sighed, adjusted his position and opened his

jacket. 'I'm trying to keep the Gods from up high off your back, Andrew. They want to bring in a team from an outside murder squad. Your ability to handle such a high-profile case is being brought into question.'

Sadie and Ziggy looked at each other, not quite believing what had just been said. Sadie clearly deciding it was time to take her leave, started to edge closer to the door, but Ziggy stopped her, gently pulling her back in the room with a look. *Oh no, you don't,* he thought.

Ziggy spoke through gritted teeth, barely able to hold back his annoyance. 'Really, sir? Well, that would be a disappointment.' Ziggy was silently seething. His team had an excellent prosecution rate and were often held as an example for the rest of the county.

'I know you're annoyed, Andrew. I get it. I've put them off for now, but I can't put it off for much longer. I need something concrete by the end of tomorrow.' Whitmore turned and opened the office door. 'I'll leave it with you, DI Thornes.'

13

Sunday, 9 June

Rachel had done a lot of thinking in the three days that she hadn't seen Scott. He'd texted an apology to her, which she considered pathetic, but after much soul-searching, she had finally replied. She couldn't pretend to understand why he had exploded the way he had. In truth, it had scared her. She had never seen that side of him, and she hoped never to see it again. Perhaps it had been a mistake asking him to move in, but he'd told her that the lease on his flat had expired now, and she felt just dreadful. He'd promised to come around today so they could talk, and he'd asked her not to make any hasty decisions until he'd fully explained things to her. She'd relented and decided to see what he had to say for himself.

Ziggy hadn't been able to have Ben again due to the investigation, but he had arranged to see him for a couple of hours later that afternoon, much to Ben's delight. She couldn't understand how Ben could be so forgiving, but then he was only seven years old, and his dad was his hero.

In her fury the other night, she had packed a few of Scott's belongings back into the boxes, and now she wondered whether she should put everything back in the drawers. She didn't want him to think that she had completely made her mind up about not living together, and she intended to let him stay until he could find somewhere else, but the guilt she felt was awful. She wondered if his boss, Jon, had been able to put him up for a few nights. Perhaps that was where he had been staying.

She toyed with the box she had carried into the kitchen and cut through the Sellotape. There really wasn't much to show for twenty-five years on the planet. A few pairs of jeans, a few shirts and toiletries. The rest of the boxes were vinyl LPs, old CDs and even a few cassette tapes. She hadn't really taken much notice of them, assuming they were part of his DJ set. Presumably the rest of his stuff was still at the flat or in storage.

Rachel folded his clothes for the hundredth time while she decided what to say to him. She loved him, of that she was sure, and they had such a great time together. He was loving and attentive the majority of the time, and she didn't expect that life would always be a bed of roses. It was true that he had swept her off her feet initially, and after years of loneliness whilst still married to Ziggy, it had been a welcome change.

Apart from his outburst the other night, she had noticed a couple of changes in him recently, but didn't everyone change once they were in a settled relationship? She knew that she had when she was with Ziggy, and God knows Ziggy had. Isn't that what couples did? They moulded to each other, took into account each other's mood and disposition?

She had tried so hard to make it work with Ziggy but his

passion, no, his personal mission, for solving injustice had become overwhelming. She couldn't understand why he didn't put her and Ben first. He couldn't understand why she was 'so demanding', as he had put it. She sighed and tutted to herself. If wanting to spend time with your husband was demanding, then she had her wires about relationships well and truly crossed. He'd blamed his upbringing, the loss of his parents when he was just fourteen. He'd told her that he felt abandoned and the only consistency in his life since then had been Lolly.

Rachel shook her head at the memory of meeting Lolly for the first time. She hadn't been anything like she had expected. For some reason, Rachel had pictured her as the academic type. She was a forensic pathologist, after all, and had spent more years at university than Rachel had worked full time. She'd been surprised to see that Lolly was a tiny, diminutive figure with the wildest coloured hair and an equally wild personality. Rachel had made the mistake of having a couple of raucous nights out in Leeds with her, and it had taken Rachel a week to recover. Ziggy had laughed and said that he had tried to warn her. He soon stopped laughing when Rachel told him she now knew how he had got the nickname Ziggy. She could only remember part of the story, thanks to the number of tequila shots she'd knocked back with Lolly, but it was something to do with the Spice Girls and Ziggy's crush on Mel B.

They had become good friends, the three of them regularly going out for meals together, and Lolly had been over the moon when Ben was born. She had absolutely doted on him, and Rachel knew that Ben missed crazy Aunt Lolly.

Unfortunately, their friendship had fallen by the wayside after the divorce. Rachel could understand it completely, but she did wish they had at least kept in touch.

She felt sad when she thought about all the good times they had had together. Maybe one day, she thought.

She heard the front door click open. Scott was standing there with a huge bunch of flowers and a very sheepish grin on his face.

Perhaps it was time to let go of the past and take a brave step forward into her future.

'Hey you,' she said, as he walked into the kitchen.

'Hey,' said Scott, thrusting the flowers in front of him.

They both started to speak at once.

'Look, I'm sorry—'

'Don't, it's—'

Rachel laughed, and took the flowers from him. She laid them on the worktop and took hold of his proffered hands.

'I'm sorry,' said Scott. 'I should never have spoken to you like that.'

'You're right, you shouldn't. You scared me, Scott.'

He pulled her in for a hug. 'I know, and I truly am sorry. Everything's just got to me recently. What with Jon messing me about at the club and moving in here. I guess I just let things build up.'

'And you took it out on me. Talk to me, Scott, we're supposed to be partners.' She laid her head against his chest.

'I know, I'm just not used to being able to share stuff, you know?'

They stood in silence for a few minutes, then Rachel gently pushed away. 'I can't have you being like that around Ben.'

'I messed up, Rachel. It won't happen again, and I'll make it up to you, I swear.' He kissed the top of her head.

'No need, just don't do it again.'

Rachel heard the thumping of Ben's feet coming downstairs and he appeared in the doorway. 'How long until Dad gets here?' he asked, heading for the fridge.

'Oh, is Ziggy coming around?' asked Scott.

'He shouldn't be long,' she answered, helping Ben reach the cheese. 'Yes, he's taking Ben for a couple of hours in between his shifts.' Rachel looked at Scott and for a fleeting second, she thought she saw a change in his eyes. 'Don't worry, he'll just be picking him up and leaving. He might not even come into the house.' Scott probably didn't want a repeat of the awkward exchange that had happened the last time they met.

'What? Oh no, it's cool, whatever.' Scott shrugged it off and took off the jacket he was wearing. 'I'm just going to get some stuff from my car. Back in a minute.'

SCOTT OPENED THE BOOT, hands shaking. 'Shit, shit, shit,' he said out loud. He couldn't exactly shoot off now. He'd have to play it cool. He retrieved his overnight bag and hoped Rachel hadn't changed her mind about him moving in with her. He'd pretty much emptied all the junk out of his flat, which was long overdue, and had given it a good clean. Jon had asked what he was doing, and he'd made some flimsy story about 'spring cleaning' even though it was June. He heard a car pull him behind him and turned around. It was Ziggy. His heart plummeted. *Great timing.*

'All right, mate?' he greeted Rachel's ex as he locked his car. 'How's it going?'

Ziggy looked over at Scott. 'All right. Yeah, not bad. You?'

They started walking up the path together, Scott letting Ziggy go first. Ben was bouncing excitedly on the doorstep.

'Dad! Come and see what level I'm on.' He grabbed

Ziggy's hand, and the two darted upstairs after Ziggy had said a fleeting hello to Rachel.

Scott stood in the kitchen with his bag. 'I wasn't sure on whether you still wanted to go ahead with the whole moving-in thing, so I've only brought a few bits.' He needed to calm himself down and act normal.

'It's fine. Let's wait until Ben is out of the way and we'll have a proper chat, yeah?'

She headed to the foot of the stairs and shouted Ben down.

After a couple of minutes, Ziggy was standing in the kitchen waiting for Ben to get ready.

'Going anywhere nice?' she asked.

'Just to the park, I think. I've only got a couple of hours, so...'

'How's the investigation going?' asked Scott as he made himself and Rachel a brew.

'Erm, yeah not bad.'

'Any leads or anything?' Maybe he could turn this disaster into something positive.

'A few but it's ongoing so I can't really talk about it.' Ziggy moved to the hallway and shouted up the stairs for Ben to hurry up.

'Poor girl, imagine being found like that.' Scott poured milk into the coffee. When Ziggy didn't answer, Scott carried on. 'Local girl, was she?'

'She was, yeah, I'm sure you've seen the news reports.'

'Oh yeah, we saw it yesterday. Terrible thing to happen. Any suspects yet, then?'

If Ziggy thought the questions were a bit odd, he didn't let anything slip. 'As I said, ongoing, so can't really say.'

'Fair enough.' He held a cup out for Rachel, desperately

trying to steady his shaking hand. Ziggy wouldn't notice, right?

Ben had finally tied his shoelaces, so after kissing his mum, they headed for the door. 'I'll have him back by four,' said Ziggy over his shoulder as they headed to the car.

As Rachel waved from the doorstep, Scott joined in bidding him farewell, relieved to see the back of him.

As ZIGGY PULLED AWAY from Rachel's place, he couldn't help but feel that the exchange with Scott had been a bit odd. The man was a bit weird at the best of times and it could be his instincts working overtime, but it was very rare that his gut feeling was wrong, and his gut was telling him that something about that man was very definitely off.

14

Monday, 10 June

I t was early, just gone half six, when Ziggy arrived at
the station, but he'd got past the point of sleep at
around three. No matter how much he'd tried, he
couldn't shake the interaction he'd had with Rachel's bloke
yesterday. A well-known saying in the police force is to trust
your gut, and Ziggy's instinct was telling him that Scott
wasn't who he appeared to be.

During the couple of hours they'd spent together, Ben
had mentioned something about his mum crying the other
day, and that Scott hadn't been around for a few days. He
couldn't ask Rachel if everything was OK – unfortunately,
they no longer had that kind of relationship – but what he
could do was check out Scott's background. It wasn't something that was technically kosher but reasoned with himself
that for the man who was now living with his son, a search
on the Police National Computer was valid. He'd still rather
not get caught.

The one thing that bothered him was trying to find Scott's surname. He couldn't remember Rachel ever mentioning it – why would she? – but he could trace him by other means.

He had a busy day ahead of him, and a full briefing at eight thirty. He swiped into the building, then headed upstairs to the incident room. There was something he liked about getting into the office ahead of his team. The relative quietness, and stillness that, although temporary, was somehow reassuring. He spent so much time in the place that it truly felt more like home than his actual house.

He opened his office door and placed the bag he was carrying on the desk. With Whitmore's ominous warning over the weekend, Ziggy was utterly determined to make a breakthrough, and had brought a change of shirt and shaving gear with him, ready for the long haul. His professional pride hated the thought of the investigation being taken over, but he was also aware that they needed to bring closure for the family, so if that's what it took – but he wanted a last crack of the whip first.

He headed to the kitchen and filled the kettle before taking his mug from the dishwasher. It had been a present from Lolly years ago and some of the writing had faded, but he wouldn't use any other. Filling his mug, he headed back into the main room and took a look at the board. When he'd left yesterday evening, they were still trawling through CCTV. The morale of the team had been low, so he'd sent everyone home, letting them replenish their reserves before tackling it all again the following morning.

Returning to his workstation, he logged into the computer and accessed the PNC. Using various search terms and calling in a few favours - namely payroll at the tax office - he finally found what he was looking for. His instinct had been right, Scott Ball had an extensive criminal record. Ziggy couldn't believe what he was reading. He doubted Rachel knew any of the information that he'd had uncovered but he needed to let her know. She wouldn't be pleased he'd run a check on her new man, but when she heard what he'd discovered, he doubted she'd be mad at him for long. He printed out the sheets of paper and folded them into his inside jacket pocket. He'd have a more detailed look later, but right now he had to prepare for the team briefing.

At 8 a.m., Sadie breezed into the office and spotted Ziggy working away at his desk.

'Morning, boss, you all right?' she asked, leaning against the door jamb.

'Hiya, Sadie, yeah not bad. You?' He stood up and they headed to the front of the room.

'Yeah, I'm great thanks. Good night's sleep and I've already been to the gym, so I'm feeling good.' She was practically bouncing with energy. He had a lot of admiration for his partner; no matter what was thrown at her, she always seemed to be in a great mood.

'Wow go you. You're going to need that energy this week, I think.'

'We must get a breakthrough soon, surely.' She folded her arms and studied the notes on the board. 'Anything overnight?'

'Thought you'd never ask. I've managed to chase Tech this morning about Claire's phone data, but more importantly, we've had a bit of breakthrough on the car that Susannah was seen getting into. They managed to sharpen the image, and it's been identified as a BMW so that definitely rules out granddad's car.'

'Woah, that's great news.'

'Potentially. I think it would be a good idea during the briefing to run through the timeline for Susannah. I know the family are desperate for updates, so it's vital we ask if they know anyone with a BMW?' Ziggy was pointing at the board as he spoke.

'Sure, Angela has been keeping them up to date, I believe.'

As he spoke, Nick and Angela walked into the room.

'Talking about me?' asked Angela as she placed her bag on her desk.

'Morning. Yes, we were just wondering if you could ask Susannah's grandparents if they know anyone who owns a BMW but I'm getting ahead of myself. Let me update you all at once in the briefing.' Ziggy asked.

Nick joined them. 'Where are we up to?'

'Morning Nick, just saying let's get all our updates together and I'll go through it all at once. Ang, before I forget, I've chased Tech for the mobile data on Claire's phone.'

'No worries.'

'Sadie, have you got a minute?' asked Ziggy, walking towards his office.

'Sure, what's up?' She followed him.

Ziggy closed the door. Sadie took a deep breath, obviously wondering if she was about to get a dressing down. Ziggy saw her face change and laughed.

'It's fine, you're not in trouble.' He sat down and Sadie took the chair opposite.

'Thank God, couldn't work out what I'd done.' She breathed an audible sigh of relief.

'It's a bit personal and I'd like your opinion.' He unfolded the charge sheet from his pocket. 'Take a look at this.'

She reached across and quickly glanced through it. She flicked through the rest of the five – yes, *five* – pages. 'Dodgy as fuck, who is it?'

'My ex-wife's new boyfriend.'

'What? Rachel? Does she know any of this?'

'No, at least I don't think so. Should I tell her, do you think?' It was a rhetorical question.

'Yes. God, I can't believe you're even asking me that. You have a duty to tell her, I would say. How did you get hold of it?'

Ziggy avoided answering her direct question knowing she would raise her eyebrows at him, 'I did it first thing.'

'Has something happened?'

'No, well not that I know of.' He updated Sadie on Scott's strange behaviour yesterday.

'Maybe he's just nervous, knowing he'd got all this in his past and you being a copper?'

'Maybe, but I don't want him round my son, that's for sure.'

'Absolutely. She needs to know.'

Ziggy took the papers from her and folded them back into his pocket. 'Thanks, Sadie. Just wanted to sense check it with someone.'

'Anytime, and look if you think it might be awkward, I can always tell her, make some shit up about him being pulled for speeding or something.'

'No, I can't ask you to do that – on the record, anyway.'

'Let me know, Ziggy, whatever's best for you and Ben.'

They left the office, and joined everyone who'd gathered by the incident boards, waiting for updates and actions.

Ziggy perched on the edge of the desk. 'I just want to cover off where we are, first, with Susannah Leibniz's murder, and then we'll review where we are with Claire Foster's disappearance.'

There were nods around the room.

'Right, so Susannah's body was discovered on Saturday the first of June, ten days ago. Post-mortem tells us that she had been dead for around twelve hours. Her grandparents, who she lived with, hadn't seen her for the four weeks in the lead-up to her death, believing she was with her family in Germany, but according to the airline she never checked in at the airport. CCTV shows nothing of Susannah, apart from her heading into Departures then she disappears. The next sighting is by Claire Foster when they met for a walk on Thursday the thirtieth of May.' As Ziggy spoke, he moved along the board, creating a timeline. 'The last time Claire saw her, she was getting into the passenger side of a car. We now know that it wasn't the car Susannah usually drove, but a dark blue BMW. We're still waiting on Tech for the details.'

Ziggy stopped and looked at the team. He saw a bank of curious faces in front of him. 'Does anyone have anything to add?'

Nick spoke. 'What about the scarf found at the scene? Is it worth tracking it down?'

Angela jumped in. 'I've tried, and I've passed it over to the research team, but I doubt anything will come of it. Even though it's an original, it could have come from anywhere.'

Nick nodded. 'What about the mention of a boyfriend, Shaun or something?'

Sadie spoke. 'He seems to be elusive. There's no mention of anyone with that name in Susannah's diary and Claire didn't know a surname, so another dead end, I'm afraid.'

'So, our priorities as far as this case is concerned are tracking down that car, and trying, if we can, to uncover where the hell she was in the weeks leading up to her unfortunate murder.' Everyone agreed and waited for Ziggy to continue.

'Now, onto Claire Foster. Claire worked with Susannah and they were also good friends. Her boyfriend returned from the pub on Friday the eighth of June and found their daughter on her own and Claire missing. He called round a few people then contacted the local police. We do not believe him to be a suspect as he has a solid alibi. No one has seen or heard of Claire since. Missing Persons have so far progressed the inquiry through the usual routes with Angela as their point of contact here. Claire's mobile was recovered and we're waiting for Tech to get the data to us. Claire's family are, understandably upset and desperate to find her. They've worked with local units to organise searches and posters, and SOCO are going through the house with a fine-tooth comb.' He paused. 'We cannot rule out that Claire's disappearance could be linked to Susannah's. Claire's parents are willing to do a TV appeal, so I'll speak with DCS Whitmore and the media team about that.

'Right, I think that should be enough to keep us going. I'm heading upstairs to update Whitmore. Keep going, team – we're so close to a breakthrough. The families are truly appreciative of your work, as am I.'

ZIGGY BRACED himself before tapping on Whitmore's door. He waited for the shout to enter, then stepped into the lion's den.

'Ah, Andrew. Where are we with everything? What happened to the update I was due yesterday?'

'Sorry sir, time ran away with us. We have several active lines of enquiry and we really are making progress. I was waiting for Tech to update on a couple of things before filing my report so you have the full picture so to speak. We're very close to a breakthrough, I can feel it.' Ziggy hoped his upbeat tone would portray an optimism he didn't feel.

'What about the missing girl? I believe the parents want to do a TV appeal – what are your thoughts?'

'I don't think it would do any harm, sir; it might just bring the kidnapper out of hiding.'

'Do *you* think the two cases are related?'

'I have a feeling they are, but we need to make sure Claire's disappearance ends in a positive result. Problem is, the perp is unknown to us so far. I'm really hoping that Tech will come up with something.'

Whitmore nodded. 'I can't delay the bosses for much longer Andrew. You must keep me updated with even the smallest detail.'

Ziggy assured him he would and eased out of the door, grateful that he'd gotten away with a slight harsh word and not a raking he'd been expecting. Sadie appeared at the end of the corridor.

'Boss, you need to come and see this.' She breathed heavily, as if she'd been running.

Ziggy picked up his pace and followed her back to the incident room. The atmosphere was tangible. 'What's going on?'

Angela waved him over to her workstation. 'We've got a partial number plate for the BMW.'

'Really? Let me see.' He leaned in and took over Angela's mouse. The rough image that had been captured had been sharpened up and though it still wasn't great, you could make out the first part. *X596*.

'It's an X reg, which puts it as two to three years old, five series,' said Nick as brought up an image of a similar car. Ziggy glanced at the picture.

'Right, that should be enough to start with. Great work, team. Let's hit the ANPR camera's and trawl CCTV. Check in with the local policing team too, see if it's familiar to them.' Ziggy felt jubilance and relief in equal measure.

15

Three days had passed and still no news. Oh, he'd read the missing-persons reports, no clues, blah blah blah... Boring.

He adjusted his dress and heard the static crackle as the silk rubbed against his nylon tights. He needed to buy some kind of underskirt, one of the pretty ones like his mother had worn. He searched through the chest of drawers, but there wasn't anything there anymore.

He piped some music through the speakers and swayed slowly to the rhythm, as he drifted away in his mind. The silk slid against his torso and he gently wrapped his arms around himself. He moved his feet and waltzed around the room. He caught a glimpse of himself in the full-length mirror and stopped to admire what he saw.

The silver sandals that encased his feet twinkled under the lights, the red silk dress floated around his legs, and clung to his hips. The fitted bodice was snug against his chest, the faux diamond pendant hanging down, grazing his breast bone. Gently touching his fully made-up face, he stroked his cheeks and then flamboyantly pushed the hair from the chestnut wig away from his eyes.

He forgot his lingering disappointment momentarily and admired his reflection. He smiled, slowly raising the corners of his mouth but not showing his teeth – he hated his teeth. He accentuated his lips to compensate, drawing a cupid's bow and filling it in with bright red lipstick.

Turning from the mirror, he noticed the time. He needed to change and get ready; places to be, people to do.

16

'So, as you can see, ANPR picks up the BMW on thirtieth of May. We can follow the car from Woodhouse Moor, and through Hyde Park, along the A58 and out through the A61 onto the dual carriageway towards Harrogate. Unfortunately, we lose it as it heads towards Harewood and starts to take local roads.' Nick moved his highlighter from the screen, swivelled round in his chair and looked at Ziggy.

'Interesting. Can we pick it up with North Yorkshire traffic?' He asked.

'They're already on it.'

'Excellent. Sadie, have you found anything on the number plate?'

'Just working through it now. Should have an answer within the next thirty minutes.' Sadie turned around and answered the phone that was ringing on her desk. Ziggy walked over to see if Angela had managed to uncover anything else when Sadie shouted him back. 'Boss!'

She had the phone hooked under her chin whilst she

furiously made notes on the pad next to her. 'Yep, sure... No problem and thank you for letting us know.'

'Go on,' asked Ziggy.

'Landlord from the Woodhouse Moor pub. One of his staff has found a bag of clothes in one of the industrial bins.' She ripped the piece of paper from her desk pad and handed it to Ziggy. 'It might be nothing, but he felt he should call it in with everything that's happened.'

'Fantastic. Has he touched it?'

'I told him not to. He said he'd moved it but stopped when he realised what it was.' Sadie put her hands on her hips. 'Shall we take a look?'

'You head over. Take Nick with you and update me when you know more.'

Nick and Sadie left the office, and Angela and Ziggy sat at adjoining workstations. He needed to find the owner of that BMW.

'I WOULDN'T HAVE NOTICED it if it wasn't for the colour,' said the landlord as he showed Nick and Sadie to the rear of the building.

'Colour? What do you mean?' Sadie was pulling on protective gloves as she spoke.

'Well, we only use white bin bags in this one for dry waste. This bag's black, so it stood out. I thought one of the staff had screwed up, so I picked it up to move it when a shoe fell out.' He lifted the huge lid of the industrial waste bin. Nick and Sadie peered in. The bag was so full it was bursting at the seams. Nick, being the taller of the two reached over and pulled the bag out, being careful not to touch it any more than he needed to. He placed it on the clean piece of cardboard Sadie had laid on the floor and opened it. Sadie squatted down beside him, and they slowly lifted some of the garments out.

'Definitely female.' Mused Nick as he pulled out a pair of French knickers.

'Look, there's a handbag.' Sadie pointed into the bin liner. She reached in, again being super careful and lifted out a brown leather bag. Using her gloved finger, she undid the clasp and lifted the flap. It was empty apart from a bus pass at the bottom. Sadie pulled it out and read the name. 'Susannah Leibniz.'

Using his radio, Nick called into control and asked for Forensics to be alerted while Sadie rang Ziggy.

'The clothes belong to Susannah. Forensics are on their way; we'll stay here until they arrive and take over.' She could hardly keep the excitement from her voice.

'Wow, I'll speak to Whitmore and get it prioritised. Thanks Sadie, let me know when you're on your way back.'

'Will do.'

ZIGGY ENDED the call and punched the air. Finally, the investigation was moving forward. He felt the boost of adrenaline surge through his veins and reinvigorate him. He relayed the news to Angela and the admin team, all of whom were equally as excited. He went into his office and rang Whitmore.

'Yes, sir, we need to make it a priority.' Whitmore, thankfully, agreed and said that he would do what he could.

Striding back out into the incident room, he re-joined Angela tracking down the BMW.

Ziggy's patience was close to snapping. His screen looked like something akin to NASA space control. Technology was not his strong point. 'This is impossible. How do I just create a list of registered owners?'

Angela smiled and leaned over to his keyboard. 'Here, let me do it.'

'Thanks.' As he waited, Ziggy looked at the whiteboards again. He rang Sadie.

'Any updates?' he asked.

'Forensics have arrived, we're just handing over,' said Sadie. 'They've already checked the bin liner for prints and it's full of them.'

'Great stuff. Whitmore's having a word, so they'll be expedited. We've whittled down the list for the BMW too. Are you heading back now?'

'Yep, unless there's anything else?'

'Head back here, let's have a round-up.'

'On it, boss. We'll set off now.'

ZIGGY WAS PACING the floor when Nick and Sadie returned. Patience wasn't his strong point, and he found he couldn't sit still for more than two minutes. Angela had sorted the names of BMW owners out for him, and one name had jumped right out at him.

'Well, well, well. Scott Ball. What have you been up to?' He strode over to Sadie, who was comparing notes with Nick. 'Look who's here.' He pointed out Scott's name.

'Bloody hell. You don't think...'

'I don't think anything right now, but I want him, and his car checked out.' He had already started to put his jacket on. He reached for his mobile phone and dialled Rachel's number.

'Ziggy?' she answered.

'Hi, is Scott with you?'

'Scott? No why?'

'No reason. Do you happen to know where he is?'

'He had to go to the club for some reason, why?'

'I'll explain later. Where's the club again?'

'Ziggy, will you tell me what's going on?'

'I will, but I need you to tell me where the club is first.'

'It's Sweet FAs in Hyde Park, but why?'

'Rachel, I want you to listen to me.' He walked out of hearing shot of anyone else. 'If Scott comes back, or if you hear from him, then call 999 immediately.'

'What the hell...?'

'Look I can't fully explain now but I promise I will.' He ended the call to stop her from asking any more questions. Sadie and Nick were waiting for him.

'Right, he's at the club – Sweet FAs in Hyde Park. Anyone know where that is?'

'Yeah,' said Nick. 'It's on the corner, opposite Sainsbury's.'

'Right, you and Sadie head over there and check out his car and where he was when Susannah was last seen. If it is his car, I want to know why the hell our murder victim was seen getting into it.'

'Why aren't you coming?' asked Nick, clearly confused about why the Deputy SIO wasn't questioning their only potential suspect.

'Unfortunately, I know him. He's the boyfriend of my ex, so I'll attend with you and hang back, but I think it's better if you make the request, and possible arrest if he gets difficult. I'm not sure how he'd react if he saw me,' He shook his head and raised his shoulders. Nick still looked puzzled. 'Don't ask, Sadie will explain it all in the car.'

. . .

FOLLOWING ZIGGY'S ORDERS, they all headed for the car park and went their separate ways. Ziggy followed them, staying close to their unmarked car, and pulled up behind the rear of the club. It wasn't immediately obvious how you entered the place. Nick assumed trashy neon signs lit up the place at night, but during the day it looked like any other drab prefab building. They eventually found the staff entrance, and sure enough, parked next to it was a dark blue BMW with the registration number that belonged to Scott Ball.

Nick banged on the door, and they waited a few minutes, but there was no response. Nick banged on the rear door again, and this time they heard a clunk as a fire exit door handle was pushed down.

A tall, dark-haired man in his mid-twenties stood in front of them, looking like he had just woken up.

'Scott Ball?' asked Nick.

The young man rubbed his face. 'Yeah, what's all this about?'

'Can we come in?'

The man looked at Nick as though he'd suggested the moon was made of cheese. 'Inside here?' he asked, screwing his face up.

Ziggy had waited in the car further down the street, to wait to see if Scott would answer. When Nick glanced over his shoulder, he nodded at him. *Yep, that was him.*

'Scott, isn't it?' Sadie asked pleasantly, pushing him backwards, less pleasantly, and walking down the corridor that led through to the bar. Scott turned and followed her, still acting dazed and confused.

'Yeah, I'm Scott. What's going on?'

Nick approached him and patted him on the shoulder. 'Just need to ask you a few questions, fella, nothing to worry about.'

He escorted Scott over to one of the seated booths in front of the bar. 'It's not bad in here, you worked here long?' he asked looking around him. It was a dump, but Nick wanted to get off on the right foot with Scott.

'Erm, just over a year.'

'Own it, do you?'

'No. If it's the owner you want, then you'll need to come back tonight.'

Sadie joined them, and Scott had to move over to let her sit on the end. 'No, it's you we would like a chat with. We're wondering if you could help us with our enquiries.'

'What enquiries?' Scott shifted in his seat, shrinking backwards.

'Susannah Leibniz. Did you know her?' asked Sadie, cutting straight to the chase.

Scott stared at her and hesitated before answering. 'Erm. Not sure.'

'OK, let's try a question you might know the answer to. Where were you last Thursday, the thirtieth of May?'

Scott swallowed and looked skywards. 'I'd have been working.'

'During the day?' asked Nick.

'Oh right, then probably not. I would probably have been here, probably.'

Nick noticed sweat breaking out on Scott's upper lip. 'That's a lot of *probably*s.'

'Well, it was a week ago, I can't really remember.' His voice went up a notch at the end.

Nick decided to change tactic. 'Is that your BMW that's parked outside, Scott?'

Scott's face went visibly pale. 'Erm, yeah. Why?'

'Scott, your BMW was seen in the vicinity of Woodhouse Moor at around the time that Susannah Leibniz – the murdered woman found in the same place in the early hours of Saturday the first of June – was last seen.'

Scott was fidgeting. He wiped his top lip and saw the sweat on the back of his hand. 'Right. That doesn't mean I know her.'

'No, you're right,' said Nick. 'But she was seen getting into your car.'

Scott swallowed. 'I... but...'

'Struggling to explain that?' asked Sadie, as they bounced the questions between them.

'No, I... I mean I might have known her.'

'Ah right. So, you did know her?'

'I might have seen her around the club occasionally.' He was being extremely evasive.

'OK. Scott, based on what you've told us, I think we should continue this down at the station, if you're willing to assist us with our enquiries, that is?' continued Sadie.

'What, now?'

'That would be ideal. Do you have some shoes you could put on?' Nick and Sadie looked down at Scott's bare feet. Bare feet, at work? They'd have to bring that up later.

'Yeah, they're upstairs. I'll go get them.' He stood up, and Sadie moved out to let him get passed.

Nick exited the booth from the other side. 'I'll come with you,' he said to Scott, following him into what looked like a store room.

ZIGGY SAT ANXIOUSLY WAITING in the car. What was he saying? What was going on? What was taking them so long? Just as his patience was wearing too thin, Sadie appeared at the back door and he got out of his car.

'What's happening?' he asked.

'Yeah, he tried to tell us he didn't know her but slipped up when we said she'd been seen getting into his car. He's just getting some shoes on.'

'Shoes?' queried Ziggy.

'Yeah, weird, right? Why would he take his shoes off at work?'

'That's odd.'

'That's what I thought. Here, they're coming out.'

Ziggy ducked back into his car and reversed into the adjoining street. When Sadie, Nick and now Scott pulled off in front of him, he followed behind.

He ran several scenarios through his mind as they headed back to the station. He was convinced that Susannah's murder was linked to Claire's disappearance, and he felt as though they were pulling at a loose thread. He felt frustrated and angry that they still hadn't made the connection. He slapped the steering wheel. What was he missing?

17

Z iggy pulled back into the station car park and dashed up the stairs. Pushing open the incident-room doors, he headed straight for the white-boards. Mumbling away to himself, he followed the timeline he'd created earlier.

Scott had picked up Susannah *after* she had met with Claire on Thursday. In the following twenty-four hours, Susannah turned up dead, and now Claire was missing. Is it possible that Scott took Claire too? His eyes once again scanned the timeline. Susannah was found on Saturday morning; Claire went missing the following Saturday. *That would work*. They needed to find out his movements during the week following Susannah's discovery.

It had just turned 6 p.m., and Ziggy was waiting anxiously in the incident room for Sadie and Nick to join him. Forensics had fast-tracked the fingerprints found on the bin bag and it was covered in Scott's prints, as were the clothes found inside it. Did that mean Scott was guilty of kidnap and murder? Ziggy just didn't know. The killer had been so careful at the crime scene, leaving no fingerprints,

DNA or anything that would identify him. Leaving finger-prints all over a bag of evidence sounded foolish, a huge slip-up. Did he act rashly in a state of panic? What had made him panic? The news reports? Ziggy didn't think so. Even taking his past record into account.

Ziggy still thought that although the killer may have been disturbed at the deposition site, he could so easily have placed Susannah in the undergrowth instead of leaving her on view, which had to him meant that the killer wanted the body to be found. It screamed the need for attention.

But she had been seen getting into Scott's car. They had followed the ANPR cameras and it was clear two people were in the car, one of them being male. The dumped clothes were the key issue. Why were they covered in Scott's prints?

The doors behind Ziggy banged open, and Nick and Sadie walked in.

'Where is he?' asked Ziggy.

'In the interview room,' said Sadie. 'Anything from Forensics?'

'His fingerprints and DNA are all over it. Let me talk you through something I was trying to work out on the way back.' He explained his thinking about the timeline. 'So, he's had plenty of time to plan his next move and take Claire and hold her somewhere.'

Nick sat forward. 'What's your gut feeling?'

Ziggy sat back. 'Just been going over that in my head that it doesn't add up. Our killer was so careful at the scene. Why would he be so clumsy when dumping the clothes?'

Sadie jumped in. 'Yeah, that's what I've been thinking.'

'I think you should lead the interview, Sadie, agree, Nick?'

'Yes, for sure. I'm more than happy to watch his body

language.' It was something that had always fascinated Nick, and it never ceased to amaze Ziggy how much he picked up on just by watching how people held themselves.

'I'll view through the two-way. I think the main strategy is establishing exactly what relationship he had with Susannah, why she was in his car and exactly where they went. Let's leave out any mention of Claire for the time being – he might slip up and mention something we can use.'

Sadie and Nick nodded in agreement.

'Let's get the details of Susannah, pin him down on that. Then, I think we can reassess and decide where we go from there, agreed?'

'Sounds like a plan to me boss,' said Sadie with her usual brightness. Aside from Ziggy, she was the most highly trained interviewer on the team. If anyone could get to the bottom of it all, it was Sadie.

'Scott, I just want to remind you that you're here to help with our enquiries and you're free to leave at any time.'

Scott was sitting scrunched up with his body pushing against the side of the two-seater sofa. The soft interview room had been specifically designed to put people at ease. Primarily used for victims and their families, it resembled an everyday living room with soft furnishings and kids toys in the corner. Sadie had found it also came in useful when they wanted to put questions to a potential suspect too when they were trying the nicely-nicely approach. Less intimidating, encouraging people to talk more freely, especially at the start of the investigation.

'Are you all right there, Scott? Can we get you anything, a drink maybe?' asked Sadie as she took the armchair opposite.

Scott was nervously bouncing his left leg up and down and wringing his hands. 'I'm good, thanks. Can we just get this over with?'

Sadie took a breath as Nick opened his notebook. 'Scott, as you're aware we have CCTV evidence of Susannah Leibniz getting into your car on Thursday the thirtieth of May. Can you tell me how you knew Susannah?'

Scott leaned forward and leant on his forearms. 'I don't know her as such, I've seen her around the club.'

'The club being Sweet FAs, where you work as a DJ, I believe?'

'Yeah. We were mates, that's it.'

Sadie noted how his story was changing already. They were 'mates' now. 'How long had you known her for?'

'Not sure, a couple of months maybe?'

'And would you say you were good friends? Did you meet outside of the club?'

'Erm... Occasionally.'

'Occasionally? What does that mean?'

'We met a couple of times, for coffee and that.'

'And that day in the park. What were you doing then?'

'We were going for coffee.'

'Where did you go?'

'Some small place in Harrogate, I don't know the name. Susie knew it.'

'After you'd had your coffee? What then?'

Nick, who had been watching Scott's reactions, spotted a change in Scott's demeanour. Scott crossed his legs and sat back. He ran his hands through his hair and folded his arms. *Defensive, keeping something back.* He wondered if Sadie had spotted it too.

In response, Sadie adjusted her position. She leaned forward, closing the space between them, waiting for an answer. She'd found that silence could be a powerful tool in these situations.

It was a few minutes before Scott said anything. He was increasingly nervous, and Sadie spotted his hands shaking. He coughed. 'Is it possible to get a drink of water?'

Stalling. 'Sure.' She stood up and went over to the water fountain and filled a plastic cup. 'Here you go.' She passed him the cup and water spilled out as his shaking hand took hold of it. Sadie didn't say anything; she simply pulled a tissue out and wiped it up.

'Sorry, what was the question?'

'After your coffee, where did you go?'

'Yeah, right. We went back to my flat.'

'Your flat, where's that?'

Scott sighed. He was folding.

'It's above the club.' Scott's tone was one of resignation.

Sadie and Nick looked at each other. 'Sweet FAs?' asked Sadie.

'Yeah, I rent the space above the club from Jon – he's the owner.'

'Why did you take her back to the club?'

'Just to chill at mine for a bit.'

'To chill?'

'Yeah, you know watch a bit of TV and that.'

'Scott, are you aware that Susannah's grandparents hadn't seen her in the four weeks leading up to her body being found?'

Scott suddenly jumped up, and Nick was on his feet in a flash, hovering close by in case Scott lashed out. Scott started pacing backwards and forwards across the room, at a furious pace. 'Fuck, man, I didn't mean for any of this to happen.'

Sadie had stayed seated, though she had been taken

aback by Scott's sudden movements. It was important that she remained calm and in control.

'Didn't mean for what to happen, Scott? Come on, sit down and tell me what happened.'

He ignored her and started mumbling under his breath. Nick slowly approached him and took him gently by the shoulders.

'Come on, lad, sit down,' he said gently. He steered Scott back towards the sofa. As they both sat down, Sadie gave him a few moments to compose himself and calm down.

'It's OK, Scott. Do you want to tell me what happened?'

Scott, whose head had been hanging down, looked up, and Sadie saw tears in his eyes.

'I didn't kill her; you have to know that first.'

'OK, just tell me what you know.'

'I did know Susie, and we did meet at the club. She had been in a few times with her mates, but one night she turned up on her own. We'd chatted briefly before, so I bought her drink and she waited until I'd finished my set.' He paused and took a sip of water. 'After the club closed, I invited her upstairs. I could see she was upset and more than a bit drunk, so I didn't want to send her home in that state. She told me she didn't have anywhere to go anyway.'

Sadie frowned. She wasn't aware that there had been any falling out with her grandparents, so why wouldn't she have anywhere to go? She let Scott continue but filed that question away for later.

'So anyway, she stayed the night and things just went from there.'

'Can you remember the dates that she stayed over?'

Scott went quiet and looked down at the floor. 'It must have been the beginning of last month, whenever the bank holiday was.'

'That's quite specific.'

'We had a club night that weekend – a foam party.'

Sadie had no idea what that was, but Scott seemed certain. She glanced at the calendar on the wall behind Scott. 6 May. That would work with when her grandparents had last seen her.

'But she was seen in your car three weeks later?'

'She stayed with me.'

Interesting, I thought he was Rachel's boyfriend. 'For three weeks? Were you in a relationship with her?'

'Yes,' replied Scott, letting out a huge sigh.

'Scott, help me to understand something. You met her on the sixth of May or thereabouts, and then she stayed for three weeks? Is that right?'

'Yeah.'

Was she there of her own free will? 'She didn't leave, go home or to work?'

'No.' He shook his head. 'I don't think I should say anything else.'

Sadie paused from writing notes and looked up at him. 'OK, that's fine. We'll take a break and continue in ten minutes.'

Scott just shook his head, took a tissue from the box and blew his nose. 'I didn't kill her...'

Nick and Sadie stood up and left one of the custody officers with Scott while they headed off to join Ziggy in the viewing room. Sadie couldn't wait to see what he thought of it all.

THE THREE OF them gathered into the small room, feeling somewhat claustrophobic.

'Nick, thoughts?' he asked.

'Interesting. His body language gave a lot away. His position, initially open and leaning forward changed when Sadie started pressing him for specifics. He leant backwards, folded his arms and of course shot up out of his seat. He's clearly holding something back.'

'I agree,' said Sadie. 'He definitely started to crumble.'

'Hmm. Where do we go from here?' mused Ziggy. 'We've established the connection with Susannah. We know they went for coffee, and Angela is still tracing the car to see exactly where they went. But she stayed at his flat for three weeks? Something doesn't add up.'

'Completely agree. I think we need to search his flat. We know Susannah was there, he's given us that much, but was she there willingly?'

'Exactly,' agreed Ziggy, waving his pen. 'I'll speak to Whitmore but can't see a problem with getting a search warrant. His car needs searching too. I think the rest of the interview should take place under caution. We have enough circumstantial evidence to proceed on that basis.'

The team nodded in agreement.

'So, Sadie, let's caution him on suspicion of kidnapping until we can establish more concrete evidence and develop a link to Claire.'

'He could go no-comment?' said Sadie.

'I don't think he will, to be honest,' Nick said. 'He seemed willing to talk but only clammed up when we probed on why Susannah stayed for three weeks. I think once he realises we're serious, he'll tell us more.'

'Let's hope so,' said Ziggy.

THEY SPLIT up and Ziggy headed to Whitmore's office. He knocked on the door and waited for the bark to enter.

'Updates for you, sir.'

Whitmore looked up from his desk and removed his glasses. 'What have you got?'

'As you know, we brought Scott Ball in to help with enquiries, and based on what he has told us, I'm changing his status from potential witness to suspect and cautioning him. We need to search his flat, and also his car.'

'What evidence do we have?'

'The bag and the clothes recovered from the pub were covered in his prints. He's admitted that Susannah was in his car and also stayed with him for three weeks.'

Whitmore raised his eyebrows. 'Willingly?'

'That's what we wondered. He stopped talking when we tried to pin him down on details.'

Whitmore crossed his hands over his stomach. 'Hmm, all circumstantial, nothing to tie him to the murder. OK, let's action those searches and see if we can find anything concrete or that links him to the missing girl. We need more than circumstantial evidence.'

Ziggy cringed inwardly. *How had Whitmore got this far?* 'Sir,' he replied and turned to leave. He closed the door behind and waited until he was around the corner before noisily blowing out a deep breath.

SCOTT HAD BEEN SHOWN into Interview Room 2. Notoriously cold, and purposely sparse, its intention was to make sure there was nothing in the room to distract the suspect. There were marks and indents all over the floor, and scratches covered the walls. A metal strip ran the entire circumference of the room with warnings not to touch it. The chair that Scott was sitting on was made of metal and bolted to the floor. The Formica table he was leaning on had similar scratches to the walls. Sadie watched as he ran his hands over the bumpy surface and gouges, as if contemplating who had gone before him.

Nick was sitting on the left, and Sadie had taken the other seat, opposite Scott. Nick explained that the interview would be recorded and that he was now under caution. Scott acknowledged that he had waived his legal right to a solicitor, and Sadie proceeded.

'Scott, when we last spoke, you said that Susannah Leibniz had been staying in your flat for three weeks prior to her body being found.'

Scott's demeanour had changed since their last chat she noticed. His expression seemed closed, showing little or no emotion. She saw him give an almost imperceptible nod as she continued.

'Searches are now taking place at your home address, that of Sweet FAs Nightclub, Hyde Park, and your car has also been seized and will be forensically searched.' She waited for some reaction, but nothing was forthcoming. 'Scott, if there's anything we need to know, now would be the time to tell us.'

'I've told you everything.' He leaned back in his chair and crossed his legs underneath the table.

Sadie made a show of looking through her notes, though she knew exactly what her next question was going to be. 'You've told us that Susannah stayed at your flat for three weeks prior to her death. What I'd like to go through with you now is whether that was voluntarily on her part or if she was kept there unwillingly.'

Scott shot forward in his chair. 'What?' His eyes were wide with shock.

That's rattled him. 'You seem surprised that I ask that Scott, why?'

'I don't understand. Did you just say I forced her to stay there? Like, against her will? No way, man, no fucking way.' He slammed the table with both hands, making everyone jump.

Nick sat forward. 'Calm down, Scott.' He cautioned.

'What the actual though? What are you saying? That I killed her? I told you I didn't.'

Sadie was still taken aback with how quickly Scott had changed. Is that what had happened with Susannah?

'If there's something we need to know, Scott, tell us.'

Scott paused though he was breathing heavily. 'She was being stalked, all right.'

'Susannah was? By who?'

'I don't fucking know, do I?'

'OK, let's take a second here. So, Susannah had a stalker, yes?'

'I just said that. I don't know who he was. That night when she came to the club, she was really upset. I only know her from the club, but we have chatted a few times, flirted, that kind of thing. Anyway, that night, the one I told you about before, she asked if there was somewhere we could talk, and cos I was working I gave her the key to my flat and told her to wait there. When the club closed, I went upstairs, and she was fast asleep, so I left.'

'Where did you go?'

'I'm seeing someone, so I went back to hers.'

Sadie made a note. 'When did you go back to the flat?'

'Most days but I just let her get on with it. She didn't want to go out very often, so I was surprised when she asked me for a lift to the park. She said she had something to tell me, so I hung around and picked her up after she'd met her friend and we went for coffee. She didn't want to go anywhere local cos she thought she was being followed.'

Scott stopped and stretched his neck from side to side and cracked his knuckles. 'Anyways, while we were having coffee, she told me about this stalker bloke.'

Nick and Sadie waited patiently for Scott to continue.

'Apparently it had started a few months ago. She'd been to this wedding fair and had a chat with some bloke about a potential collaboration. They'd swapped phone numbers and then he began to bombard her with messages and calls. She changed her number but then she said he started to follow her. She was scared when she spotted him waiting opposite the bus stop outside work a couple of times.'

'Did she tell you a name, give you a description at all?' asked Sadie, intrigued.

'No, she never mentioned it. Then odd stuff started to happen. Clients started cancelling appointments or making bookings and not turning up. It was really doing Susie's head in. She couldn't tell anyone cos she couldn't prove it. She thought she was going mad.'

'But why did she want to talk to you? She had other people in her life that she was close to.'

'Cos I wasn't *involved* in her life, really. She asked if she could stay for a while in the hopes that the stalker would lose interest.'

'And she stayed for three weeks?'

'About that, yeah. I had somewhere else to stay, so it didn't really matter to me.'

'Why did you dump her stuff?'

'I panicked. I saw the news and knew how it would look so I dumped it.'

'Don't you think the better option would have been to come to the police?'

'I know that now, course I do, but at the time it was all about self-preservation. Plus, if my girlfriend found out I was cheating on her, she'd give me the boot.' For the first time, he looked genuinely remorseful.

Sadie needed a couple of seconds to wrap her head around everything Scott had just said. Thankfully her brain worked like a filing system so she could easily store and retrieve even the tiniest snippets of information.

'So, the searches that are currently taking place will show Susannah Leibniz's DNA all over your flat, and car?'

'I would have thought so. I mean I cleaned the place, but she was there so...'

'You mentioned that you were in a relationship with someone else besides Susannah?'

'Yeah.' Scott looked down at his clenched hands.

'Right, so your girlfriend can vouch for you on the nights you stayed with her rather than Susannah then?'

'I mean... if she has to, I guess. Does she have to?'

'I'm afraid so. We need to substantiate what you're telling us.'

'Oh God. She's going to go mad.'

'That's not our problem, Scott. We'll need her details.'

'Well, she shouldn't be that difficult to find. She's the ex-wife of your boss.'

'We'll still need you to write them down.'

Sadie suspended the interview and left the room, with Nick following her. Ziggy was anxiously waiting in the corridor for them.

'He claims she was there voluntarily,' stated Sadie as they moved out of earshot.

'So why was she there?' asked Ziggy.

Sadie went on to relay the latest.

'And she told him nothing about the so-called stalker? Not even a description?'

'Nope, not a thing. Just that she seemed scared and

wanted to hide until he lost interest.' Sadie shrugged her shoulders. 'It just gets more complex.'

They headed back up to the incident room whilst they talked.

'Where are we with the search?' Sadie asked.

'Nothing so far. The car has been transported to the garage and they're working on it now, but it will take a couple of hours. I've asked them to look for any blood, any ropes or restraints. They'll get back to us as soon as.'

'What about the flat?' asked Nick.

'Same. Anything obvious. They're testing for blood stains with Luminol, usual stuff. No sign or evidence of Claire Foster, unfortunately.'

They all looked at each other.

'We need to ask him about Claire,' said Sadie.

'Go back in and show him her picture, see what his reaction is.'

THE MINUTES that passed as Ziggy waited for them to return were agony. 'Well?' he said as they strode back into the incident room.

'Nothing, refused to talk and turned the image over.'

Ziggy closed his eyes and shook his head. 'How long have we got left to hold him?' he asked rhetorically, looking at the clock on the wall. It was just gone ten. Another late night. 'OK, let's keep him overnight until the searches are complete, and depending on what they find, we'll pick it up again in the morning. A night in the cells might shake things up. Not much more we can do here now. Head home everyone, back here for eight am sharp.'

18

Claire was shaking, or maybe shivering. She couldn't tell the difference any more. Periodically, she twisted her wrists, clenched and unclenched her fists in an attempt to trigger the blood flow back into her fingers. Each time, her wrists tightened the rope and pinched her already raw and bruised skin. Her legs were lashed at the ankles to the crossbars at the front of the wooden chair, and she could no longer feel her toes. The tightness she could feel in her chest was unrelenting, making her breath come out in short, gasping breaths. Her head ached, and each time she lifted it up, it felt as though her brain was freewheeling inside her skull. For long periods of time, she sat still, with her eyes closed and her chin tucked into her chest. It alleviated the pain somewhat as she slipped in and out of consciousness.

When she was awake, she was weak and confused. She had tried desperately to string together the sequence of events that had placed her here, but she would get so far and lose her thread and end up more confused. She swallowed. Her throat, raw from screaming, felt like she had hundreds of tiny shards of glass trapped down it. She was desperately in need of water. Her captor had been back on occasion, allowing her to sip water from a plastic cup, which she gratefully took despite the fact she suspected it was drugged to keep her in this woozy state.

Her thoughts scared her. She couldn't let her life end like this. She kept seeing images of Susannah in her mind's eye. Is this how her life had ended? Her captor had once called her Susannah, and she had shivered in fear, feeling physically sick. She was in no doubt that she had been taken by Susie's killer, but what she didn't know was why. She had asked him that question each time, but he never answered.

She had asked about her daughter, but he never answered.

She had told him she knew who he was. He still didn't speak.

She was lost, alone and scared beyond measure.

19

Tuesday, 11 June

Scott pulled the thin blue blanket around him. How the hell had he ended up here? He'd spent a sleepless night going over everything he had already said, trying to remember what order he had said it all in. He was cold, hungry and wanted more than anything to get out of there. He couldn't do more time inside. It had nearly broken him last time.

He thought of Rachel and wondered what she would make of it all. His past would definitely come out, and he doubted very much that she would want anything to do with him. Shame. He really liked her, and they could have had something really special. If he could just explain stuff to her, she'd see it from his point of view, surely? None of it had been his fault.

He'd have to move again, just when he thought he'd got settled. *Fuck's sake*. He was tired of moving around. He'd tried to make it work when he was in Ibiza, but look how that had panned out. Going abroad again was definitely out of the question. He could try Scotland, he supposed. He'd never been there, and it had a lively nightlife. Or Newcastle. He'd met a couple of lads from Newcastle when he was in Ibiza and had their numbers somewhere.

What was he thinking? He wanted to stay with Rachel and the little lad. Get respectable. Perhaps, deep down, he did want routine – something he'd always hated, which is why he'd never fared well in prison. Everything was so regimented. But a domestic routine. That would be different, right? A regular job, washing the family car on a Sunday morning. Going home to someone and having tea at the table. Holidays, weekends away. Maybe he wanted all that. Life was so un-fucking-fair. He thumped the wafer-thin mattress, exasperated.

Eventually, he lay back down on the cold, metal bench that passed for a bed. 'Fuck my life,' he said and turned his back to the door.

He'd just got a few moments respite when he was jerked from his sleep. 'Scott?' shouted the custody sergeant through the access panel on the door.

Scott opened one eye and turned over again.

'Breakfast.' The officer placed a tray through the door. 'Tea or coffee?'

Scott stood up and took it from him.

'Erm, coffee, please,' said Scott, shuffling back over to the bench and assessing his breakfast. He was just about to take a mouthful of scrambled egg when the door opened.

'Morning, Scott.' It was the detective from yesterday.

'Morning.' *What is she so cheerful about?*

'Back in the interview room when you've had your breakfast. Is someone bringing you a drink?'

'Yeah, a coffee.' *Ah, she's playing nice cop – whatever.*

She left the cell, and he finished his breakfast. He had

woken from his brief sleep with a new determination. He wouldn't be played for a fool.

The trackie bottoms he'd been issued were two sizes too big, so when he stood up, he had to grip them by the waist. He used the chemical toilet, washed his hands and sat back down. His coffee arrived and he was taken back to the same, draughty room as before.

'Why is it so fucking cold in here? Don't you lot pay the heating bill?' He asked his escort as he took a seat.

Receiving no answer, Scott pulled the sweatshirt sleeves down over his hands. He didn't know why they'd taken his own clothes. It wasn't like there'd be any DNA or whatever on them. He sipped his coffee and nearly spat it back out. It was cold.

He was about to shout a complaint when the door opened, and the detectives walked in. They did the usual introductions, and when he moaned about the coffee, they arranged a fresh one for him.

'Let's just get this over with. I need to get out of here,' he said.

'So, do we, Scott, trust me,' said the female – Sadie he thought she was called. He couldn't remember the bloke's name.

'Did everything check out yesterday then?' asked Scott as Sadie shuffled some papers in front of her.

'Sorry, did what check out?'

'Did you speak to Rachel? Bet she vouched for me, didn't she?'

'Oh that, we're still chasing it up. We'd like to talk to you about something else today, Scott.'

Shit. 'Yeah, like what?' *What the fuck do they have?*

'Are you familiar with the name Claire Foster?'

She was staring hard at him, as was the bloke next to her.

'Who?'

'Claire, Claire Foster.' She pulled a photograph out of the folder and passed it to him.

He looked at it properly this time. The picture was of a young blonde woman, holding the hand of a little girl who couldn't have been more than two years old. They were standing on a beach, with the sea in the background. It was the same image they'd briefly shown him yesterday. 'Never seen her.' He pushed the image back across the table, turning it over as he did so.

'Are you sure? Look at it again. You've never seen this woman before?' She'd turned the photo back over, and he couldn't help but stare at it.

He gulped. He had seen her before, course he had. 'What's she done?' he asked, stalling for time, though he knew it was pointless.

'Have you seen her recently?'

Scott paused and sat back in his chair, brain working overtime. 'I think I'd like a solicitor now.'

The two detectives looked at each other. Scott took a little pleasure in seeing the disappointment on their faces.

He had no choice. He wasn't saying another word until he'd had legal advice. End of.

ZIGGY KNEW he needed to speak to Rachel. He'd had a couple of missed calls from her, but however inadvertently, she was now involved with Susannah's case, so he had put off calling her back. Now he had no choice. If he didn't call her, she'd hear of Scott's arrest either through the media or from one of his team. Despite everything that had passed between them, he wanted her to hear it from him first.

Whilst Sadie and Nick were tying up Scott's interview and requesting legal representation, he took himself out into the car park, hoping for some privacy.

'DI Thornes, isn't it?'

Ziggy turned around. *Oh, for God's sake*. 'I have nothing to say to you.' Mack the Knife along with her photographer were right behind him.

'Is it true you've made an arrest in connection with Susannah Leibniz's murder?'

Ziggy walked over to his car and clicked the key. 'I've told you I have nothing to say.' He climbed into the driver's seat and started the engine. She was standing directly in front of the bonnet. He was tempted to slip it into first gear. Instead, he beeped his horn and drove forward. She moved, and he exited the car park. He drove around the block and pulled into a side street. He made a quick call to the front desk to let them know vultures were hovering, then steeled himself to call Rachel.

'About bloody time, Andrew, what's going on? Why were you asking about Scott? Is that why I can't get hold of him now? Have you scared him away or something?'

It all came out in one continuous screech, and Ziggy had to hold the phone away from his ear. He waited a second or two to see if she had finished.

'Hello to you too,' he said.

'Don't start. What is going on?'

He could hear Ben in the background; it sounded like they were at the park. 'I'm sorry I haven't called you back. I've been tied up at the station.'

'You're always tied up at the station.'

'Rachel, just listen a second. Scott has been taken in for questioning.'

There was silence for a moment, and he wondered if she'd heard him.

'What? Questioning? About what?' came the reply.

'The case I'm currently working on, the murder case.' He waited for the explosion he knew was about to come, and sure enough...

'Murder? Scott? What the hell are you talking about?'

'Look, there's no easy way to say this, and I would rather you hear it from me than the media, so if you'll calm down a second, I'll explain everything.'

He heard her ask one of the other mums to watch Ben. He assumed she was moving out of everyone's hearing. 'Go on.'

'Scott has told us that he was in a relationship with Susannah Leibniz for about three weeks before she was murdered. A bag of her clothes had been dumped in a rubbish bin and it was full of Scott's fingerprints.'

Silence.

'Rachel? You still there?'

'Yes, I'm here. I don't understand. He's been with me. How would he be able to see anyone else?' She sounded confused.

'Did you know he has a flat above the nightclub where he works?'

'Yes, but the lease has run out, that's why he's moving in with me.'

'Well, Susannah had been staying there.'

He waited whilst his words sank in. He could picture her walking backwards and forwards, shaking her head and chewing her lip as she did when she was upset.

'I'm sorry, Rachel, I really am.'

'Er... That's a lot to get my head around. And he's told you all this?'

'Yes. Well not me, Sadie and Nick interviewed him due to my connection with you, so...'

'Did he kill her, Ziggy?' He could hear Rachel was fighting back tears.

'Honestly? We just don't know, and I've probably said more than I should. Listen, he's asked you to provide alibis for the times he alleges he was at your house, so someone will be in touch and inviting you into the station. I'll see if I can ask Sadie to talk to you – I know you get on well.'

'Right. Oh God, what has he done?'

'I need to tell you something else as well.'

'Jesus, what else can there be?'

'Did you know he has a criminal record?'

'What? What the hell for?'

'It's quite a long list to be honest, but primarily domestic violence. Two of his previous partners have injunctions against him.'

'What?'

'I'm so sorry, Rachel. I only found out myself yesterday and...'

'You knew yesterday and didn't think to tell me?'

'I've had my hands full, in fairness, plus Scott was here so I knew you were both safe.'

'This is too much; I can't take it in.'

'I know, I'm sorry Can you go to your mum's or something?'

'I don't know, Ziggy, oh God.'

He heard her sobbing, and it sounded as though one of the other mums had seen her distress. Not quite knowing what to do, he hung up and headed back into the station.

He'd ask Sadie to give her a call and see if anyone was free to call round.

BACK IN THE BUILDING, he headed to Whitmore's office. A press appeal for Claire Foster had been arranged for later that afternoon, and Ziggy wanted to update him before he went back to the incident room.

'Sir?' Ziggy tapped on the door and poked his head round. Whitmore was in there with a guy from the media team.

'Ah, Andrew. Perfect timing. You know Thomas from the press office – we're just going over the strategy for the press appeal.'

Ziggy shook hands with the young man and took a seat.

'We were just discussing what we should say about Claire's disappearance being linked to the recent murder case?' asked Thomas.

Ziggy coughed. 'Well, we don't know for certain that they are linked, and I wouldn't want to risk taking away any attention from the urgency of finding Claire, if that's what you mean?'

Whitmore interrupted. 'Oh, absolutely. No, we were talking about the Q and A session afterwards.'

'Oh, I wasn't aware that there would be questions after.'

'Yes, yes,' said Whitmore. 'It's a good time to update the press with where we are with everything.'

'I disagree, with all due respect, sir.'

The young PR guy blushed, and a palpable silence built in the room.

'And why is that, Andrew?' asked Whitmore, frowning. He interlinked his fingers and leant forward on his huge mahogany desk.

'Surely the purpose of the press appeal is to raise aware-ness for Claire? If we then do a press briefing on Susannah, first the press will tie the cases together, and second it takes the spotlight away from Claire.'

Thomas spoke up, rather nervously. 'That's what I was trying to say, but maybe I didn't put it as well as that.'

'It's not a press briefing on Susannah specifically, but we're bound to get asked questions, so it would kill two birds with one stone.'

'No, sir, by all means have a press briefing but on a different day.' Ziggy was adamant. 'If we get asked questions today, just tell them we have no further comment to make.' He had to leave before he said something regrettable. Standing up, he made for the door. 'If you'll excuse me, I need to get back.' He walked out before Whitmore had time to call him back.

Once he was back in his own office, he sat down, placed his elbows on the desk and rubbed his face. He thought he'd done really well to curb his temper, but he did question just how Whitmore had landed that role, and whose palm had been greased in return.

There was a light tapping on his door. 'Come in,' he said wearily. 'Ah, Sadie. Sit down.'

'Everything all right?' she asked, placing a drink on his desk.

'Thanks. Yes, it's fine.' He couldn't even be bothered to explain his run-in with Whitmore. 'I've spoken to Rachel. She's willing to come in and answer any questions, but I did say you would ring her. Is that all right?'

'Course, no bother. Did you tell her about Scott's record?'

'I did. She sounded pretty shocked and upset, of course.'

'I'm not surprised. Wolf in sheep's clothing, that one.'

'Indeed. Is his legal rep here?'

'Yeah, she's just arrived. It's Carol Wood, we've worked with her on a couple of cases. She's just in with him now. I've handed her our briefing notes.'

'Great. I'll be out in a second, just need to get my head together.'

'Don't worry. We're on top of everything.' Sadie left the office and quietly closed his door.

THE INCIDENT ROOM was a hive of activity. Nick was briefing one of the support staff on something as Sadie walked over.

'Got a second?' she asked, tapping him on the shoulder.

'Yeah sure.' He shoved his hands in his pockets and followed her to a corner of the room. 'What's up?'

'Ziggy's coming out in a minute. He's spoken to Rachel, so we'll get her in for questioning. Do you have a list of the dates we need covering?'

'Yeah, it's on my desk.'

'Great. We need to look at how we're going to continue with interviewing Scott. The search team haven't found anything either in the flat or his car linking him to the murder, though obviously her fingerprints and DNA are everywhere but he's accounted for those.'

Ziggy walked over and joined them.

'Boss, we're just going over interview strategy,' she said.

'Hmm, no trace of Claire found in the flat or his car, I hear?'

'Nope, just Susannah, which as I was just saying to Nick, he's fully accounted for.'

'Well, he's had plenty of time with his brief, so I'd say get back in there and see what he has to say for himself now he's had some advice.'

·   ·   ·

WHILST NICK and Sadie headed back downstairs, Ziggy made his way to the viewing gallery. He stood in front of the two-way mirror and switched on the volume.

Scott entered, with his legal rep Carol, and they both took their seats on the far side of the table. Nick and Sadie joined them moments later. Once the preliminaries were done, Sadie began with the questions.

'Scott, when we last spoke I showed you this image of Claire Foster.' She slipped the photograph across the table again.

Ziggy watched Scott's face closely, but he didn't see even a flicker of acknowledgement.

'Can you confirm if you know the person in the photograph?' asked Sadie.

Scott looked directly at Sadie, grinned and answered. 'No comment.'

Ziggy slammed his hand against the wall in anger. 'For fuck's sake,' he raged. He carried on listening as Scott's solicitor read the prepared statement, silently seething. They'd missed their chance, and he knew who would be dragged over the coals for it.

20

As she came back into awareness again, Claire slowly lifted her head and opened her eyes. She had no idea how long she had been out. The light never changed in the room. It was a constant dim light, like the nightlight in Zoe's bedroom. Thinking of her daughter, she felt a resolve grow inside her. She *wouldn't* let her life end like this. Zoe needed her. She had to escape. Her despair turned into anger and fuelled her need to stay awake. But as her eyes started to close again, she dug deep into her slender reserves and forced them to stay open. Tears were flowing down her cheeks, and she licked the saltiness from her dry, cracked lips. She focused on the tiny drops of moisture in her mouth, rather than the pain.

She needed a plan. First, though, she had to work out where she was. The room was so poorly lit that she couldn't make out any shapes. She wiggled in the chair that held her. She could feel that the bindings on her wrists were made of a thick rope, presumably the same as those that tied her ankles. Looking down, she could see that there were a series of complicated knots. Even if her hands were free, she doubted she would be able to undo them. Shuffling her bare feet backwards and forwards as much as she could, she could feel the surface of the floor was like the linoleum Lee had laid in the kitchen at home. Straining her neck as far as she could, she spotted a small window at the far end of the room. It was covered with what looked like a metal grill. She hadn't heard any footsteps other than those of her captor, so she was somewhere remote or deserted; perhaps both.

She glanced around her. Twisting her head from side to side created a tidal wave of pain in her head, neck and shoulders. She rested for a second until the pain subsided slightly. All she could see were bare brick walls. She couldn't smell any damp or feel any draughts. There was no other noise than that of her own breathing.

Feeling despondent, she pushed back in her chair in frustration. She was instantly alert to a creaking sound. She propelled herself forward, only a fraction, but as she pushed back, she heard the noise again. There was a weakness in the chair. She repeated the action over and over, creating a rocking momentum. She could feel something behind her giving way with each movement. It was the back support of the chair. Almost giddy with excitement, she rocked harder and finally, after what felt like hours and huge physical exertion, she heard a loud snap. She collapsed onto the floor with the chair in bits around her. Her arms were tangled up in the broken support, but she quickly shook herself free. The rope slipped off over her hands. She rubbed her painful, bruised wrists, and flexed her fingers. Using her now free hands, she slipped off the rope that had been holding her legs in place. Tears of joy streamed down her face, and she laughed maniacally. She was getting out of there. She tried to stand, but immediately fell to the floor, her legs too weak to hold her. She clawed her way back upright and tried again. Slowly, slowly, so painstakingly slowly, she crawled over to the stairs where her captor entered and left each time. Placing her hands on the steps in front of her, she dragged her legs behind her and started to ascend them.

The door above her flew open, bringing a flash of light that blinded her momentarily. She felt an almighty crack to her jaw and the whole room somersaulted around her as the world went black.

ow dare she. *He took in the scene before him.* How had she managed to escape? *He descended the stairs and saw the broken chair and her discarded bindings.*

'Bitch!' *he screamed at the prone body on the floor. Enraged, he lifted his foot and stomped hard on her ribs in his high heels. He felt something give way as the steel stiletto punctured her skin. There was a spurt of blood that splashed onto his silver shoes. He was incensed.* 'How dare you?' *He grabbed her by the hair and dragged her across the floor. He would need another chair now. His rage was palpable.*

Heart pounding, he stormed back upstairs and locked the door behind him. She wouldn't move, but the little bitch had shown herself to be resourceful, and that just wouldn't do. It wasn't how proper girls behaved. He stormed across the floor and retrieved another chair. Metal this time. The little bitch won't get out of this one. *Opening a cupboard, he dragged out the heavy-duty rope and headed back into the basement.*

She was right where he had left her. He threw the rope down the stairs and dragged the chair down behind him.

He checked her pulse. Of course, she was still breathing, but there was blood everywhere. Good. *Now he could really make her suffer. He picked her up, threw her battered body over his shoulder and pushed her into the chair. He tied her up once again, ensuring that knot was sufficiently tight.*

Going to the tap in the corner, he picked up the bucket he had been letting her use as a toilet and filled it with ice cold water. Carrying it back over to the chair, he threw it over her.

She screamed, instantly awake.

He leaned in closer and stared at her, making sure she was fully conscious.

'What the fuck do you think you're doing?' He snarled.

His guest shivered and let out a groan of pain.

'Did you think you could leave me now?'

No answer.

He slapped her hard across the face, her head violently twisting round and spilling blood from her lips.

'You had plenty of chances to ask me for forgiveness, but no. You chose to ask stupid questions about your child. Well, she's dead. I killed her.' Let's see what she does now.

He stared down at her and saw tears escaping from her eyes. Good.

'Nothing to say?' His rage was building again. It always started at the pit of his stomach and turned his insides into an oozing blackness that he could feel working its way throughout his body. As it reached his face, he felt his temperature rise and he started to sweat. He had to find a release.

'This is not how it happens. You don't tell me what to do,' he threatened, slapping her again. This time she moaned louder.

He stepped away, breathing heavily. He angrily paced back and forth as he thought through his next move. He couldn't understand it. His intuition was rarely wrong. He'd have to get rid of her now and move her later. He couldn't afford to leave it any longer, though again he had hoped for more time with her. Where was he going wrong? Maybe she hadn't been the right one after all.

Leaving the basement, he headed back to the cupboard and removed a silk scarf. Walking back into the room, he approached his guest and pulled her head back by her hair. Her eyes flew open and the look of terror he saw there pleased him greatly.

'I'm having to bring our little meeting to an end.'

He laughed as she started to beg for her life. 'No, please don't,' he mimicked. 'If you hadn't been naughty, then I wouldn't need to, would I?'

She recoiled, scrunching her eyes closed.

'Open your eyes, bitch,' he snapped. He wanted to see the life leave them.

He slipped the silk scarf around the back of her neck and crossed the two ends over. He gripped them tightly and pulled.

He laughed as her eyes bulged and she struggled for breath. She was trying to thrust herself away from him, but he was far too strong for her. Mere moments later, he achieved his wish and watched the life drain from her eyes.

22

'Can I get you a drink or anything Rachel?' asked Sadie as she opened the door to the soft interview room and guided her in.

'No, thank you, but I'm fine.'

'Is Ben with his grandma?'

'Yeah, she's having him until we're done here. I thought that was for the best.'

Sadie could tell that Rachel was understandably nervous and upset, so she tried her best to put her at ease. Offering to take her coat, she invited Rachel to sit on the sofa. Sadie took the chair opposite and smiled.

'First and foremost, you must understand that you're only here to help with our enquiries, which I believe Ziggy has explained to you?'

'He did, but to be honest I didn't take everything in. It was such a shock.'

'I can imagine.'

'Plus, I was at the park with some of Ben's friends, so it wasn't ideal timing.'

Sadie smiled again. 'Yeah, not the best. So, as I briefly

said over the phone, we just need you to verify some dates, if that's OK?'

Rachel looked at Sadie with tears in her eyes. 'Is the other thing true? About the domestic violence.'

'It is, I'm afraid. I'm so sorry.' Sadie reached over and touched Rachel's hand. She pushed the tissues in her direction. 'We'll take this at your pace, Rachel.'

Rachel took a tissue and blew her nose. 'No, it's fine. I just can't believe I was taken in by him. And to think I let my son near him.'

'You weren't to know – don't blame yourself. You know now, that's what matters.'

'Yes, that's true. So, what do you need me to do?'

'Scott states that he was with you on certain dates, that either he stayed over at your house or you were together during the day. I'm going to pass the list of dates to you, and if you could confirm that would be great.'

Sadie opened the folder that she was balancing on her knee and found the relevant paperwork. She placed it on the table in front of her. 'If you could just go through and mark which dates are accurate.' She passed Rachel a pen. 'I'll leave you for a couple of minutes to go through it. If you need anything, I'll be just outside.'

'Oh, OK. Thank you.'

Sadie made sure Rachel had everything she needed and stepped out of the room. She used the office downstairs to call Ziggy.

'Hiya. Rachel's here. I just wondered if you wanted to see her or anything.'

'No, it's fine I'm sure she doesn't want to see me right now. I'll give her a call later. Thanks though.'

Sadie rang off and headed back into the room. 'How are you getting on?'

Rachel was sitting with her phone and a paper diary in front of her and was marking her place on the sheet of paper. 'Getting there. It's all accurate so far. I've kept a diary for work for years, old habits die hard, I guess.'

'I'm super impressed. If I didn't have to log my shifts, I don't think I could remember where I was yesterday, never mind seven or eight weeks ago.'

Rachel smiled for the first time in days. 'There you go. He's right about every date.'

'OK, that's great. Thank you for coming in.'

Rachel was surprised. 'Is that all you need?'

'Yes, for now. You've been a great help, thank you.'

'What happens now? With Scott, I mean?'

'He's still here whilst we carry on with our enquiries.'

'And what if he gets out? What should I do?'

'He knows you've been in here, and that you're aware of his criminal record, so I would maybe stay with your mum for a few days, just until everything settles down?'

'Right, OK.' Rachel paused and chewed her bottom lip. 'Sadie, tell me honestly. Do you think he killed her?'

'Ah, Rachel, it's not that simple, love. If only it were.'

The two women hugged, and Sadie promised a girls' night with her as soon as she could.

RACHEL LEFT the station and headed for her car. The lights flashed as the car unlocked and she stepped into the driver's seat. Once the doors were locked, she placed her head on the steering wheel and let out the sobs that she had been holding in all day.

. . .

'WHAT DID CPS SAY?' asked Sadie once she was back in the incident room.

'Not enough to charge on either account. No evidence of kidnap or being held against her will.'

'Damn. What now?'

'Release on bail pending further enquiries.'

Ziggy saw the shoulders of the team drop. They'd worked so hard to build a case against Scott Ball. Ultimately, in his opinion, as much as he hated to admit it, the CPS had made the right call. Everything they had was circumstantial. There was nothing to tie Scott directly to the murder, and no evidence had been found in his flat or car that would suggest Susannah was held against her will. His prepared statement had indicated that he had seen Claire with Susannah on the day he had picked Susie up, but there was no other link to the missing girl.

'Shit. Where do we go from here?' asked Nick, as he swung from side to side in his swivel chair.

'Let's look at what else we have.' Ziggy turned to Angela. 'How did the press appeal go?'

'Just awful. I mean it was emotional to say the least, those poor parents, but they held it together well.'

'What about the boyfriend, how was he?' asked Ziggy.

'He didn't want to go on camera, so he stayed away. He's at his mother-in-law's with the little girl.'

'Interesting. Have we spoken to Family Liaison? How's he been, do you know?'

Sadie cut in. 'What are you thinking, boss?'

'Not sure, just trying to explore all angles. Experience tells us it's usually someone close to the family.'

'But we've already spoken to him, he seemed genuine and looked gutted,' commented Nick.

'Hmm, maybe. I'm going to go and have another chat

with him, find out if he knew Scott Ball. There must be a connection there somewhere. Nick, can you hold the fort here? Anything crops up give us a call. Sadie, with me.'

'Yeah, no problem. I'll speak with the neighbourhood teams and see how the ground search is going on.'

'Good idea. Angela will bring you up to speed.'

'How was Rachel?' Ziggy asked Sadie as he started the car. She may be his ex-wife, but she was still the mother of his child and despite everything, he cared about her.

'Yeah, not great but she's a tough cookie. She'll get through it.' Sadie fastened her seatbelt. 'I told her to stay with her mum for a few days. She seemed worried about what would happen if Scott was released.'

'I don't think he'll go anywhere near her; he's a coward, and I would imagine he isn't one to face up to his failures. He could be completely innocent, of course – let's not discount that option – but even so, she knows about his past now.'

'Yeah, I told her we'd have a girls' night out when everything had settled.'

Ziggy laughed. 'She'd probably appreciate that.'

They continued the rest of their trip in silence. Ziggy silently vowed to spend less time at work and more time with his son after this case. He couldn't imagine how it must feel to lose a child or not know where they were.

Pulling up outside Claire's parents', they saw Lee playing in the garden with Zoe. They were throwing a frisbee around, with Zoe missing more than she caught. The officers exited the car and walked up the driveway. Ziggy had chosen not to phone ahead to let them know they were calling in. He wanted to catch Lee unawares.

As soon as Lee saw them, he stopped playing and stared at Ziggy.

Sadie spoke first. 'Hi, Lee,' she said pleasantly. 'And you must be Zoe?' She squatted down so that she was level with the little girl.

Ziggy stepped forward and held out his hand. 'Hi, Lee, we haven't met before, but I'm DI Thornes. I'm working with DS Bates on Claire's case.'

They shook hands and Ziggy noticed that Lee's palms were sweating. It could be down to the frisbee activity, but he also felt a slight tremor as well.

'Oh, hello. Sorry, I didn't know you were coming.' He looked around for Zoe, who was clinging to his legs and hiding behind him. 'Zoe, darling, why don't you go find Gran and ask her for an ice cream?'

Zoe went tripping off up the driveway, excited at the prospect of a treat. Lee spoke again. 'Is there any news?' His eyes filled with tears.

'No, I'm sorry, Lee, there's nothing as yet. We'd just like a quick chat with you if that's OK?' Sadie was gentle with him.

'Sure, let's head inside.' Lee turned and headed towards the back door.

Claire's mother was in the kitchen, clearly alerted by Zoe that Daddy was talking to someone. Lee introduced the two detectives after telling her there was no news. She covered her face with her hands and shook her head.

'They just need a chat – can we use the dining room?' asked Lee.

'Of course, can I get you a drink or anything?' she asked, wiping her tears away with the apron she was wearing. 'My husband isn't here – he's out with the search team. I was just making some cookies to thank everyone for helping.'

'It's fine, Mrs Foster, we won't be long.'

She turned back to the worktop as Lee led Sadie and Ziggy through to the dining room just off the kitchen. They sat down, and Sadie took out her notebook.

'Lee, I know this is a really stressful time for you, but I would like to ask you a few more questions, is that OK?' asked Ziggy.

'Sure, but I don't know what else I can tell you that I haven't already said.' He was pulling at the skin around his fingernails. Ziggy could see that they were bitten to the quick and looked sore.

'As you know, Forensics managed to retrieve the data from Claire's phone, but it didn't reveal a great deal to be honest. Do you know if she had a second phone?'

'No, not that I'm aware of. The one she has is pay-as-you-go. We didn't want to get tied in with a contract.'

'OK. What can you tell me about Claire's friends? I know you've been over this before, but just to make sure we've covered all angles. Who were her friends?'

'Well, there was Susannah obviously. She was mates with a couple of girls at the salon, but they're all into partying and nights out. Claire isn't like that. She likes to stay home with me and Zoe.'

'But if Claire was going on a night out, for someone's birthday, for example, where would she go?'

'Not sure. Possibly Sweet FAs, but she didn't like it there – the DJ gave her the creeps, apparently.'

Sadie made a note.

'When did she tell you that?'

'Oh, it was months ago. Susie really fancied him, but Claire said he loved himself more than anyone else.'

Ziggy already knew from watching the interviews that Scott was a narcissist, so it didn't come as any surprise. 'Did she know the DJ outside of the club?'

'No, not as far as I know.'

'Did she mention the DJ's name at all?'

'No, I'm not sure she knew his name to be honest.'

'Lee, do you know anyone called Scott?'

Lee thought about it for a second. 'No, don't think so.'

Ziggy was getting nowhere fast, so he changed the line of questioning. 'How did Claire seem in the days leading up to her disappearance? Was she acting differently?'

'No. I've wracked my brains, but I honestly can't think of anything. It was all just normal, you know?'

'Let's talk about her friendship with Susannah. When DS Bates and I spoke with Claire at the salon, she said that they were good friends but didn't live in each other's pockets. Is that your impression?'

'I think maybe Claire was playing it down. They were really good mates. It was one of those friendships where they might not hear from each other every day, but when they spoke, they just picked up where they left off. Claire was a little worried when she didn't hear from Susie, but she just brushed it off. I remember her telling me how guilty she felt.'

'Guilty? About what?' asked Ziggy.

'That day they met in the park. She said she'd wished she'd done something different, asked her to come back to ours for dinner. Maybe she wouldn't have been killed then.' He faltered over the last sentence and sniffed loudly. He looked down at his hands.

'Ah, she must have taken Susie's death hard?' Sadie said sympathetically.

Lee nodded. 'Yeah. She was going to call you on the day she disappeared.'

Ziggy and Sadie looked at each other, then looked at Lee.

Ziggy spoke. 'Call us? Why?'

'Claire had been beating herself up since you spoke to her. Susie was apparently on her phone the whole time they were out and seemed on edge. She thought she might be in trouble for not having said anything, but I think she was still in shock.'

That was news to Ziggy and Sadie. It tied in with Susannah being wary of a stalker following her and despite extensive searches, they hadn't managed to locate Susie's phone either.

Reaching the same conclusion that Nick and Sadie had in their initial visit, Ziggy also felt that Lee had nothing to do with his girlfriend's disappearance. They were clearly a hardworking young couple.

They were just wrapping up when the dining-room door burst open and little Zoe came charging in with her face covered in chocolate sprinkles and ice cream running down her arm. Lee was immediately on his feet. 'Zoe, don't touch anything!' He exclaimed, trying to protect Grandma's furniture from being covered in sticky ice cream. Seconds later, Grandma appeared at the door with a face cloth.

'Come here, monkey, let me wipe your face.' As she approached the toddler, the girl squealed and shot off, Grandma close on her heels.

Ziggy and Sadie laughed and stood up. 'Thank you for taking the time to talk to us, Lee, I think we've covered everything.'

Sadie nodded in agreement. 'We will be in touch but if you need to know anything in the meantime, you can speak to your family liaison officer.'

'Right, thank you. I'm hoping the press appeal will give us something.'

'I'm sure it will. It will run again on every bulletin,' confirmed Sadie as they turned to leave.

OUTSIDE THE HOUSE, they walked down the path and climbed into Ziggy's car. They were just about to set off when there was a tapping on the passenger-door window.

Sadie buzzed her window down. 'Hi, can I help?'

'Hello. I'm not sure to be honest. You're police officers, yes? Looking into Claire Foster's disappearance?'

Sadie confirmed that they were.

The elderly gent continued. 'I live just down the road from Claire and Lee, and I wondered if you might have a minute.'

Sadie looked at Ziggy and he nodded whilst shrugging his shoulders. 'Sure.'

They climbed back out of the car.

'What can we do for you?' asked Ziggy after the introductions had been made.

'I mean, it might be nothing, but I thought I'd better mention it.' The neighbour looked as though he was having trouble standing upright.

'Do you live far? Shall we go to your house?'

'Oh yes, I live just down here.' He pointed his walking stick in a general direction up the road.

They walked a few minutes and Mr Burnell let them into the small two-bedroomed bungalow. They followed him into a cosy living room and he motioned for them to sit on the old-fashioned sofa that was covered with a colourful throw. A Jack Russell terrier didn't seem keen on sharing his space, until Mr Burnell brushed him onto the floor.

'So how can we help you, Mr Burnell?' asked Sadie. The

house had the smell of stale pipe tobacco and she quite liked it.

'That poor wee lassie, it's such a shame. And they have that gorgeous little girl too.'

'Yes, but we're doing all we can to find her. Did you have some information you wanted to share?' Sadie knew Ziggy's patience would be wearing thin, so she tried to speed things along a bit.

'Oh yes, sorry, silly me. I've been watching the news and following the story.' Mr Burnell rubbed his chin with heavily nicotine-stained fingers. 'It must have been about ten thirty that Friday night cos the news had just finished, and that dreadful Jonathan Ross was about to start. Anyway, I was closing my curtains when I heard a really loud noise. I thought it was race boyers.'

Ziggy glanced at Sadie questioningly. 'Boy racers,' she mouthed.

'Anyway, I couldn't see anything at first, but just as I was drawing the curtains, a car went speeding out of the road at a ridiculous speed. I didn't have time to see it properly, it went that fast, but I thought I'd tell you about it, you know, just in case.'

Ziggy scratched the back of his head. 'And did you see anything of the car, Mr Burnell?'

'Only the colour, I think it was dark blue but then it was dark out so who knows.'

'You didn't catch the number plate or anything?'

'No, I'm sorry. I did see a badge on it, though.'

Ziggy perked up. 'Really? What kind of badge?'

'Here, I'll show you.' Mr Burnell stood up and headed into the hallway. He came back with a pen and a piece of paper. Sitting back down, he pulled over a small side table and started sketching out what he had seen. 'Here.'

He passed the paper over, and they both looked at it. It was a BMW badge.

'Does anyone in this street own a BMW, Mr Burnell?' asked Ziggy.

'Oh, is that what it is? I can't think of anyone.'

'Have you seen this particular car before?'

'Not that I remember, but my memory's not what it used to be.'

'Mr Burnell, that's been really useful. Thank you so much. If there's nothing else, we won't take up any more of your time,' said Ziggy, standing up. His full height seemed exaggerated in the low-ceilinged living room. Sadie joined him, and they left Mr Burnell to settle down the Jack Russell who clearly didn't like visitors.

Once they were out of earshot, Ziggy asked Sadie what she thought.

'It's odd that it was a BMW. Could be coincidence, but we all know there's no such thing,' she said.

'But Rachel has said she was with Scott that night, or was he working at the club?'

'I can't remember offhand. I'd need to check the records.'

'Come on, then. Let's go see if Nick has news.'

23

S cott waited on the corner, looking for any signs of Rachel. He'd lost his house key somewhere in the last twenty-four hours, so he had knocked on the door but there had been no answer. He knew she must be due home soon, as Ben would be out of school, so he had decided to hover nearby. He had no idea what kind of reception he would receive, but she had confirmed his alibi, so she must know he wasn't involved. He could talk his way out of the whole cheating thing – it had been nothing after all, so he wasn't fussed about that. As for his past, well, everyone had one of those. No, he was convinced, none of it mattered.

The weather had been naff all day, even though it was June. It was cloudy and looked as though it might rain again. He pulled up the collar of his leather jacket and shoved his hands deeper into his pockets. He leant against the wall and waited. He hoped he could make it work with Rachel. He really liked her, and she had a few bob behind her too, which always helped. Obviously, things weren't going to work out at the club. He doubted Jon would let him back in the place after the police would have been all over the place. It didn't matter. He could find another job or sign up with an agency. That's how he had met Rachel in the first place, before he'd started at Sweet FAs. She had needed a DJ for the local hotel she worked at, and he had been allocated the job via the agency. It was a good gig too – Christmas Day and New Year's Eve, so double rates; he'd been quids in. Yeah, he would just sign up with them again.

He was about to walk to the shop and see if he could blag himself a drink when Rachel's car pulled around the corner. He stayed out of sight until she had pulled onto the drive. She got out of the car on her own and headed for the front door.

Even better, the little one wasn't with her.

She let herself in, and Scott approached the house. Rachel saw him through the kitchen window, and he could tell by the look on her face she was shocked to see him. He strode up the path just in time to hear the door locking and the chain being slipped over.

He banged on the door. 'Come on, Rach, let me in.'

'Go away, Scott.' Her voice sounded firm but there was a nervousness to it.

'Aww, babe, I only want to talk.'

'I don't have anything to say to you. Go away.'

He banged on the door again. 'Just let me explain—'

'No!' Rachel was shouting now. 'No, Scott, there is no explanation. Go away and leave me alone.'

'You don't understand.'

'What? That you think it's OK to batter women?' She yelled through the locked door.

Scott looked around him. A couple of the neighbours had come out to see what all the noise was about. He pressed his ear against the door and spoke in a low, menacing voice. 'Rachel, let me in and I'll explain everything.'

He heard a rustling sound from the other side. *She must be leaning against the door.*

'Come on, baby, you know me. I'm not like that.' He kept his voice low, stroking the door as he spoke. 'We've got something really special. Let me in so we can talk.'

'No, Scott. It's over. I'll send your stuff round to the club,' said Rachel through her tears.

He was trying so hard to keep his temper in check, but he could feel his blood pressure rising as his breathing accelerated. 'Last chance, Rachel, let me in.'

When he didn't get an immediate reply, he stood back from the door and took a deep breath. He tried the handle, though he knew it would be locked. He walked around the side of the house, heading for the back door. As he passed the kitchen window, he saw Rachel sat at the table. He tapped, and she jumped.

'Hey, come on. It's been a hellish twenty-four hours, babe. Just give me a chance.'

She stood up and folded her arms. 'No, Scott. Please leave me alone. I've nothing to say to you. If you don't leave, I'll call the police.' Her hand was shaking as she held the phone to her ear.

'You don't want to do that, babe. Put the phone down,' he threatened.

She turned her back to him and left the room.

'Rachel!' he shouted, banging on the window. 'Rachel!' he shouted again.

He stormed back to the front door and started hammering both fists on the top panel. 'Last chance, Rach. Open this door and let me in, or I swear I will kick it in.' He raised his right leg and booted the bottom panel. It was made of UPVC and didn't move an inch. He heard her yelp inside as he booted it harder.

'The police are on their way,' she yelled.

The neighbours were still watching the fiasco. One of the men, who was built like a brick outhouse, started to walk forward.

'I'd stop that if I were you, mate.'

'Oh, fuck off and mind your own business,' snapped Scott, sweat pouring down his face.

'Big man, aren't you, threatening women? Why not try someone your own size?'

Scott had had enough of the jumped-up little shit. 'If you don't fuck off, you'll be next.' He booted the door again, putting all his weight behind it. The bottom panel creaked and with one more swift kick it cracked and caved inwards. Scott knelt down and hooked his arm inside, trying to reach the door handle. Rachel screamed and ran upstairs.

Scott suddenly felt himself being yanked backwards and felt a blow to the side of his head. The sound of approaching sirens faded as he lost consciousness.

ZIGGY WAS SITTING NURSING a cup of coffee as Nick updated him with the search details. 'NPAS is out and the dogs are searching in Middleton Park.' NPAS was the National Police Air Support, often used in the search for missing persons.

'But still nothing?' asked Ziggy.

'Nope. Working on the theory that she's being held somewhere – all empty buildings are being searched. Honestly, every angle is being covered. I'm not sure what more we can do. It's like she's just vanished into thin air.'

Ziggy stood up and walked over to the whiteboards. Once Scott had been released, there wasn't anything else to add to it. The appeal for Claire had brought in several sightings of her all over the country and all of which were currently being followed up.

'The neighbour reckons he saw a BMW, but the house-to-house hasn't had anyone else say anything about it,' Ziggy said.

Sadie joined them. 'Have you told Nick what Lee said about the DJ at Sweet FAs?'

'Oh yeah, apparently he gave Claire the creeps.'

'Scott gave me the creeps too. No offence, Ziggy, but I do wonder what Rachel see's in him.'

'Horses for courses, isn't it, I guess?'

Ziggy felt his mobile phone vibrating, so fished it out of his trouser pocket.

'Rachel?'

'Please Ziggy send someone.' His ex-wife sounded hysterical before she let out an ear-piercing scream.

'Rachel? Rachel? Are you OK?' He pinned the phone to his ear.

'He's breaking in. Please send someone.'

'Who is Rachel? Is it—'

'SCOTT!' She shouted, and the line went dead.

'That bastards turned up at Rachel's.' Ziggy was already halfway across the room. 'Get control to send a unit, I'm heading over there now.'

Sadie chased after him. 'Hold up,' she shouted. 'I'm coming with you.'

24

H e watched the emotional press appeal as he dressed
Claire for her outing.

'Please, Claire, if you're watching this let us
know you're OK. If you can, call one of us. Either your mum
or me, or Lee. We all love you and want you home safe.'

*The camera panned over to the mother's face, which was
stained with tears.*

*He grabbed Claire by the hair, lifted her up and turned her
lifeless body towards the TV screen.*

'See that, Claire? Your family wants you to call them.' *He
dropped her again as he started laughing, a deep belly laugh that
he couldn't control. Tears were streaming down his face but for
very different reasons. He lifted her left hand and moved it to her
ear.* 'Mummy, it's me. I'm dead.' *He cackled.*

*Still chuckling to himself, he moved her body and laid her out
on the polythene sheeting that covered the room and looked at
her. It hadn't ended how he would have liked, but never mind. At
least he had the time he needed. He'd taken off the trashy clothes
she had been wearing and placed her into a tea dress. It was a
pretty blue colour with a lace Peter Pan collar. It buttoned*

through the front and after much hefting and adjustments at the back, he'd managed to squeeze her into it. He'd seen it in a charity shop a few weeks ago. It had been in the window as part of an Alice In Wonderland scene and he thought it was just perfect.

He wriggled her feet into the short white ankle socks and folded them over, so the bows were showing. Next was his favourite part. Her hair.

Every Friday, before she had fallen ill, his mother had a regular hair appointment. He would go with her while she had her regular set and blow-dry. He enjoyed going, watching his mother become a model again, as she once had been. He liked looking at the other ladies too. As he grew older, he always made sure he was around for the Friday trip.

When she had become more fragile, at first someone had called at the house to do it for her, but he'd stopped that. He did it for her himself. He'd seen it being done for such a long time he knew exactly what was needed.

He dragged Claire's body backwards by the shoulders, then sat her in the chair. Dead bodies were funny things. Once the initial stiffness had dissipated, all that was really left to deal with were the bodily fluids. It could get messy (if you were an amateur) but he'd learnt over the years what you could and couldn't do with one.

He stroked her long blonde hair gently, wishing he could enjoy the feeling of it against his skin through his gloves. He imagined it was so soft. If it wasn't for the terrible stench emanating from her, you would probably think it had been freshly washed. He took the brush and carefully ran it the full length, curling it under gently at the ends. He looked around for the blue headband he had set to one side especially for the occasion. Finding it, he looped it underneath her hair and carefully tied it in a bow at the top, leaving her blonde tresses to fall around her shoulders. He moved around to the front and admired his handiwork. *All that was left now was the lipstick, the most important part. He took the Chanel Rouge Coco lipstick and applied it to her lips. It was unfortunate she had a cut, but he could cover that up.*

Once he'd finished, he stepped back again. Pleased with his efforts, he smiled. He'd sleep down here, next to her, tonight and move her tomorrow.

25

Rachel was shaking from head to toe. She felt physically sick as she watched the paramedics work on Scott. The neighbour who had delivered the damaging blow was speaking with the uniformed officers who had arrived on scene within minutes. Rachel was wrapped in a blanket that had been provided by the medic and clutching a mug of hot sweet tea. She placed her cup on the kitchen table with a shaking hand.

'Rachel?' called Ziggy as he came through the broken front door. He took one look at her face and immediately wrapped his arms around her, whispering words of comfort as she sobbed against his chest. 'Hey, hey, hey. He's gone, it's OK.' He stroked her hair, and she felt her crying slowly subside.

'Ziggy, I was scared for my life.'

'I know, but you're OK. That's what matters.'

'Ben's still with my mum, can you ring her for me?'

Sadie had been hovering by the door and now stepped forward. 'I'll give her a call, don't worry.'

Rachel pulled away from Ziggy's embrace and wiped her tears away. 'Thank you, Sadie. Has he really gone?'

'Yeah, he's on his way to the hospital, but he's been arrested for criminal damage, so he won't be back anytime soon.'

Rachel sat heavily on the kitchen chair. 'Thank God I'd left Ben with Mum. I've never seen anyone so angry.'

Ziggy sat opposite her. 'You'll need to make a statement, when you're feeling up to it. I assume you're going to press charges.'

Rachel sniffed. 'God, yes. He's a monster. I don't know what he would have done if he'd have got in.'

'Thank goodness for your neighbour. That was one hell of punch.'

Rachel smiled through her tears. 'I don't even know him. He lives over the road. I think he was the one that called 999.'

'I just heard him say he owns the local gym and runs a boxing club, which is always handy,' said Sadie, before ducking out to make the call to Rachel's mum.

Rachel turned to Ziggy. 'I'm sorry for all this.'

Ziggy reached his hands across the table, taking her fingertips in his hands. 'You don't have anything to apologise for.'

'I can't understand why I couldn't see him for what he is.'

'Sociopaths are very good at hiding their behaviour,' he said. 'There wasn't anything you could have done differently.'

'When Nick rang to tell me he'd been released, I honestly didn't think he'd come around here. I thought he'd be too ashamed,' said Rachel.

'His moral judgement isn't the same as yours or mine.

But he won't bother you again,' said Sadie. 'I've spoken to your mum. She's understandably worried about you.'

'Thanks, Sadie. I'll give her a ring in a bit. Do I need to make a statement today?'

'No,' replied Ziggy. 'It can wait until tomorrow. I can call in and see Ben. Do you want me to drop you off there?'

'No, I'll drive over later, when the door's been fixed. I'll stay there tonight, but if he's locked up, we can come back here tomorrow.'

After making sure she was really OK, Ziggy and Sadie headed outside.

ZIGGY AND SADIE drove back to the station and updated the team who were shocked to hear what had happened.

'Bloody hell, makes you question everything we know about him, doesn't it?' said Angela.

'Yeah, thankfully she's pressing charges, so we'll see where that leads. At least he can't hurt or threaten anyone else,' commented Sadie.

'Where does that leave us?' asked Nick, looking at Ziggy.

'Back at square one, pretty much.'

Ziggy's mobile started ringing, ending the conversation. As the team watched, his face visibly paled. He ended the call, and the team waited with bated breath.

'A body's been found.'

26

Wednesday, 12 June

All there was left to do now was wait. Wait until she had been found. Wait until he watched as the investigation team struggled to put the pieces together. Wait until his next guest showed themselves to him.

He sat back and looked at the room around him. He'd cleaned up after himself (his mum would be proud) and finally the smell had dissipated. The enclosed space only had a small air vent, but it was also sealed, so the sickening smell of death had an annoying way of permeating every space. That's why he didn't keep them for too long. Plus, he got bored easily. There was only so much you could do with a dead body.

He'd been more careful this time. The moon had been full, which wasn't ideal, but he'd been extra cautious. She wasn't as visible as the first one had been, but he was confident it wouldn't be too long before she was found. He giggled to himself and wondered what that detective would make of the scene. He'd left her dressed in the Alice In Wonderland outfit. She looked sweet, and the setting he'd left her in was quite *fitting. In amongst the trees, with late-blooming spring flowers. He'd made sure she was south-facing, so the early-morning sun would rise on her face as she leant with her back against the tree. For all the world, it looked as though she was just resting her head for a few minutes – if you looked past the bruises and cuts.*

Once he'd finished, he watched from a safe distance. The park was always busy in the early mornings, filled with joggers and dog walkers. To find her, you would need to step right into the woods, as she was off the beaten path. He hadn't needed to drag her this time. He'd simply carried her in his arms. She weighed next to nothing. He'd adjusted the bow in her hair as it had slipped during the short journey, but everything else was pristine. He himself had dressed carefully for the occasion too. His black overalls had served him well, but he needed to dispose of them in the canal on his way back. A few heavy stones in the pockets would make sure they sank; they hadn't found the others, not yet anyway.

He sat low down in his car, resting his head on his hand so it looked like he was dozing. An early riser, or a late night that had led to a few too many causing him to sleep in his car. That's what he'd say if he was challenged, but he doubted he would be. He used false plates and been careful to use local B roads, avoiding the ANPR cameras. Not that it really mattered. The car he used wasn't registered to him.

He had glanced up and seen a group of joggers heading towards the woods. He watched as one of them broke away from the rest and jogged into the copse. As the unfortunate man prepared to relieve himself, he looked over to his left. He clearly spotted something, and after adjusting himself, he cautiously made his way over. The jogger spoke, but the watcher couldn't hear what was being said. The jogger pushed the blue sleeve of the dress, and it slumped to one side. Unsure of what he was looking at, the jogger returned to his friends who all came over to take a look.

One of them reached into their pocket and took out a mobile phone.

He'd seen enough. She'd been found, and that pleased him greatly.

Carefully, quietly, without drawing attention to himself, he had slowly pulled away from the kerb.

Time to find his next guest.

27

A large crowd had already gathered by the outer cordon when Ziggy arrived on the scene, and a tent had been erected to hide the body from view; the crime scene manager wasn't taking any chances.

'Hey Lolly,' said Ziggy as he entered the tent, stomach filled with dread as to what was going to be revealed to them.

Lolly was standing at the side of the body as photographs were being taken under her direction. 'Female, mid-twenties, I'd say. Haven't had a chance to take a close look as yet, just got here myself.'

The body had been blocked from Ziggy and Sadie's view as they entered, but Lolly now moved to one side. Sadie did a double take, while Ziggy inhaled sharply.

'What the hell?' he gasped.

'Precisely. What the hell indeed,' said Lolly, adjusting her face mask.

'Is she in fancy dress?' asked Sadie, taking a small step closer.

All three looked at the body, taking in the macabre sight

in front of them. The victim was leaning over to the left, though the witnesses had said that when they first saw her, she was sitting with her back against the tree. What they hadn't seen was the two meat hooks that had been gouged into her shoulder blades, enabling the cadaver to remain in an upright position. As she had been pushed, the hooks had broken away from the skin, leaving tissue and muscle dangling. The blue dress she was wearing had two slashes in the back to allow for the hooks without disturbing the fabric from the front, which pulled in tight over the waist and breasts.

Looking at the face, Ziggy was appalled with what he saw. A heavy layer of garish make-up had been inexpertly applied. Rosy red cheeks had been painted on, using a bright red cosmetic, and the eyes had exaggerated lashes that looked as though they had been drawn on by a five-year-old child.

But it was the lips that were the most horrific. A black lip liner had been used to create a cupid's-bow pout, which was then filled in with a bright red lipstick. It gave the overall image of some kind of perverse doll.

As Ziggy squatted down to take a closer look, he could see that underneath the foundation the face was heavily bruised, and the bottom lip had a huge gash.

Now he was closer he could smell the scent of death, but it mingled with something else, as though someone had tried to mask it with perfume. He motioned to Sadie, who was standing just behind him.

'Here, what can you smell?'

She carefully leaned over and inhaled through her nose. 'Rotting flesh?'

'No, beneath that. There's another smell, slightly floral, woody?'

Lolly came over to join them. 'Yeah, I can smell it. It's perfume, but I don't know which one.'

Sadie sniffed again. 'Nope, can't get past the smell of death.' She stepped away.

Ziggy stood up. 'Well, at least we have an ID this time. It's definitely Claire Foster.'

'Yeah,' agreed Sadie. 'Her poor family.'

'Well, if you two will excuse me,' said Lolly, making her way around them, 'I need to make a start.'

'Sure thing. Can you let me have the PM results as soon as?'

'Of course,' she replied. 'We could do with a catch-up at some point too.' She spoke directly to Ziggy and looked at him pointedly.

He knew he was going to be in trouble when he told her about the whole Scott and Rachel situation, and he felt a twinge of guilt. 'Yeah, I'll call you later.' He promised.

Once they had spoken with the crime scene manager and made sure the witnesses were giving their statements, Ziggy thought it best to deliver the bad news to Claire's family before anything could be leaked to the press so they headed to his car.

As Sadie rang Nick to coordinate the house-to-house and various activities, Ziggy made a quick call to the family liaison officer to find out where Lee was.

'Lee's still at his parents-in-law's. I've asked them to stay at the house until we get there,' He relayed to Sadie as they both climbed in his car.

'It never gets any easier, does it? I think they were clinging onto the hope that she would be found alive.'

'I think we all were. We don't know cause of death as yet, so we'll play it by ear and just let them know we've found her. Angela can work with the FLO and arrange a viewing, if Lolly thinks that's OK.'

THEY DROVE in silence and pulled up outside Mrs Foster's house a short while later. As they exited the car, Lee stood on the doorstep waiting for them.

'Is it her?' he asked as they approached.

'Let's go inside, Lee, it's better that way.' Said Ziggy.

'Oh God, it's her isn't it?'

Ziggy took him by the shoulders and steered him through to the family living room where Claire's mum and dad were seated along with the FLO. The local lunchtime news was playing, and sure enough, there was the intrepid reporter relaying the very little information they had. Claire's dad turned the TV off as Lee sat down with Ziggy and Sadie. Both of the parents looked at them with expectant eyes.

For once, Ziggy couldn't think of anything to say. They'd seen the news report, and the FLO had advised them that the detectives were heading their way. It didn't take a great amount of surmising to put the pieces together. Instead, he just offered his sincere apologies, after uttering the words no family ever wants to hear.

Mr Foster sat quite stoically in his armchair, gripping the armrests and clenching his jaw. Mrs Foster collapsed into Lee's arms on the sofa and wept uncontrollably.

'How did she die, officer?' asked Mr Foster.

'We don't have full cause of death at present, but it would seem that she was murdered,' said Ziggy gently.

'Did she suffer?' he asked through gritted teeth.

'The post-mortem is due to take place later today. We'll know more then. Your family liaison officer will keep you updated, and a member of the inquiry team, DS Sadie Bates here, will keep you up to speed as well.'

There was a moment of silence as the news settled, then Claire's mum asked, 'Can we see her?'

Sadie nodded. 'I'm sure that will be possible but as DI Thornes just said, it may be tomorrow, but we will let you know.'

Lee blew his nose and asked, 'Is it the same bastard that killed Susannah?'

Ziggy paused. The truth was, he just couldn't say. The position of the body and the area it had been found in were the same, but he really didn't know much more than that. He told Lee so, and once again promised to keep them up to date with everything as soon as they knew more.

Leaving their heartfelt condolences, Ziggy and Sadie left the grieving family. Ziggy dropped Sadie at the station to collect her car and with strict instructions to head home.

28

Thursday, 13 June

Z iggy hadn't slept, nothing new there. It was a perpetual circle that he knew wouldn't end until the killer had been caught. The stakes were higher than ever with the threat of another team being dragged in to replace him, and he already had a missed call from Whitmore. He was due into the office at eight, despite having left at eleven the previous evening, but he had an important visit to make on his way in.

He'd spoken to Rachel at length on the phone when he'd finally arrived home. It was the most they had spoken since they had divorced. Most of the conversation had been about Scott and what would happen next, but they had also talked about Ben. How it may affect him with Scott no longer there, but they both agreed that it was for the best; for obvious reasons, neither of them wanted that kind of influence around their boy. They both knew that Ben was a tough cookie who digested information, thought about it and then asked questions later. He had a well-adjusted head on his young shoulders, more like Ziggy than he knew. Ziggy had said he would call in before Ben headed to school the following morning for two reasons. Primarily to reassure him that he wasn't to blame for any of the arguments he may have heard, but also Ziggy knew that the double murder investigation would demand all of his time and attention and so he didn't know when he'd be able to find the time to see him again until the case was solved.

HE DROVE to Rachel's and pulled up alongside the kerb. Walking up the path, he could see the front door had been completely replaced. He was about to knock when Ben opened the door.

'Dad!'

'Hey, buddy, how are you?'

'Have you come to have breakfast with us?'

'Yep, your mum has promised me pancakes with blueberries.'

They walked into the house and headed into the kitchen. Rachel was wearing an apron over her clothes as she prepped the batter for the pancakes.

'Good morning,' she said brightly, though Ziggy could tell it was forced.

'Morning. That coffee smells good.'

She laughed. 'Help yourself. Do you have long?'

'About half an hour.'

'Can you pass me the blueberries out of the fridge, please?'

Ziggy did as he was asked, and their fingers brushed as he passed them to her.

'Thanks,' she said, casually.

Ziggy poured himself a coffee as Ben excitedly told him

about the upcoming sports day at school. Ben was taking part in the sack race, which made his dad laugh; Ben was so clumsy and could fall over his own feet at the best of times without the aid of a sack.

Rachel piled the stack of pancakes onto a plate and placed it in the middle of the table. Ziggy ate until he literally couldn't eat any more and checked the time.

'I need to get on, I'm afraid.'

'No problem. Ben, say goodbye to your dad.'

Rachel and Ben walked Ziggy to the door. He lifted Ben, covering his face in raspberries and ruffling his hair.

'Smell you later, alligator.' Ziggy laughed, standing his son back on his feet.

'Not if I smell you first!' shouted Ben as he scooted off down the hallway.

Ziggy and Rachel laughed. 'Thanks for breakfast,' he said.

'You're welcome, we should do it again.' Rachel pushed her hair away from her face.

'I'd like that,' he said, then he had no idea what came over him, but he leaned in and kissed Rachel on the cheek. Surprising himself, he took a quick step back. 'Erm, I'll see you later.'

If Rachel had been shocked, he couldn't see any signs of it on her face. He started the car, feeling a little confused. Why had he done that? Why had Rachel let him?

He brushed it off. He didn't have time to think about that now. He had a killer to catch.

ARRIVING AT THE OFFICE, Ziggy checked in his pigeonhole and could see he had messages from Whitmore and several from various media outlets, even though they knew they should contact the media team. He threw the unwanted messages in the bin as he made his way to the office. Sadie and Nick were already there. Angela was starting later as she had volunteered to accompany Lee and Claire's parents to the morgue so that they could say a final goodbye to Claire.

Extra resources had once again been drafted in and units from other stations close by had been called on, so the room was filling up, and along with it the noise levels.

Ziggy, Sadie and Nick retreated into Ziggy's office so that they actually could hear themselves think.

'Briefing in ten minutes. Do we have anything to add from overnight?' asked Ziggy.

'Just waiting for further forensics. They're hopeful they might get some latent evidence from the clothing, but if it's a fancy-dress costume that's been worn by loads of people, I've no idea how useful that will be. They're also looking at footwear marks that were left in the flower beds – again could be from the witnesses, so we'll see.'

'Speaking of the witnesses,' Nick interjected, 'all have given their statements and been ruled out.'

'Typical. Have either of you spoken to Whitmore?' he asked.

'Nope, we thought we'd leave that pleasure to you,' said Nick, with a sly grin on his face.

'Gee, thanks.' There was no way Ziggy could avoid it, but it would have to wait until after the briefing. 'Good to see every resource being thrown at this.' He indicated to the extra bodies that were seated in the room.

'Yeah, North and South Yorkshire, and I believe a few from Derbyshire as well.'

'Fantastic, let's get to it then.'

The three of them left the office and headed to the front

of the room. Ziggy said a hello to a few familiar faces, then waited until silence fell before he began.

'For the benefit of those I haven't met as yet, I'm DI Andrew Thornes, lead on Operation Silk. This is my deputy, DS Sadie Bates, and alongside her is DS Wilkinson.' He walked across the front of the room so that everyone could see him.

'As you may know, Operation Silk started a little under two weeks ago with the discovery of our first victim, Susannah Leibniz. Her body was found on Woodhouse Moor on the first of June, after she hadn't been seen by her grandparents, who she lived with, for three to four weeks. Cause of death was asphyxiation. She had also been bound with some kind of rope, restrained, and had several cuts and bruises all over her body. We've established that during the weeks since her grandparents saw her last, she was staying at a friend's flat.' He paused to let that sink in and took a sip of the water that Sadie had passed him.

'During the investigation into Susannah, we met with Claire Foster, who was one of Susannah's work colleagues and close friends. Claire Foster went missing on Friday, the seventh of June. Her body was found yesterday, again on Woodhouse Moor. Post-mortem results have just come in and they show that Claire was also strangled, had several cuts and bruises to her body and had been similarly restrained with some kind of rope. She was also found to have a puncture wound that appears to have been done by a stiletto heel.'

The only sound that could be heard was the scratching of pens on paper as everyone took notes.

Ziggy continued. 'There is one major critical factor that differentiates these cases. In the first case, Susannah was dragged to the deposition site whilst she was still alive.

Claire wasn't. She was held somewhere and then dressed in an *Alice In Wonderland*-like costume.'

The door at the back of the room open and Whitmore walked in. Ziggy nodded in acknowledgement but continued with his hypothesis. 'The working theory is that our killer is getting more organised. His deposition of Susannah although clearly planned was sloppy, haphazard, whereas Claire was placed, her position staged much more carefully.'

There were nods around the room. 'Our job now is to thoroughly explore every avenue and make sure we leave absolutely nothing to chance.'

Ziggy saw a hand tentatively raised. 'Yes, go ahead.'

'Morning, sir, wasn't someone arrested for this and released?' PC Jones asked.

Ziggy flinched inwardly. He knew this would raise its head. 'Yes, we arrested someone but there wasn't enough evidence to prosecute. He also had solid alibis for the times we are focusing on. In the briefing notes, you'll find all the details. We haven't completely discounted him from our investigation but it's looking unlikely. He has been subsequently rearrested for causing a disturbance and criminal damage, so he's currently being held in remand.' The room didn't need to know it was his ex-wife that the offences had been committed against.

'One final thing before we organise into working teams. DCS Whitmore and I will be holding a press conference later on today. Until then, there is a complete media blackout. I do not want anyone speaking to the press. Is that clear?'

There were nods all around the room. Sadie took over organising the various teams, so Ziggy walked over to Whitmore.

'Shall we go into my office, sir?' asked Ziggy as he opened the door.

Whitmore followed him in. 'So, have we discounted your suspect from the inquiry?'

'We've not entirely ruled him out, but as you know, there isn't any evidence against him and considering he was locked up when Claire's body was left in the park, I think it's safe to say he wasn't involved.'

'We're throwing everything at this now, Andrew, is there anything else you might need?'

Ziggy had to stop himself from doing a double take. *Is Whitmore offering to spend money on an investigation? Wonders will never cease.* 'Not as yet, though I expect when the full forensics come back, we may need to run a reconstruction and early-morning patrols stopping traffic to see if anyone remembers anything.'

'You've got it. Anything that needs doing. We have to solve this.'

'Sir, there is no one more than me that wants to get to the bottom of this.'

'What about a profiler? I know sometimes they're frowned upon, but it may give us the upper hand?'

'Not just yet. Again, let's see what forensics brings. I'm certain something will come up. Our perp went to great lengths to create the scenario we found in the park, but I don't see how he could possibly have gone to all that trouble without leaving any trace evidence or DNA.'

Whitmore was nodding along in agreement. 'Yes, absolutely. For the press conference, same as before? I'll read the prepared statement and you answer the follow-up questions?'

'Can't see a problem with that.'

'I can see a few, just remember to curb your delivery, eh?' Whitmore smiled and winked.

'Yes, sir,' said Ziggy. *Did he just smile and wink at me?* He had no idea why he triggered that reaction, but it was better than the usual snarky comment he received and all thoughts of moving him off the case were rescinded.

Once Ziggy had caught up on all his reports and urgent paperwork, he let Angela know that he was heading out. He didn't want to say where he was going. It wasn't strictly protocol, but he never let that stop him. He just couldn't sit with Whitmore breathing down his neck until the press conference. He checked his watch. He had an hour until he needed to be back. As he left the building, the press had started to gather in the car park, so he dodged out of a side door to avoid them.

'I can tell you for certain that it's from a heavy-duty boot, fairly new, size eleven.'

Ziggy looked at the forensic footwear specialist. 'Anything unique or distinguishing marks?'

'Hmm, not really. It's Timberland, which is a popular brand. Hundreds of thousands of pairs sold every day, I would imagine.'

Ziggy peered from the plaster cast to the digital replica. 'Isn't it the wrong sort of weather for such heavy boots?'

'Not if you work in the ground-keeping industry. This could have been made by one of the Leeds City Council workers that maintain the grounds of the park.'

'Damn. So not much use then?'

'Nothing to identify it as belonging to a specific individual.'

'Fuck's sake, will we ever get a break in this case?'

'Sorry. Have they finished with the fabric analysis yet?'

'That's my next stop. Thanks, Matt.'

Ziggy was at the forensics lab in Wakefield, West Yorkshire. Being sat in the office frustrated him, and house-to-house had once again turned up nothing. CCTV had identified a car leaving just minutes before the body was discovered, but the plates weren't registered. It was lost on the B roads heading out of Leeds city centre.

He returned to the reception area and asked if he could see Joanna, who was heading up the fabric analysis. The receptionist buzzed him through, and he once again donned the paper overalls that were obligatory to stop any contamination.

'Hey, Jo.' He waved at Jo on the other side of the lab.

'Now then, DI Thornes, it's been a while,' said a cheery Jo. Their paths had crossed on quite a few occasions when she was on shift with the mobile forensics team, but now significantly pregnant, she had opted to remain lab based.

'It has. You're looking extremely well. How long to go?' he said.

'Thanks. Feel crap, look great. Another two months, but this little one seems keen to get here earlier.'

'Oh gosh. I hope you're taking it easy?'

'As easy as I can – we're snowed under at the moment. Then your lot come in, jumping the queue.'

Ziggy knew she meant it in jest. Any major investigation takes precedence based on the severity of the crime, and this was about as severe as it got.

'Anything for me?'

'Come here, I'll show you.' She walked over to her bench. 'I'm going to be honest with you. There is a lot of evidence, but before you get too excited most of it is useless.'

Ziggy hadn't expected anything less, if he was honest. 'Nothing about this case has been straightforward, Jo.'

'It's interesting though. The clothes that were submitted – the dress, sock, shoes, underwear – were all pretty much invalid. It had hundreds and hundreds of DNA profiles, and unusually it had been dry-cleaned even though it was cotton. That would tell me that it was bought from a charity shop. Not exclusively but primarily charity shops steam clean their clothes using a spray filled with dry-cleaning fluid. If it had been in a machine, it would be consistent throughout the fabric, but it isn't. It's irregular, patchy, so not much use forensically.'

'OK, and what about the shoes and socks?'

'Generic underwear, Primark labels in both. Same applies to the shoes.'

'Hmm, again not much use. Too generic. And, of course, no unidentified fingerprints?'

'Nope. There is something though, and that's what I wanted to show you.' She spun round as best she could and pulled over her microscope. 'I've found a strand of hair.'

'What? Really?'

'Don't get too excited. I asked one of my colleagues to take a look, and she'll send you across the official report, but it's synthetic...'

Ziggy jumped in. 'From a wig?'

'Exactly.'

Ziggy's mind was working overtime. He had no idea how useful that information was, but it was more than they currently had.

'Also, Ziggy, did you notice the smell?'

Ziggy clicked his fingers and pointed at Jo. 'Yes! Lolly thought it smelled like a perfume?'

'That's what I thought. We've managed to isolate it. It's

Estée Lauder Youth Dew. Quite an old-fashioned fragrance, but you can still buy it in the big department stores.'

Ziggy could have kissed her. 'You, my love, are a bloody genius.'

Jo laughed. 'To be fair, it wasn't me, it was the rest of the lab. But I'll be sure to pass your thanks on.'

'Please do, and if the reports could be sent...'

'We're on it. We've given it top-priority, so with any luck they'll be in your inbox when you get back to the office.'

Ziggy said his goodbyes and left, feeling more enthused than he had for days. Could they really be closing in on the killer?

29

J o had been true to her word and by the time Ziggy arrived back at HQ, the results were waiting for him, albeit abbreviated but enough for him to share with the team.

'The perfume's intriguing isn't it?' commented Nick as he read through it. 'Isn't that something an older person would wear, like your granny or someone?'

'Possibly, but it is widely available. Might be worth checking with the clothes belonging to Susannah that were dumped.' Sadie said, thinking aloud.

'Good point, Sadie. I'm heading into the press conference, so I'll catch up with you afterwards,' said Ziggy as he hurried off.

The room where press conferences were held was on the ground floor and at the far end of the building. He was already running late, thanks to his impromptu lunchtime visit, but he figured it had been worth it. He arrived just in time to spot his superior running through the press release with Tom from the media team.

'All set, boss?' he asked Whitmore, smoothing the front of his shirt.

'Where have you been? I've been looking everywhere for you!' Whitmore looked flustered.

'Out for lunch, sorry about that. I do have some updates for you though.'

'Quickly then, they're like a baying pack in there.'

Ziggy ran through the forensics as they headed towards the conference room.

'Great news. And when's the next briefing?'

'I've asked for everyone to update by six, and those that can make it back into the office to do so.'

'Brilliant. Right, let's do this.' Whitmore took a breath and readied himself. As he and Ziggy walked into the room, flashes went off and a few people shouted out questions. Whitmore waved his hands up and down, urging everyone to be silent.

'I understand you're all eager to hear the latest updates, but we have a press release and that will be followed by a question-and-answer session, though I should remind you that this is still an ongoing investigation.'

The crowd settled down, and whilst cameras still flashed, they were quiet in the main. Once Whitmore had finished the official release, he passed the microphone over to Ziggy.

'I'll now take questions,' he said, with a sense of dread in the pit of his stomach. He'd already spotted Chrystal Mack, and she looked like she was out for blood. Surprisingly, she wasn't the first to ask a question. That honour came from the *Leeds Weekly News*.

'Can you confirm the two cases are linked?'

'Yes. We believe they are linked.'

'Do you have any suspects being questioned?'

'We have a suspect firmly in our sights and expect arrests to be made imminently.' Ziggy was pushing the truth in the hopes of unnerving the killer. Misleading the press wasn't the ideal strategy but it if it triggered a mistake by their perpetrator it was a chance he was willing to take.

'Chrystal Mack, *Yorkshire Post*. What happened to the arrest that was made last week?'

Bitch. 'The suspect was released without charge.'

'But he has been charged subsequently, I'm led to believe?'

'On an unrelated matter. Next question, please?'

She persisted. 'Didn't he attack your ex-wife in her own home?'

The room fell silent and Ziggy wished he could be really rude and tell her where to go. Instead, he schooled his face into an impassive expression. 'As I said, it was an unrelated matter.' He shot her a look that dared her to ask anything else. Instead, she looked down at her pad and notes.

'Is he still a suspect then?' asked another reporter.

'Investigations are ongoing,' said Ziggy noncommittally.

'What can you tell us about the killer? Do you think he's likely to strike again?'

'Whilst these incidents are linked, we have no reason to believe he, or she, will act again. As always, everyone should take care when walking through the Hyde Park area of Leeds and try to be in a group where possible.' He looked around the room, hoping the questions would now stop.

'You say *she*, could this be a female?'

Shit. 'We are looking at every angle. Now, thank you for your questions. If there's anything else, please speak to the media team.'

· · ·

WHITMORE CAUGHT up with him as he headed back to the office.

'What was that about? "We have a suspect firmly in our sights." Really? Because that's news to me.'

Ziggy knew he was going to get grief from Whitmore but what the hell. In truth, Ziggy was certain that if the perpetrator wasn't caught quickly, there was every likelihood he would strike again. His MO was escalating, and for that reason alone, Ziggy believed he was growing in confidence.

30

'I'd like us to take a closer look at another potential key piece of evidence that was found in the post-mortem of our second victim, Claire Foster.' Ziggy glanced down at the full post-mortem report in front of him. The outline of a female body was relayed onto the big screen so that the crowded room to see it for themselves.

'You can see here,' he pointed to the screen and then at a photograph next to it. 'Just above the rib cage, there is a puncture wound. Dr Turner indicates that it is similar to a wound made by a stiletto heel. As yet, we have no idea how significant this is, but we need to look at it.'

'Could it be a woman we're looking for?' asked one of the seconded detectives from South Yorkshire.

'We can't discount that possibility. We also have the synthetic hair fibre, which we believe to be from a wig.'

Sadie was sitting near the front. 'So where does that leave us?'

'I believe initially the key to all of this will lie with CCTV, so we need to focus on that. The car that was seen pulling away from Woodhouse Moor in the early-morning hours on the day of Claire's discovery needs to be identified and allocated. On the forensics side, I want every council worker who has worked at Woodhouse Moor questioned and their boots, or footwear examined. We know the dress came from a charity shop, so I want every charity shop within a twenty-mile radius of Leeds city centre questioned and shown the image. Again, high-street CCTV may hold the key.

'Look, I know this case is frustrating when all we want to do is provide justice to the families, and, of course, the victims, but we must be meticulous in how we proceed. Good old-fashioned police work is how we are going to solve this case, and I urge every single one of you to keep the victims' faces front and centre with every enquiry we make.'

Everyone dispersed and the room filled with a renewed sense of purpose. Ziggy clarified a few points with the team that would be heading up the high-street enquiries, then turned to Nick and Sadie.

'I'd like to go back to Woodhouse Moor, just to take in the scene again. I know it's early evening, but it might give us some idea of who frequents the park at that time, give us a bit of a feel. I don't know, maybe I'm just puffing hot air here. What do you think?'

'I can see the sense in that, though the local teams have been very thorough. I guess it could give us a fresh perspective. Want me to come with you?' asked Sadie.

Nick butted in. 'I'm happy to head into the high street with the neighbourhood team. Don't mind a bit of door knocking. It's how I started back in the day.'

'Great, Nick, I was going to ask you. Angela is knee-deep with the indexing and managing the incident room, so I don't want to interrupt her. Let us know if anything comes up, but if not, then back here in the morning for the eight o'clock briefing.'

THE SUN HAD STARTED to set as Ziggy and Sadie pulled up into the car park at Woodhouse Moor. They had deliberately parked away from both deposition sites so they could take in the full setting. Though it was early evening, the park was alive with groups of people gathering to enjoy the unusually warm day. Families were picnicking, and a team of students were in the throes of a football game that had accumulated a crowd of spectators.

'I just don't understand how such a popular place hasn't turned up any eye witnesses.'

They saw the blue police A-board, which detailed the incident time and dates along with an incident number.

'It does seem strange, but our perp is devious,' commented Sadie as they wandered down the path that led to the other side of the park. The grounds were well kept, being council owned, with regularly cut lawns and neatly tended flower beds. As they approached the edge of the park, they turned to walk in the direction of where Susannah had been found. If it wasn't for the floral tributes laid by family and friends, a passer-by wouldn't know anything had happened; the grass continued to be cut, borders were weeded, and paths kept free of litter.

They stopped and looked at the flowers.

'Do you think he was disturbed?' asked Sadie.

'What literally or mentally?'

'Well, I think we can safely say he has some kind of mental disorder, but the scene?'

'I'm not sure. I don't think Susannah was his first victim,' Ziggy said. 'I think he's killed before. There's no sexual motive behind either attack and that's where I'm struggling. What's his motive?'

'That's what the team have been struggling with too. There must be a motive.'

Using his amateur profiling skills, learnt over the years from studying criminal profiles, Ziggy voiced his thoughts, 'If you put together what we have already – hair fibre, stiletto heels, mid-twenties females, same location, same or at least similar MO – I think we're looking for someone in their late forties, early fifties. Probably lives on his own or with his elderly mother. I don't think he's married. To keep someone alive for a few days is a difficult thing to do, let alone with your spouse wondering where you keep disappearing off to,' mused Ziggy.

'Unless they're in on it too? I can't help but wonder if there's more than one person involved. Why the wig, and the stiletto heel?'

'That's very true and is a definite possibility.'

Sadie shrugged her shoulders to indicate she was happy to go with Ziggy's suggestion.

Ziggy knew most behavioural profiling was based on guesstimates and presumptions but that coupled with years of experience and intuition, he had always been able to build up a fair picture of their potential killer or killers. He'd already written all of his thoughts in his daily reports and had shared it with the team, but it helped to be here, at the scene to crystallise his thought process.

He turned around and looked at the distance from the tarmacked path to the path where Susannah had been dragged. It wasn't a huge distance, just a few feet, so why didn't he use the proper path. 'So why here, Sadie, do you think?'

'Not sure, was he in a car? He must have been driving or using some mode of transport. But you're right, why here?'

'And why was she dragged?' asked Sadie.

Ziggy walked off in the opposite direction.

'If we retrace the potential steps that he might have taken.' He put his hand up to stop Sadie from interrupting him. 'I know, I know. SOCO have covered all this, but let's work on the hypotheses of where she was dragged. Where would he potentially park the car?'

They spent the next hour or so working on the theory, walking the scene and voicing their thoughts. By the time they had exhausted every possible avenue, they were still no closer to a conclusion. At ten o'clock, the park almost empty, they called it a day. Ziggy phoned into the incident room but with nothing urgent having surfaced, he decided to head home.

31

H e couldn't believe his luck. She'd been delivered directly into his path again. For various reasons, he knew this one was the right one. This time, she really was.

He had spotted her a week or so ago at the local park. She had been with a gaggle of other mothers, any one of which could have been his next guest, but she had stood out. She was tall, with long dark hair and a tanned complexion. She was slim, dressed in what he'd call 'smart casual,' with dark jeans and a plain white T-shirt. She'd taken a call on her mobile phone and had literally been a few feet away from him. As she'd turned to walk back to her friends, he saw that she had a beautifully made-up face, with perfect red lipstick.

He'd wanted to reveal himself to her right then, but he had learnt his lesson and would bide his time.

He'd followed her as she walked home afterwards and watched as her slight hips swayed as she walked with her little boy. They were holding hands, like he used to with his mum. He envied the small boy. He wanted his mum back so he could do that again.

He immediately shrugged off the thought, remembering the evil that had been hidden within her. Lying bitch whore.

He had hidden over the road, out of sight as she had opened the front door and she and the boy had headed inside.

It had been a couple of days later that all the pieces finally fell into place. He'd arrived early morning, wanting to get to know her routine so he could time his appearance to perfection. From his spot, he saw a car pull up alongside the kerb and a figure had exited the vehicle and walked up the path.

He knew that face, but how?

He thought for a minute or two then it occurred to him. Then he heard the little boy shout, 'Daddy!'

Perfect.

32

Friday, 14 June

R achel hadn't slept properly since the incident with Scott. She had replayed everything over and over in her mind until she'd driven herself crazy with it all. She knew there wasn't anything she could have done differently. As Sadie had pointed out, Scott had hidden his behaviour behind a loving facade, and the more Rachel heard about his past record, the more she realised that she wasn't his first victim.

His boss, Jon, had called to the house to find out what the situation was. He hadn't sounded best pleased that Scott had been arrested, but there was very little Rachel could do. She got the impression that Jon was familiar with Scott's past, though he didn't say anything directly, because he didn't seem shocked when she told him about it. Scott had said that he had very little time for his boss, and Rachel could see why. A lanky, wafer-thin man with a pinched face who looked in need of a good meal. His long grey hair hung in greasy strands down either side of his face and was tied loosely at the back with an elastic band. His skin was pock-marked with acne scars. He'd made her skin crawl. Rachel couldn't fathom how this man had run a nightclub success-fully for years. She reasoned that Jon had used Scott to front the business, for his looks and the type of crowds he would attract.

Exhausted, she dragged herself out of bed, ready to start her day. Ben would be going to school soon, and she was due to start work at the hotel at ten and she wanted to get some shopping in first. Stretching and yawning, trying to remove the last remnants of sleep, she grabbed a towel from the radiator and headed into the bathroom. Once she was showered and dressed, she headed into Ben's room, to find him already awake and glued to his Nintendo.

'Hey, you, you should be getting ready for school, not playing games,' admonished Rachel, snatching the game controller out of his hands.

'Aww, Mum,' he moaned.

'No, Ben, you can play after school, but we need to get ready. Now,' she said right in his ear. He pushed her away and continued to roll onto the floor in an exaggerated fashion.

'Come on, lazy bones, teeth brushed, please, and get dressed.'

Rachel headed downstairs and switched the coffee machine on before pulling various cereal boxes out of the cupboard and placing them on the table. Ben eventually made it downstairs, and once they'd had breakfast, she grabbed his school bag and headed for the door.

'Aren't we going in the car?' Ben looked appalled as Rachel walk passed their car and onto the pavement, shaking her head.

'Nope, I thought we'd walk this morning. It's a lovely day

and some fresh air will do us both good.' She grabbed a hold of his hand and they headed up the road. Ben's school was only a twenty-minute walk away, and she had plenty of time to walk back home and pick up the car for her drive to work.

As they ambled along, happily chatting about the day ahead of them both, Rachel felt herself relaxing for the first time in days. She was glad to be going back to work, hoping that the comfort of routine would settle her anxiety and lead to better sleep.

She waved her son goodbye at the school gates and turned to head home. She felt her mobile ringing in the back pocket of her jeans.

'Hey, Ziggy,' she answered cheerily.

'You're sounding bright and breezy. Sleeping better? I tried you last night but there was no answer,' Ziggy asked.

'Not really, but I've just walked Ben to school and it's really lifted my spirits. I feel quite good.'

'That is good to hear. Are you working today?'

'Yes, thankfully. Hoping the routine will lessen my anxiety.' She'd spoken to Ziggy a couple of times in the last few days. It was nice to finally just chat and not argue over every little point. She'd confided in him about her fears over Scott reappearing, but he had reassured her that there was no chance of that happening.

'Let's hope so. How's Ben doing?' he asked.

'He's fine, he's got a spelling test today, but he's confident he'll ace it. How's the investigation going?'

'Slow but lots of activity going on as you can imagine. I don't think I'll get much of break over the weekend, sorry.'

'I understand, don't worry. Just call Ben after school and if you get a chance, pop round.'

'I will and thank you for understanding, Rachel. I appreciate it.'

She knew that a double murder investigation would mean everything was on the line for Ziggy, and if she was being honest with herself, she wanted to keep Ben around her as much as possible. 'Don't worry. Just catch the bad guys.' She laughed, using the catch phrase that Ben always used.

Ziggy laughed too, and they ended their call amicably. Even that made her feel better about life. She hated all the sniping and arguing between them. She still stood by her reasons for leaving Ziggy, but she vaguely wondered sometimes if she shouldn't have been more understanding. She shrugged it off. She was in such a good mood and refused to let her mind travel down roads that led nowhere.

Arriving at home again, she took her car keys out of her bag and opened the door. *Yes,* she thought, *today will be a good day*.

HE WAS glad he'd parked his car out of sight. He hadn't expected her to walk this morning. That was a change in routine. She was smiling and laughing as she walked along, which made him happy too. He wanted her to be happy. It was important to him that she was happy. When people were happy, they let their guard down, became careless, and he relied on this to find out more about her.

He already knew her name, and he liked the sound of it as it rolled off his tongue. He wondered how his name would sound on her lips. He wondered how her skin would feel in his hands. How her hair would smell. The thought sent shivers down his spine and brought goose bumps to his skin. This one would be very special; he was sure of that.

He slumped further down in the driver's seat as he saw her walking back towards him. He had a baseball cap pulled firmly down on his head and, for once, his sunglasses didn't look out of place as the sun rose higher. He'd left the engine idling as he'd waited for her, and as she pulled out of her drive, he waited about half a minute or so before pulling away. He followed her through the town centre, keeping a careful distance. She passed through the high street and headed out onto the A roads towards Harrogate. After another twenty minutes, she turned left and pulled into the car park of a hotel complex.

'You're going to work,' he pondered aloud. Now that was convenient; working in a hotel. He wondered what role she played. He didn't see her as a cleaner or chambermaid. Perhaps she worked in the back office, accounts or something like that. With looks like that, she should play a front-of-house role, he felt. Hiding her away in the back was such a waste of her beauty. There was only one way to find out. He needed to visit the hotel. He couldn't do it today – he looked a mess – but he'd think of something. He always thought of something.

33

D CS Steve Whitmore stood at the head of the incident room, with the chief constable at the side of him. Ziggy wondered what that was all about. It was rare to see his boss's boss in the middle of an ongoing investigation.

Before he had a chance to speak, Whitmore stepped forward.

'Ah, good morning, Andrew.' He thrust his hand forward for shaking.

Bit formal. 'Morning, sir.' Ziggy returned the shake, frowning as he did so.

'I'm sure you've met Chief Constable Hartley before?' Whitmore turned towards him.

Hartley stepped forward. 'Morning, DI Thornes.'

'Of course. Morning, sir.'

'Good, well that's the formalities out of the way. Chief Constable Hartley will be staying for the briefing, so that we're all on the same page, so to speak.'

Ziggy knew the 'higher-ups' would be keeping a close eye on proceedings and he sincerely hoped it would motivate the team rather than make them feel they were letting the side down.

The office had started to fill up behind them, and there was a low buzz of activity as the gathered detectives and support staff exchanged greetings and compared notes. Ziggy acknowledged his own small team and saw that they were all surprised to see The Boss in the room.

'No problem, we'll start in five minutes.' Ziggy removed his jacket; it was already looking like the British summer had reluctantly arrived.

He caught Sadie's eye and with a quick, slight flick of his head, he nodded towards the kitchen. Sadie followed him, practically bursting through the door.

'What's going on?' she asked breathlessly.

'No idea. Hartley's staying for the briefing.' Ziggy poured hot water into his mug.

'Are they moving us off the case?'

'No, I wouldn't have thought so. It's probably just a show of support.' He stirred his coffee, adding an extra sugar.

'For God's sake, we're working twenty-four seven – what more do they want?'

'Don't worry about it, but don't shoot off after the briefing – let's see what he's got to say.'

They both headed back into the room and Ziggy walked to the front. Whitmore introduced Hartley – not that it was necessary, but there were mumbles of 'sir' throughout the room. Whitmore handed over to Ziggy.

'Let's go around the room, how did the door-to-door go yesterday?' Ziggy looked over at Nick, who had spent the day pounding the streets.

'We hit the charity shops on the high street, nothing pertinent turned up but British Heart Foundation took the photograph and said they'll circulate it on the national forum they have. All the charity shops, regardless of who they are raising money for, frequently use it to share intel about shop lifters, that kind of thing. The majority of the stores also have CCTV, but unless we can pin down a time and date, we're looking at thousands of hours of footage.' Nick closed his notebook.

'Great work, thanks, Nick. Let's stay on that. If we need to widen the search, let's do it.' He turned to the group of detectives gathered in front of him. 'How is the search for the car going?' Ziggy was referring to the car seen pulling away from the second victim's crime scene.

DC Dove stood up. 'We've made a few developments. We can say with certainty that it is a BMW five series. It was travelling on false plates, so we're working with neighbourhood teams to try and locate it in the area, but as you can imagine it's taking a while. ANPR loses the vehicle shortly after it leaves the scene, so that's been exhausted. We're putting more resources on the streets, so hopefully something will turn up soon.' She sat back down.

Ziggy had been hoping there would be more positive news. He knew that everyone was pushing for results, not least Hartley and Whitmore, plus the other powers that be. It was turning into the biggest murder investigation for West Yorkshire in the last twenty years. Right now, even he would welcome outside help, albeit reluctantly.

He knew he had to pull something out of the bag. Taking a deep breath, he voiced his opinion that he believed Susannah wasn't their perp's first victim. He saw a few nods around the room from the older, more experienced detectives.

'So, I think we should extend our search perimeters.' He looked across at Angela again. 'Can you cross reference any missing women that fit the profile, but go back even further, say twenty years? Stay within the West Yorkshire region for now but broaden the area if need be. I firmly believe whoever did this knows the Leeds area like the back of his hand – how else would he know which B roads to take? I don't think he's the sort to use a satnav – he's too prepared.'

He glanced over at the DCS and Chief Constable Hartley. 'Anything to add?'

Hartley shook his head, folded his arms and looked over at Whitmore, who said, 'I just wanted to say that you're all doing an excellent job. Keep going, the killer *will* slip up at some point. Let's do our best for the families of Susannah and Claire.' With that, the briefing drew to a close.

'Your office, Andrew, please,' directed Whitmore as everyone began to disperse, CC Hartley following closely behind. Whitmore took Ziggy's seat, forcing him to stand awkwardly at the side of his own desk. He stood straight; hands crossed in front of him as if he was on parade.

'How can I help you, sir?' asked Ziggy, heart pounding slightly.

It was Hartley that spoke. 'I asked DCS Whitmore if I could be in on the briefing. As I'm sure you're aware, we have unrestricted support and resources at your disposal, and I have to report back to *my* superiors as to the progress of the case.'

'As you can see, sir, we are utilising every resource—'

Hartley raised his hand. 'Yes, I can see that everyone is working to capacity. I'm satisfied that the investigation is progressing, though I would have hoped there would be at least a suspect at this point.'

'We did make an arrest, but unfortunately we weren't able to proceed with charges as all the evidence we had was circumstantial. The suspect is now in custody but on an unrelated matter.'

'Yes, I'd heard about that, most unfortunate. And have you discounted him now?'

'Not completely, no. I'm hoping we can prove links with him and the BMW that was seen. When we arrested Scott Ball, he was driving a BMW and although forensically nothing was produced, it seems too much of a coincidence that the same type of car should be seen at the second scene.'

'Ah yes, I heard that mentioned.' Hartley turned to Whitmore. 'I'm happy to report good progress. Keep me in the loop. Any major turn of events, let me know ASAP.' As he stood up, Whitmore followed suit and they both headed for the door.

Hartley left, and Whitmore turned back to Ziggy. 'Good job, Andrew. Pass my comments onto the team and keep me up to speed.'

Ziggy breathed a sigh of relief. 'No problem, sir, and thank you.'

He felt blood return to his face, and a huge boulder lifted from his shoulders.

Sadie and Nick walked over.

'Everything OK?' asked Sadie, eyes wide in anticipation.

'Yeah, it's all good. They just wanted updates. I imagine a bean counter somewhere needed to clear the additional costs and they needed to check that we weren't wasting it.'

'What the hell?' Sadie couldn't hide her reaction. Her short tether with the big wigs when it came to the budget aspect was well known. How anyone could put a cost on hunting a killer seemed callous to her. But Ziggy had made her all too aware that she needed to get past it if she was to achieve her career goals.

'It's fine, I half expected it, in all honesty.' He took in the look on Sadie's face. 'Don't let it bother you, at least we're still on the case.'

'Look, let's just get on with what's happening in the real world,' Nick said. He was too long in the tooth to let any of it get to him. He was as committed as the rest of the team to reach a result, but he accepted that things took time.

'Absolutely,' agreed Ziggy. 'I've got a day full of catch-up meetings with the various teams, but I will say this. Sadie, you're doing an outstanding job under enormous pressure. We are getting somewhere, I assure you.'

'Thanks boss, needed to hear that.' The smile came back to Sadie's face.

'Oh, and Nick? You're not too bad.' Ziggy reached behind him to grab his notes as Nick flipped him the two-finger salute.

THE NEXT TIME Ziggy looked at the clock, it was past four in the afternoon and his head was ready to explode. He needed to grab five minutes of fresh air. He'd been in meeting after meeting, strategising, making sure every single angle was covered. He poured himself a cuppa and headed to the rear entrance of the building. Primarily used by the few smokers that remained, he was surprised to find it empty. He crossed over the car park and leant against the fence, feeling the sunshine on his face for the first time that day.

34

Saturday, 15 June

Ziggy headed into the office early to speak with Sadie about interviewing Scott Ball again. He was convinced that he was somehow involved in the whole tangled mess and was just missing a vital piece of the information jigsaw. They'd made the request for Scott to be brought back to the station for further questioning.

As Ziggy pushed the office door open, he was pleased to see Sadie was already at her desk. They exchanged morning greetings, and once they each had a coffee, they sat in Ziggy's office.

'He's in custody downstairs. He's being quite pleasant, apparently.'

'Probably grateful for being out of prison for a short while,' said Ziggy.

'True. So how do you want to go about this?'

'Let's keep it brief and to the point. All we want to know is about the car. How did it come to be in his possession?

When did he get it? How did he pay for it? Just fill in the gaps.'

'OK, are you coming in with me?'

'I don't see why not. It's nothing to do with Rachel's case, so...'

Sadie collected her notes and stood up. 'Shall we crack on then?'

'Scott, we'd like to ask you a few further questions in relation to the BMW you own.'

Scott looked over at his solicitor. She'd advised him to help out and answer as much as he could. She had told him it would work in his favour in the long run. 'Yeah, what about it?'

'How did you come to own that car, the BMW five series?'

'It was a gift.'

Sadie hadn't expected that answer. She waited to see if he would anything else.

Scott continued. 'Well, I say "gift". It came with the job.'

'What job?'

'At the club. Jon, my boss, gave it to me as part of the deal. I needed wheels, and he wasn't using it, so he gave it to me on the proviso that should I quit, I gave it back.'

'Wow, that was pretty generous.'

'Yeah well, I did a lot for that club. Made it a name, somewhere to be seen.'

Sadie struggled not to laugh. She, for one wouldn't be seen dead in there. 'I see. And how long had it been in your possession?'

'Since the beginning of the year. New Year's Eve. It was a sort of bonus.'

'Very generous of him.'

'Do you have any more questions for my client, Sergeant?'

Sadie looked at Ziggy. 'No. I think we're done here.'

THEY HEADED BACK UP to the incident room and filled in the few team members that were there with the latest.

'It's a weird one that's, for sure.' Ziggy was pacing the floor, arms folded as he processed everything. 'I think we need to speak to this Jon character. Was he there when you first picked up Scott?'

Sadie shook her head. 'Not that I'm aware of.'

'Right, Sadie and I can head over there now and have a chat. Angela, can you stay on top of SOCO and let us know when we hear anything back?'

'Course.'

ZIGGY PULLED his car alongside the kerb outside of Sweet FAs but didn't move immediately. 'It's a bit of dump, isn't it?'

'Well, it's not exactly The Ritz, is it?'

He leaned forward and looked down the road. It looked as though at some point it had been a working men's club. A 1960s prefab building that had had various extensions added over the years. The outside looked neglected, run-down and in dire need of a lick of paint at the least. They exited the car and walked round to the front. A garish pink neon sign hung down at an angle, with one *E* missing out of *Sweet*. The entrance had a weather-beaten porch, with faded green paintwork. Ziggy knew he wasn't exactly the desired demographic, but he failed to see why the hell anyone would visit the place.

'Needs a tidy-up,' Sadie commented as she flicked loose paint from the door.

'Is this the main entrance?'

'I think so. When we came last time, we entered from the other side, so we didn't really see this.' Sadie indicated to the back of the club, which was overgrown and littered with empty beer bottles. A steel fence closed it off from the main road on one side.

'Do we knock or what?' asked Ziggy.

'You can try it, but maybe the back entrance would be a better bet?'

Ziggy knocked and they waited. When there was no answer, they made their way round to the rear. The old cellar door was raised with the steel access door bolted shut, Ziggy almost tripped over it in his haste.

The padlock was off the gate that took them through to the door they could see, so they approached it and Ziggy knocked again. They heard some scuffling, and a few swear words before the door finally opened.

'Can I help you?'

'Hello there, Jon, is it?' asked Ziggy. He and Sadie produced their IDs. 'Would it be OK if we came in for a chat?'

'Yes, yes, of course. Come through. You'll have to excuse the mess – the cleaners haven't been yet.'

Jon led them down a dark corridor that opened up to a wide room with low lighting.

Ziggy looked around the room, taking it all in. There was a bank of booths, covered in black leatherette and studded with faux jewels. Each booth had a black circular table nestled within it, and clear curved plastic separated each seated section. Ziggy walked over to the bar area and saw a huge dance floor with a stage at the back, which had, what he assumed were, pole dancing poles. Glitter balls hung down from the ceiling, and a complicated rig of speakers and struts led back to a DJ booth.

Sadie explained why they were there. Jon offered them one of the booths and they took their seats. It was a little awkward, as Jon had slipped into the booth first, leaving him sat at the back whilst Sadie and Ziggy sat at opposite ends. Ziggy started with the questions.

'We're here regarding an employee of yours, Scott Ball?'

'I did wonder when you might come around. I spoke to the officers that searched the flat, but I haven't heard anything since. I had no idea of his background, I can assure you.'

'I understand. We'd like to chat with you about the car you gave Scott.'

Jon shifted uncomfortably in his seat. 'What would you like to know?'

'Scott claims that it was given to him as part of his employment package, is that correct?'

'Yes. He was a much sought-after DJ and had a few offers on the table, so I thought the car might sweeten the deal so to speak.'

'Did you buy the car for him?'

'No. I wasn't really using it, so it was no skin off my nose to change the ownership over to him.'

'That was a very generous gift, Mr... I'm sorry I don't know your surname?' asked Sadie.

'It's Mason, dear, but please call me Jon.' He laughed and gently slapped Sadie's knee.

'Right, thank you. You felt such a generous gift was acceptable for a DJ?'

'Oh, Scott was more than a DJ. He was the face of the club. He brought a lot of business with him.'

Ziggy was listening closely, paying attention to Jon's body language. He wasn't sure what he'd been expecting in a club owner, but Jon wasn't it. Maybe his view was old fashioned, but he had pictured a heavy smoking, large set man and Jon was just the opposite. Something just didn't add up. Ziggy could imagine him floating around in a silk kaftan, smoking a cigarette in a silver holder. He was actually dressed in a pair of work dungarees that were covered in dirt and grass stains and looked decidedly uncomfortable in them.

'Have we interrupted something, Mr Mason?' Ziggy nodded to his attire. 'You look as though you were in the middle of gardening or something?'

'Oh no, dear, I was just clearing up from last night. The agency DJ wasn't all that good, and the crowd he attracted were a bit rowdy, as you can see from the rubbish by the back door.'

Ziggy nodded and asked Sadie if she had any more questions. 'No,' she replied. 'I don't think so.'

Ziggy decided to take the opportunity to quiz Jon on another issue. 'Jon, as I'm sure you're aware we are currently investigating the murder of two women. We know Susannah, the first victim stayed here in the weeks prior to her being discovered, and that she had a connection to the second victim Claire Foster.'

Jon had his hands on the table in front of him and knitted his fingers together. 'Yes, I had heard about it, dreadful business.' He looked down at his hands.

'Did you know Claire Foster at all?'

Jon looked over at Ziggy. 'No, Inspector, I don't believe I did.'

'Her boyfriend said that she would come to the club on occasion.'

'That's as may be, but I don't remember every face that comes through the door, I'm afraid.'

Realising that he wasn't going to get anywhere, Ziggy ended the conversation, and they each shuffled out of the booth. As Jon directed them to the back door, Ziggy took a final look around. 'What kind of clientele does Sweet FAs attract?'

'Students mostly, nowadays,' replied Jon. 'Scott ran themed nights and that kept us ticking over.'

Ziggy nodded, thanked Jon for his time, and they headed out to the car.

As they fastened their seatbelts, Ziggy couldn't shake the feeling that something just didn't add up, but he couldn't quite put his finger on it.

'What did you make of that?' he asked Sadie.

'Thought it was a bit odd, to be honest. Wasn't what I was expecting. I got the impression that this place is just a bit of a hobby for him. Seemed happy to let Scott run things.'

'Yeah, me too. Let's do a search on our Mr Mason when we get back. There's definitely something not right there.'

35

Sunday, 16 June

The irony wasn't lost on Rachel as she put the finishing touches to the carefully staged wedding breakfast. With one divorce and a shattered relationship behind her, she was finding it hard to drum up her usual enthusiasm for the wedding fair. It had been planned for ages, and at first, she had been excited at the prospect of helping excited couples organise their dream wedding day, but the events of the last couple of weeks had started to take their toll. She was tired, overly emotional and desperately looking forward to having the day off the next day. Ben was staying with his gran, so Rachel could indulge in some quality time to herself.

She took one last look around and headed back to man the reception. She peeked out of the front door and saw a queue of keen brides-to-be already forming, even though the doors weren't due to open for another thirty minutes. Sitting at her desk, she looked through the list of couples that had pre-registered. A couple of names were familiar to her – she had shown them around the venue at some point – so she was hopeful of a few bookings.

She prepared her list, and right on time, she opened the doors and started checking people in. Her mood and spirits lifted as the excitement from the brides and grooms filtered through.

She handed out another flute of champagne. 'Hi there, welcome. What name is it, please?'

'Sheila Vincent. I'm probably not on there – it was all a bit last minute.'

Rachel looked at the woman and smiled. 'That's no problem. Just sign in here please.' Rachel passed the clipboard and pen over. Sheila took it from her, and Rachel couldn't help but notice the beautifully manicured hands. 'Wow, your nails are fabulous.'

'Oh, you're too kind, thank you.'

'You're welcome. Just head through the double doors and follow the signs.' As Sheila walked away, Rachel caught a faint whiff of perfume that reminded her of something, but she couldn't quite put her finger on it. Shrugging her shoulders, she continued checking in the other brides.

By the time, the clock struck four, she was exhausted. Her feet were killing her, and she had a headache from all the talking she had done. Overall, it had been a success with three bookings taken, a record according to the sales manager.

All she had to do now was grab her coat, then head home and soak in a long, hot bath. She closed her locker in the staffroom and headed back to reception. The remaining team congratulated each other on a successful day and went their separate ways, leaving Rachel to lock up the staff entrance. It had started to rain lightly, and she hadn't brought a coat, so she hurried across the car park.

As she clicked the remote key for her car, a face appeared in front of her and stopped her in her tracks.

'Oh, gosh, you scared the life out of me. Are you OK? What are you still doing here? Sheila, isn't it?' Rachel pulled her bag further onto her shoulder.

'Yeah, I was waiting for a lift, but I think I've been forgotten,' Sheila said, gesturing to the empty car park.

'Can I call you a cab or anything?' offered Rachel. She unlocked her car and threw her bag onto the passenger seat. Turning around, waiting for a reply she saw that Sheila appeared to be upset. 'Are you OK?'

'Oh yes, thank you, dear. I'm sure he'll be here any second.'

The rain had started to fall heavier, and Rachel noticed that Sheila was only wearing a thin dress.

'Would you like to wait in my car?' she offered.

'If that's not too much trouble for you?' Sheila had already walked around to the passenger side and opened the door.

A little taken aback by Sheila's decisive actions, Rachel climbed into the driver's seat. As she turned to reach for her seatbelt, she felt a sharp scratch on her neck but before she even had time to react, everything turned black.

36

H e'd learnt his lesson. He knew she was special, and he wasn't about to make the foolish errors he had before. This time he was prepared. He was ready. He'd rearranged the basement so that she could live in relative comfort for her stay. She had a bed, a toilet and even a wash basin; absolute luxury compared to the others.

He carried her limp and unconscious body down the steps, treading carefully as he went. He gently laid her on the camp bed, confident that she would remain in her drug-induced slumber for at least another hour. That would give him time to change into his regular clothes and prepare all the equipment he would need. He'd reinforced the locks on the door, so even if she roused, she wouldn't be going anywhere.

He gazed down and studied her face. She really was delicious with her glossy auburn hair and tanned complexion. She had been wearing the red lipstick he loved so much but it had long since worn off. He glanced over to the side of the wash basin where he had set up a little dressing table and mirror. The Chanel lipstick was there, all ready for her to apply when she woke. As his gaze drifted across her, she reminded him of a sleeping princess. She was a princess in his eyes, anyway. He could tell by the way she treated her little boy that she had a pure soul. He bet that she didn't harbour an evil grudge against her son. He imagined that she loved him without the conditions his own mother had applied to her love for him.

Lying bitch whore.

If it hadn't been for his mother, he would have lived a normal life. He doubted that his childhood would have ended as catastrophically as it had done, and so suddenly. He had just turned sixteen when he discovered the truth. She had spun a web of lies that had unwittingly included him. It was after her passing that it had all unravelled. Until that point, he'd loved his mother above all else. Everything he had done in his life was for her. He had believed that she had always put him first; he believed they were a little unit, a team. It had always been just the two of them, his father having left shortly after he was born. Not that that was his fault, his mother had sought to reassure her son on several occasions. She had told him what his father was like, and he hated him as much as she did. Still, she had done her best to raise him with proper morals and values.

When he started school, he slowly realised that things were different in other people's homes. Not all mothers stayed at home all day as his own mum had done. 'More's the pity,' she had said when he asked her about it. He'd asked her once what she did all day and that had been the first time she had slapped his face. He soon learnt never to ask again. He heard the rumours at school that men were always in and out of his house during the day, but he hadn't dared ask why after the slap.

Needless to say, he didn't have many friends at school. He was socially awkward and hated putting himself out there, expecting to be ridiculed at every turn. His classmates were cruel, but he knew he was destined for better things. That's what his mum had told him all the time. He was better than them. He had been raised properly.

Then she had died suddenly just after his sixteenth birthday. His world had been ripped apart. He had to leave the house they'd always lived in. With no relatives that he knew of, he came to the attention of the local authorities. They rehoused him in a poky flat where damp ran down the walls. He lived amongst drug addicts, ex-prisoners and 'women of ill-repute', as his mother had called them. He only learnt what that was when one kind neighbour took pity on him. She would turn up at his little flat with food and treats for him. He had liked her; she was glamorous and always perfectly made-up. She had taught him so much; much more than she realised. Using what she had told him, he worked out that his mother had been a prostitute. Lying bitch whore.

His new friend, his only friend, had opened his eyes to a way of living that his mother would have scorned. But even his friend had lied to him. He had sneaked into her flat one time, only to discover that she was a he.

Intrigued with what he had found, they had shown him how they transformed from male to female. He was fascinated as he had watched the transformation. She was beautiful, and he felt his body respond in ways that he previously had been led to believe were immoral.

One night, no longer being able to contain his self-control, he had attacked her. That was his first. The thrill he felt had been overwhelming. As the dead body lay prone on the floor, he had wept inconsolable tears; for what he'd done, for what he'd lost. As his tears subsided, he felt an enormous sense of release. He felt free from the chains of his mother. He realised that he didn't need to stay in the body he felt so uncomfortable in. He could recreate himself. Have a new, separate persona.

At first, he'd experimented in secret but as time went on and he felt more self-assured he would occasionally dress up as Sheila, and in the dead of night he'd take a walk. He loved the feeling of freedom, of no one knowing who he really was. He'd walk through parks and public gardens with his high heels tapping across the pavement. He soon discovered a new world, where he could meet people that wouldn't look down on him but accept him for what they saw. He fell in love with this new world and knew that his mother had been right. He was destined for better things.

After spending a few years on the club circuit, he had been given the opportunity to start his own place. He'd invested the nest egg he had saved into the club. He wasn't quite ready to face the world fully as his alter ego, but the club would give him a place to socialise without revealing everything. That had been the plan anyway.

Then Scott came along. He'd needed to take a step back from the club so he could pursue his alter ego and all that entailed, and Scott had seemed perfect at first. Good-looking, sociable, outgoing and definitely knew how to run a club.

But he grew to despise him. Scott's massive ego and sense of self-importance disgusted him. He had hidden his hatred well, he thought. Always trying to include Scott in decisions and show an interest. When Scott had met Rachel, Jon could barely contain himself. He'd only met her once or twice as Jon, but it had been enough to tell him all he needed. She needed the love of someone who would value her. An egotistical cretin like Scott was nowhere near good enough for her.

And now he had her. His heart skipped several beats at the thought of spending precious time with her. He couldn't wait to see her face when she realised who he was.

37

At first, Rachel couldn't feel her legs. She tried to open her eyes, but the lids felt heavy and reluctant. Her mind was fuzzy, brain sluggish and confused. She lay still, trying to remember where she was. Snippets of images flickered through her mind; the wedding fair, rain, car. Had she driven home and fallen ill? Where was Ben? With that thought, she forced her eyes open. After several rapid blinks, she managed to open them fully and took a look around her. She didn't recognise where she was. She sat up, hearing the squeak of the bed springs as she did so. There was an old-fashioned, knitted blanket over her legs and it fell to the floor as she swivelled round. *Where the hell am I?*

Panic started to build in the pit of her stomach and creep slowly into her chest. She stood up, legs feeling weak, but at least they were working. She felt a chill in the air and looked down to see that she was wearing an old-fashioned cotton nightgown with a frilly collar that was buttoned right up to her neck. She still had her underwear on, but her feet were bare, and she felt the cold floor seeping into her toes. She looked around for her own clothes and saw them folded neatly on a makeshift dressing table. She grabbed them and hastily pulled on her jeans. It was the clothes she had been wearing at the wedding fair. Completely confused, she sat back down and rubbed her hands over her face before cradling her head.

'Think, damn it. Think.' She could remember leaving the hotel and locking up. She could vaguely remember getting into her car. Wait, hadn't she met someone in the car park? She sat back, mind clearing as the fog lifted and she saw everything with crystal clarity.

Sheila! She shot upright. *Sheila got in the car. She stabbed me.* Rachel felt her neck and there was a small, tender lump just below her left ear. *She injected me.* Rachel walked over to the steps that led to the only door in the small room. She rushed up them and dragged on the door handle but there was no movement. That's when she spotted the heavy-duty lock. She looked around for a key. Nothing. Heading back down the steps, she went over to the dressing table she'd seen earlier and swiped her hand across, hoping a key would appear. No luck. There was a wash basin, some kind of toilet, a camp bed and a metal chair, but nothing else.

There must be a window. She walked to the far end of the room, which was only about ten feet wide and the same in length at the best, she estimated. She ran her hands over the brick walls, hoping to find a hidden window or door, but again, nothing. Looking up in the far corner, she could see a window with a wire grill over it, but it was too high for her to reach. She took a step back and tried to see if there was any way she could reach it. She went to grab the metal chair, but it was bolted to the floor.

'What the hell?'

Feeling desperate, she started yelling for help. Her

words fell dead in the room, not even the faintest echo came back to her. She ran up the steps again and hammered on the door, pleading for someone to help her.

After several minutes, she fell onto the bed, exhausted and terrified. She still felt woozy from whatever had been injected into her and before long she cried herself into a restless sleep.

ON WAKING FOR A SECOND TIME, Rachel's head was clearer and she was able to think more rationally. Sheila had, for some reason, injected her and was keeping her locked in a cellar or basement of some kind. However strange that sounded to her logical brain, she couldn't think of any other scenario. She had no idea why. Perhaps something to do with the wedding fair? Rachel went over to the little wash basin and splashed her face with cold water, swallowing gulps of it to try and get rid of the dry mouth she had. She reasoned there was no point in trying to figure out the why, what she needed to do was figure out where she was.

She remembered the little grilled window and went to inspect it as best she could. It was high up, and beyond the metal grill, there appeared to be glass. It had been dark outside when she had seen it before, now there was a faint glow of daylight. She couldn't hear anything outside, no cars or footsteps passing by. A scent came to her again, familiar but just out of grasp as to why it was familiar. Inhaling through her nose, she tried to track the smell down. There were overtones of bleach, so it made it harder to pinpoint. Eventually, it led her to the dressing table. Then she saw a bottle of Estée Lauder Youth Dew. It was dated; the box worn and yellowing. She took the bottle out of its box. Heavy glass, the contents inside nearly gone. She pressed the pump and a tiny squirt vaporised in the air. She sniffed. It was definitely that that she could smell, and now she remembered why. Sheila had been wearing it at the wedding fair.

She took the bottle and sat on the edge of the bed, cradling it in her hands. Was it heavy enough to hurt someone? Could she throw it when Sheila appeared, assuming she would?

As she looked around for something more substantial to use as a weapon, she heard the locks unfastening on the door. She was instantly alert. She stood up, holding the bottle behind her back. The door opened and footsteps descended. It wasn't Sheila.

'Jon?' asked Rachel, confused. The light from the torch he was holding shone directly into her eyes. She held her arm across her eyes, trying to shield the glare.

'Ah, you're awake.' Jon came down after securely locking the door behind him. 'I do hope you had a nice sleep? And you've got dressed, excellent. I'll be bringing more clothes later.'

Rachel was utterly confused. His voice was jovial, as if finding her held captive in a basement was the most natural thing in the world. 'I... I don't understand.'

'No, dear, I wouldn't expect you to.' Jon walked over to the wash basin and filled a glass he had been carrying with water. 'It's only cold water, I'm afraid, but you should be comfortable.' He also pulled a towel from a bag that had been slung over his shoulder. He placed the bag down and unloaded a cheese snack pack, an apple and a protein bar. 'Not much for now, but it should keep you going,' he said as he laid everything on the dressing table for her. 'I'll see if I can find a small table for you to take your meals at.'

Jon stood up and looked at her confused face. 'Everything all right, dear?'

Rachel had been watching in disbelief. 'I don't understand.' She was struggling to find words.

'I know, dear. You've already said that.' He took her by the shoulders and guided her to the metal chair. 'Sit there a minute, you look a bit pale.'

Rachel reluctantly sat down and continued staring at Jon.

'It's rude to stare, Rachel, didn't your mother teach you that?' He stood in front of her with his hands folded in front of him. 'Now, is there anything else you need before I head off?'

'I, I... Where am I?' she managed to stutter.

'Well, you're my guest for a short while. Don't worry, everything will become apparent in due course. Oh, and the door will stay locked, so you needn't worry about that.'

'But where's Ben? Why am I here?'

'Ben, I believe, is with his grandma. As to why you're here, well, I thought we'd get to know each other a little better.'

'Where's Sheila? Why did she take me? Are you working together?'

Jon let out a disturbing raucous laugh that sent shivers down Rachel's spine and made her flinch at the sudden change in volume. Jon didn't answer her. He walked up the steps, still laughing, and locked the door behind him.

Still clutching the perfume bottle, she threw it in his direction, but it shattered on the steps before it could reach its target.

38

J on was still chuckling to himself as he made his way into his office. It was so convenient having an old, disused basement right beneath his feet. With Scott now out of the way, he once again had free run of the place and no longer had to keep looking over his shoulder. Scott getting arrested had been the stroke of luck he needed. He knew the dirty lech would take girls back to the flat, and it had worked brilliantly for a while. Now, Jon had his modus operandi down to a fine detail, meaning he could execute his plans without interference.

He wondered how long it would be before anyone noticed Rachel was missing. He figured Rachel's mum would probably be the first to raise the alarm. He'd overheard Rachel talking at the wedding fair about having a few days off, but he wasn't sure what the arrangement was. No doubt Rachel's mum would contact Rachel's ex-husband. Shame he was a police officer, but it couldn't be helped. He'd be long gone before they found her, and even then, they'd be looking for Sheila.

He looked at the bag that was on the floor, his 'work kit',

as he called it. It had everything he needed to ensure that Rachel had a pleasant stay. He wanted to get to know her better. He wanted to find out more about her son, Ben; what did they do together, what were his hobbies and favourite foods? He whimsically wondered if they were the same as his. He really hoped she wouldn't be reluctant to share. Although he had the necessary tools in his work kit, he really didn't want to use them on her. He wanted them to be friends. Maybe he could even meet Ben one day – they could become a little family.

He was getting ahead of himself. He had plenty of other things to do today, so for now Rachel would have to wait. He was sure she would understand. He secured his bag back in the safe and went upstairs to what had once been Scott's flat. Jon had cleaned the place and put all of Scott's belonging's in bin liners and placed them in the loft. He wouldn't be needing them for a while, he'd reasoned. He had considered keeping Rachel up here, but it wasn't secure enough and he didn't want to take any chances. Instead, he'd turned it into a dressing room. All of his/Sheila's outfits were together in one place, and he could dress up to his heart's content. He looked along the clothing rail, his hands gently touching the various fabrics; velvet, silk, sequins, all in a variety of colours. All were long, flowing evening gowns that swept along the floor as he walked, just the way he liked them.

When he'd created Sweet FAs, it had been his intention for Sheila to be the hostess. It had worked at first. Sheila became a popular character with locals. Clubgoers had flooded in from all over the region. Sweet FAs became *the* place to see and be seen. Sheila hosted regular drag nights, and they had been a massive success, to begin with.

As the club and its reputation for the weird, wild and wonderful had grown he found it almost impossible to live a double life as more demands were made on his time. Scott was supposed to solve all that, but he'd grown too big for his boots. The drag nights had fallen out of favour as Scott introduced a new crowd, new music and Ibiza-themed nights. Jon had been side-tracked, wrapped up in quenching his own needs and desires that didn't involve Sweet FAs. He'd taken his finger off the pulse, and by the time he'd realised, it was too late. Takings in the club were down, the interior was dated and tired. He had lost interest, and no longer cared what happened to the place.

He'd kept his role up at the salon as a way of maintaining the release he had found. It had stopped the urges for a while, for a long time in fact, but as with all things he coveted, eventually it hadn't been enough. He'd felt the tension and urges start building in him again as he had watched the lovely Susannah running make-up sessions. She had awoken something in him that he thought he'd conquered. He knew now Sheila wasn't who he was meant to be. If he wanted a future with Rachel, he would have to remain true to himself, and convince her that they had a future together.

But for now, until he was truly ready, he could still play. He pulled a scarlet gown from the rack and held it up against himself. He turned to the full-length mirror and admired himself, but it wasn't quite the same when he wasn't wearing the wig, heels and make-up. In a fit of pique, he threw the gown onto the floor.

He would give up Sheila, surrender her, although reluctantly. He loved the escape it gave him, but he needed to do whatever he could to keep Rachel. He saw that now, but it didn't make him happy. He felt tears building up at the thought of sacrificing the only love of his life, all for her. His thoughts rampaged at the prices he was prepared to pay, wondering if Rachel appreciated any of it.

Frustration, hate and resentment converged to make his blood boil. Anger flooded through him. He needed to vent. Heading over to the safe, he retrieved his work kit and headed to the basement. He would show her how far he was prepared to go to give them the perfect life together.

RACHEL HAD BEEN PACING the floor, trying to think of a way to escape. The glass splinters from the perfume bottle were still on the steps, but she'd looked at them and none were big enough or strong enough to do any harm. She'd searched for her mobile phone even though she knew it was pointless.

She had given up and sat on the camp bed in tears when she heard footsteps approaching and the lock turn in the door. Instantly alert, she was determined not to play the part of the victim that she was sure her captor wanted. She stood up straight, defiant.

Jon entered the room and Rachel instinctively picked up on his change of mood. There was a tension around him, an energy, a bad energy. She braced herself.

Jon dumped his bag on the floor and glared at Rachel. 'Sit down,' he instructed, pointing to the metal chair.

Rachel faltered for a second, and he was on her, right up in her face.

'Sit. The. Fuck. *Down!*' he yelled at her, spittle flying everywhere.

Terrified, Rachel did as she was told, all thoughts of defiance gone.

Jon rummaged around in the bag and produced a rope.

'I didn't want to do this, but you've given me no choice.'

He forced her arms behind her back and roughly tied her hands together. He moved round to the front and as he tried to pull her legs forward, she kicked out, catching him on the jaw with her bare foot.

Incensed, Jon rapidly recovered and punched her hard in the face. Her nose broke instantly with blood billowing out and running over her lips. He stood back, breathing hard. 'Now look what you've made me do.'

Rachel was dazed and in pain. She couldn't wipe the blood away as it ran down her face and over her chin. She cried, trying to form the words she wanted to say, but she felt sick and all that came out was a bloody gurgle.

Jon started pacing backwards and forwards. 'Why did you have to do that?' He turned and stared at her. His eyes were bloodshot and bulging out of their sockets. 'All you had to do was be nice. How many times have you told me, speak when you're spoken to? If you can't say something nice, don't say anything.' He spoke in a high-pitch, shrieking voice. He took a silk scarf out of the bag and started twisting it round in his hands. 'I won't let you do this to me this time. I'm tired of all your shit.'

Rachel had put her head down, sobbing. Jon forced it roughly backwards. 'Look at me when I'm talking to you.' He slapped her hard across the face, spinning her head to one side.

Rachel groaned and pleaded with him to stop. 'What do you want?' she spluttered through her tears, tasting the metallic tang of blood on her lips.

'What do I want? Ha, that's a laugh.' He snorted. 'You've never asked me that before. My needs, *my* wants have never been *your* concern.' He punctuated each word with a sharp jab of his finger to Rachel's face.

She flinched, trying to pull away. 'But I don't know you. I don't know what you mean?'

'What I mean is your wicked ways.' Jon stood back, folding his arms as if he had revealed a secret and was waiting for a response.

Rachel could barely see, but she knew he expected her to show some kind of reaction, but all she felt was utter confusion. 'I... I don't understand.'

'It's simple. I know what you've been doing.' He walked over to her and squatted down so they were face to face. He poked her cheek. 'What do you think to that?' He grinned; his pointy features amplified by the cruel curve of his lips.

Rachel didn't know what to say so remained silent.

'Not so quick with your slaps now, are you, bitch? Tell me, how long have you been a whore?'

Rachel was violently shaking and shook her head from side to side. 'I... I'm not a whore.'

'Yes, you are. And you lied to me.'

'No. No, Jon, I've never lied to you.'

Another slap to the other side of her face.

'Yes, you have. You've lied to me my whole life. All I ever wanted was your love.' Jon sat on the edge of the camp bed, in tears now. 'Everything I did, everything I've done has always been for you. I killed my best friend, for you. And how did you repay me? You were a whore. You opened your legs to any man who knocked on our door.' He was still twisting the scarf between his fingers, edges now frayed as he tugged at the seams. He sniffed, tears falling, he breathed deeply and looked up. 'What did I do wrong? How did I let you down?' He stood up and walked away from Rachel towards the bottom end of the room.

Rachel shifted in her seat. Her arms were aching, her nose

was throbbing and the nausea she felt was overpowering. Her brain was desperately trying to process what Jon was saying. Who did he think she was? His mother? She watched him closely, fearful of what he would do next. He stood silently with his back to her. She took it as a chance to try to placate him.

'Jon?' she whispered, trying to soften her voice. 'Jon.'

He turned and looked at her. 'Yes?'

'Please, come here and sit down. Let's talk.' If she had to be his mother, so be it.

Jon shuffled forward, his shoulders slumped, anger spent. As he made his way over, Rachel forced herself to smile. 'That's it, sit down just there.'

Jon sat on the edge of the camp bed, just at the side of her.

'Now. Let's start again, shall we? Tell me why you're angry Jon, so I can understand?' As much as it pained her to be nice, she could see a softening in his features. 'Why don't you blow your nose and wash your face? Maybe help me... Mummy with her face too?'

Jon stood up and retrieved tissues from the dressing table. He cleaned his face, then rinsed a face cloth under the cold tap and wiped Rachel's face so gently it felt featherlike. All the time he was apologising and whispering platitudes of regret and begging forgiveness.

Once they were both tidied up, Jon sat on the edge of the bed again.

Rachel started again. 'What would you like to talk about?'

'Tell me how much you love me?' Jon looked at her with a childlike expression.

Going along with the game, Rachel answered. 'To the moon and back.' She smiled at him.

'That's good, I like that.'

Rachel felt a glimmer of hope. If she could talk him round, he might let her go, or at least leave her alone until someone found her.

'Would you like a hug?' she asked.

For the first time, Jon's eyes lit up. 'Oh, that would be wonderful.'

'You would need to give Mummy her arms back to do that.'

'But I can hug you, anyway.' He approached her and she tried to recoil and stop herself from vomiting as he placed his arms around her shoulders. Her head rested on his shoulder and he squeezed, hard. She let out a little squeak as her arms were pushed hard against the metal chair.

'Oh, I'm sorry, Mummy.' He let go and stood up. 'Are you OK? Did I hurt you?'

Rachel played down the pain. 'It's fine. That was a lovely hug, thank you.'

'I've wanted to do that for so long.' Jon was smiling. 'Are you hungry? Shall I make us some lunch?'

Sensing she could get a few minutes of respite, and despite feeling sick she agreed that food would be good. Jon left the room and Rachel leaned back into the chair, tipping her head back and let out a silent prayer.

'Please, for the love of God, someone save me.'

39

Monday, 17 June

Ziggy stood at the front of the investigation room waiting for everyone to file in. He noticed the drooping of their shoulders and muted voices. It had been two weeks since the discovery of Susannah Leibniz's body, a week since Claire Foster had been found, and they were still no further forward.

He knew how the team felt. He felt it too; frustrated, demotivated and tired. They had put so many hours of overtime in that he had insisted on splitting the team so that they all had some rest, promising that things wouldn't look so bleak come Monday morning. He had been wrong. He'd spent the majority of his weekend going over each case from start to finish, trying to figure out what they had missed. He'd scoured through every report from CCTV to forensics and still didn't have any answers.

He acknowledged Sadie and Nick as they took their places, each clutching a much-needed boost of caffeine. Ziggy had already worked his way through more than his usual share and could feel the slight jitter as it surged through his veins.

With everyone seated, the room held at least seventy additional officers of various rank and division, all of which had been drafted in to close the case as quickly as they could. Some of them he knew and had worked with previously. Others were new faces to him. All of them looked at him expectantly. He stepped forward.

'Morning everyone. We're moving into the almost third week of the investigation, and it's imperative that we keep up the pace. We need to continue reviewing the CCTV from the high streets, keep searching for the second BMW and I want to see if we can focus in more on Claire. We've been over her movements for the twenty-four hours leading up to her disappearance. Let's go further than that. Sadie, speak to her boyfriend again. I know it's a long shot, but he's the closest person to her that we have right now. Also, the link between Susannah and Claire seems to be the salon. What do we know about the clientele? I noticed they offer a barber service – could our killer be a customer? Whoever the perp is, he was known to our victims.' Ziggy took a sip of water before continuing.

'I know you're all frustrated, trust me I am, too but we're this close' – he pinched his thumb and forefinger together – 'to getting a breakthrough, so dig deep, girls and boys, we will get there.'

The team split up and went about their various duties whilst Ziggy, Sadie, Nick and Angela headed into their office.

'Do you really believe we're that close?' asked Sadie.

'Yes, absolutely I do. The breakthrough will come from the most unexpected place I feel, which means we have to make sure we stay on top of everything.'

'It's true,' commented Nick, the longest serving member of Ziggy's team. 'How many killers have been pulled up for traffic offences, only for the police to find dodgy equipment in the boot of their cars? Peter Sutcliffe, for example.'

'Well, we're working like pack horses in the incident room. I think a few came in over the weekend just to make sure the index was up to date,' said Angela.

'Thanks, Ang, you're all doing a brilliant job,' acknowledged Ziggy.

'Do you want me to talk to Lee again this morning, boss?' Sadie asked.

'Please. It seems odd that there was so little on her mobile phone. I know she was a dedicated mum, but she had clients, wouldn't they message her or something?'

'I don't message my hairdresser,' queried Nick, raising his eyebrow.

'You mean you get those three strands on top of your head trimmed?' joked Angela, and she received a faux box around the ears.

Ziggy laughed. 'She's got a point, Nick. Angela, I'll review the CCTV footage today. No harm in a second pair of eyes going through it. If you could ask them to isolate the charity shops on the high street for the two weeks running up to Claire's last day at the salon, that would be great.'

Angela glanced at the others, who had raised their eyebrows. 'We've been very thorough, boss, there's really no need.'

Ziggy spotted the looks between the team. 'I know, I know what you're all thinking but it's an itch I need to scratch.' He looked around. 'Any questions? No? Right. Let's get to it. Another briefing at four, please.'

. . .

Four o'clock came around sooner than expected. The update had been limited with new information, and conscious of the overtime bill mounting up, he sent the majority of the team home. He knew it wouldn't be long before more eyes were focused on the ongoing costs of the investigation.

Deciding there was little more he could do at the office; he rang Rachel's mobile to see if there was a chance he could pop in and see Ben on his way home. He hadn't had any real time with him in three weeks, and guilt was overwhelming him, along with everything else. When he didn't receive a reply, he tried the landline, but again, it clicked through to the answerphone. He tutted and shook his head. Of course, Rachel had been running a wedding fair at the hotel on Sunday, and Ben was staying with his grandma, in light of Ziggy working, so Rachel was probably out having some me-time. He liked his former mother-in-law; she wasn't one to interfere and always put Ben first. Scrolling through his phone, he found her landline number and hit dial.

'Hey, Val. It's Ziggy. How are you?'

'Hello there, it's been a while, hasn't it? I'm good, thank you. Did you want Ben? I have him here with me.'

Ziggy could hear cartoons playing in the background. He smiled. 'In a second, do you know where Rachel is?'

'I'm hoping she's on her way to collect Ben.'

That would explain her not answering her mobile; she was driving. But Val continued, 'She was supposed to be here this morning, but I didn't hear anything, so I took him to school. I walked up at pick-up time to see if she was there, but I ended up bringing him home with me when there was no sign of her. Maybe she's just running late after work.'

'Have you tried calling her?'

'I've tried a few times. I just assumed she'd had a busy day at the wedding fair and had slept in to be honest.'

'Seems a bit strange. I've tried her landline and mobile, but there was no answer from either.'

'Oh my. I'll try her again and let you know if I get hold of her.'

'Please. I'll pop round to the house on my way home and see if she's in.'

'OK. Here's Ben for you.'

Ziggy heard the muffle of the phone as she passed the handset to his son. After catching up on his day's news – everything was boring, and the teachers had given him even more spellings to learn! – Ziggy ended the call with the promise to see Ben soon.

Rachel didn't live too far from him, so the diversion on the way home wasn't a pain, but as he pulled up alongside her house, he noticed there were no lights on, and her car was missing from the drive. He walked around the house, checking through the windows but it was clear that she wasn't home and there was no sign of a break-in or any kind of scuffle. Though he wasn't truly satisfied – maybe she was on her way to Val's or shopping – there seemed very little he could do. He put in a request that local patrols keep an eye on the place, and then headed home, picking up a pizza on his way.

JUST AS ZIGGY was preparing for an early night, his landline rang.

'Andrew, it's Val. I'm sorry to bother you but Rachel still hasn't been for Ben. I don't mind keeping him, of course, but I thought you would want to know. Do you think we should be worried?'

Ziggy's heart skipped a beat. 'Have you tried calling her?' He had taken the call in his bedroom and was already pulling on his jeans as he spoke. Something wasn't right.

'Yes. I've been trying both on and off since about seven, but no reply.' There was a nervousness in Val's voice.

'I'm sure it's just something simple, Val. Maybe if she knew you were having Ben, she booked herself a night away.' Even as Ziggy said this, he knew it couldn't be true. Rachel was a creature of habit; she planned everything.

'Hmm, I don't think so. I'm worried, Andrew. Did you call at the house?'

Ziggy could have kicked himself for not taking action sooner, but at the time he assumed Rachel was just on her way to Val's. 'I called round, but all the lights were out, and her car wasn't there, so I assumed she was driving to yours, like you said. I did ask local patrols to keep an eye out.' He wasn't sure why he felt he had to justify himself.

'OK, well, I'll try phoning her friends but it's a bit late in the evening, isn't it?' asked Val.

'I'm sure they'll understand when you explain. I'll take another look around the house and see if I missed anything. I'll give you a call in an hour unless you hear anything first then call me.'

Ziggy completed dressing with an urgency he hadn't felt since Rachel had gone into labour with Ben. Slipping his feet into his trainers by the front door, he shrugged into a jacket and fished his mobile out of his pocket.

'Sorry to bother you, Sadie, did I wake you?'

Sadie sounded bleary eyed. 'I'm awake now. Wassup?'

Ziggy felt guilty for disturbing her, but he wouldn't rather have anyone else with him on this one. 'I'm so sorry. Rachel's mums phoned me.' He went on to explain the situation. 'So, I was wondering if you could meet me at Rachel's house?'

'Of course. Give me twenty minutes and I'll see you there.'

'You're a star, Sadie, thank you so much.'

THEY'D CHECKED round the house, front and back but there was still no sign of Rachel. Ziggy had peered through the downstairs windows, but everything looked as it should.

'Do you want to call Traffic?' asked Sadie, tentatively.

'I think we should, and check with hospitals?'

'Let's do Traffic first, then hospitals,' Sadie said decisively.

Ziggy wasn't thinking clearly; of course, that was the logical way to approach this. One would lead to the other. He scratched his chin and rubbed his hands over his hair. How would he approach this if it wasn't Rachel?

The first question he'd ask was if the missing person was at risk. *Is Rachel at risk?* He didn't believe so now that Scott was safely behind bars awaiting trial. Ziggy wasn't aware of anyone else that she had been involved with, and after the messy break-up with Scott she had given Ziggy the distinct impression that she was off men for a while. He knew she wouldn't just leave Ben; he was her world.

Wait, where had he heard that before?

Claire! Lee had said it about her.

'Oh my God, Sadie, you don't think this is linked to the missing girls, do you?'

Sadie was on her mobile and held up a finger as she listened to the speaker on the other end. 'Right, no traffic incidents reported within the area so that rules out any road traffic accidents. I've asked local patrols to take the route that Rachel would take from both the hotel, and also from her mum's, just in case.'

Ziggy was pacing back and forth. 'Did you hear what I said?' he snapped.

'I did, and I chose not to answer so there's no need to snap. We'll find her, Ziggy. She may have popped to the supermarket for all we know.'

Ziggy looked at Sadie apologetically. 'I'm sorry for biting your head off. It's just you know...'

'Yes, I know. It's different when it's your own.' She climbed back into her car.

'Where are you going?'

'To the hotel. Make sure she left the event OK on Sunday.'

Ziggy thoughts were all over the place, and he could have kicked himself. Why hadn't he thought of that?

Sadie leaned over and opened the passenger door. 'Come on then, are you getting in or what?'

He did as he was told, glad for once that someone else was making the decisions, at least for now.

SHORTLY AFTERWARDS, they pulled up outside the main entrance of the hotel where Rachel worked. It was nearly eleven and the car park was fairly quiet. During the week, the hotel attracted mainly business people travelling in and out of the area. They headed to reception, where a rather bored-looking young man was busy playing on his phone. They waited a second or two for him to look up and when he didn't, Ziggy slapped his hand down on the counter. The lad nearly jumped out of his skin.

'Ah, erm... Sorry. Can I help you?' he stuttered, straightening his hair.

'Yes. I'm DI Thornes and this is DS Bates. We're looking to speak to a manager please, with a view to looking at your CCTV.'

'A manager? At this time of night, you'll be lucky.'

'It's concerning an employee, so if you *could* find a manager that would be really helpful,' Ziggy snapped at him.

On hearing Ziggy's tone, Sadie raised her eyebrows and stepped forward. 'As my colleague said, it is in relation to someone who works here so if any one of a senior level is in, that would be great.'

They both expected the young man to go off and find someone or make a few calls, but he just stood there, not speaking.

'Is there a problem?' asked Ziggy, his infamous thin patience being pushed to the extreme.

'Erm, if it's about that weed, then it was for personal use.'

Ziggy exhaled loudly and walked away.

He breathed deeply and heard Sadie take over. 'No, it isn't. Could you just go get a manager or someone of seniority, please?' It seemed that even Sadie's endless patience was being tested.

Finally, the receptionist picked up the phone and called someone, who was clearly as perturbed as he had been by the distraction from his phone.

'He'll be along in a minute.' The lad sat back down and picked up his phone again.

Sadie walked over to where Ziggy was standing staring out of the window. 'Someone's coming.'

'Thank God for that. How do these people keep their jobs?'

Sadie was about to reply when a heavy set, jovial-looking man came through the double doors. He had obviously been woken up, his appearance dishevelled and unkempt.

'What can I do for you, officers?'

'I'm DI Thornes—'

Unkempt Manager interrupted. 'Yes, yes, I know who you are. What can I do for you?'

Rude. 'Is there somewhere we can talk?' asked Ziggy, looking around for a side room.

'Depends on what you want?'

This man was really getting to Ziggy. 'We'd like to chat to you about one of your employees, so if we could do that in private it would be better.'

Unkempt showed them into a side room, which Ziggy realised was where they kept the IT hardware, with racks of servers and fans going constantly. He managed to keep his short temper in check.

'On Sunday, you held a wedding fair here. Rachel Thornes was running it. I'd like to see the CCTV for the car park from after the event. Please.'

'Don't you need a search warrant for that?'

'Only if a crime has been committed and we won't know if one has until we view the CCTV.'

The man looked at Ziggy with questions written all over his face. But it seemed that he had worked out that the sooner he gave them what they wanted, the sooner he could go back to bed.

'Follow me.' He held the door open so that Ziggy and Sadie could pass by him, where they waited for him to re-lock the door. He then led them along the hotel corridor to another small, poky room. In there, they could see banks of screens showing CCTV footage, focusing on all areas of the hotel.

'What did you want to see?' asked Unkempt, fiddling with a mouse.

'Just the CCTV from the end of the wedding fair, the one that shows the car park, please.'

'Do you know what time it ended?'

Ziggy didn't have a clue. He looked at Sadie, who shrugged her shoulders. 'What time would these things usually end?' he asked, clueless.

'Depends. Sometimes they run over as late as seven in the evening.'

Ziggy really was at the end of tether. Was this man being deliberately obtuse? 'Can you look from say five p.m. onwards?'

While Unkempt jiggled the mouse about and tutted, swore and generally made it absolutely clear this was a ball ache, Ziggy and Sadie stood right behind him. After ten awkward minutes, Unkempt swung round in his chair, almost knocking Sadie off her feet.

'Oops, sorry, here you go. Shouldn't take you too long if you watch it on high speed.' He stood up and pushed past them both. 'If there's nothing else?'

The officers looked at each other, appalled by the shoddiness of the night manager.

'No, I don't believe there is. Thank you for being so helpful,' said Ziggy. Then, just as the manager had walked through the door, he shouted him back. 'If we want to take this with us, do we have your permission?'

The manager shrugged his shoulders. 'Makes no odds to me.' And with that Unkempt shuffled off, clearly heading back to bed.

'Pleasant fellow,' commented Sadie as she took the vacated seat and started the video running.

'Seriously, how do these people keep their jobs?' Ziggy pulled up an empty chair.

'It's a mystery for another day.' She wiggled the mouse and the car park CCTV lit up like a Christmas tree. 'Here we go.'

They both leaned forward, but the quality was exceptional compared to what they were used to. They watched closely as couples and groups of young girls came and went from the hotel to the car park and vice versa. Just before 6 p.m., they saw Rachel by the back entrance, locking the staff access door. She stood still for a minute or two, saying what looked like goodbye to the staff, then turned and headed to the area where her car was parked. They saw her take a few steps forward before a figure stepped in front of her.

'And who are you?' asked Ziggy, leaning in closer. They let the video play and saw Rachel open her car door, and the figure walk round to the other side. As they dipped their head to get into the car, their faces were directly towards the camera.

'Pause it.'

Sadie did so and zoomed in. 'Who is she?'

'We've seen her before.'

'Bloody hell, it's Sheila from the salon.'

Ziggy squinted a little to try and get more focus on the image. 'Do you know, I think you're right. Now what would she be doing at a wedding fair?'

'More importantly, why was she getting into Rachel's car?'

40

Z iggy and Sadie had returned to HQ and had briefed the few remaining staff on Rachel's disappearance. Ziggy had spoken with Missing Persons to ensure her disappearance was registered on the national system. There was no telling where she might be, but he wasn't taking any chances.

'We need to find her car. Can we run the reg through ANPR, see where it's been picked up on the cameras? And register it as of interest on PNC.' This meant any force that happened to check on the vehicle would know that it was of interest to West Yorkshire Police. Ziggy wracked his brains, well-known procedures momentarily slipping from his mind. 'And financial checks, has she used her bank card at any point?'

'On it, boss. Here, I'll grab us a coffee and take a minute, shall we?' Sadie suggested.

She headed to the kitchen and switched the kettle on. She knew Ziggy's break-up with Rachel hadn't been exactly amicable, but she was genuinely worried about him.

Knowing him as she did, Sadie knew that if he took a few minutes and detached himself from the emotion, which they all had to do at some point, he would start to think objectively and switch back into DI mode.

Sadie passed Ziggy his coffee and sat down. She swivelled her chair around to face her desk and logged in.

'Did we do the search on the club owner, Jon Mason by any chance?' asked Ziggy.

'I'll have a look; do you think it's relevant?'

'Something was odd about him and it's bugging me.'

'Yeah, I agree.'

Ziggy leaned over her shoulder and watched as she searched for 'Jon Mason'.

'Nothing,' Sadie said.

'Nothing at all? OK, let's pass that on to someone else to do the digging while we focus on Rachel. Let's see if ANPR brings up anything.'

In between all the activity, Ziggy kept trying to call Rachel's mobile, but it was clicking straight to answerphone, so it had either been turned off or the battery had died.

'Can we trace Rachel's mobile signal?'

'Depends. I'll have a word with Tech.'

Ziggy left Sadie and walked into his office. He debated on whether or not to call Val back. She'd called him after they'd left Rachel's house, once she'd finished calling Rachel's friends, to say no one had seen Rachel.

He had tried to track down Sheila from the salon, but all they had was her name, which hadn't shown anything, not even the electoral register. The salon wouldn't be open for another – he checked his watch – eight hours. It was just past midnight on Tuesday which meant Rachel hadn't been seen since Sunday evening. He knew she wouldn't just disappear. He felt in his gut that it was somehow connected to the other girls. The wedding fair had played a part in it. Wait, hadn't Susannah been stalked by someone after visiting a wedding fair? The woman they had seen in the car park was definitely Sheila, without a shadow of a doubt. At least they had a definite connection between Sheila and Susannah.

But we've had that all along, thought Ziggy. He placed his elbows on his desk and rubbed his face and the top of his head with his hands. Though he was in very familiar territory, he felt like an outsider looking in, watching things take place. He couldn't do that. He had to take control. He needed to find the mother of his child.

His internal phone rang. He snatched up the receiver. 'Yep?'

'We've had hits on ANPR.'

Standing up, he took deep breaths, pulled his shoulders back and headed into the office to let Sadie know. She already knew and was waiting for him.

'Her car was picked up by the cameras driving through Leeds city centre,' said Sadie.

'She wouldn't take that route home,' mused Ziggy as they headed to the incident room where the ANPR reports were being followed.

Rachel worked at Blythe Manor, a seventeenth-century building that had once been the home of a successful industrial mill owner. It had been many things over the years but had stood the test of time as a renowned wedding venue since the early eighties. It was approximately fifteen minutes by car from Rachel's home in Holbeck, and although she could take the journey through the city centre, it made no sense as the A roads were always quieter and would cut her journey time.

They stood either side of the PCSO who had been tasked with the job.

'So, we can follow the car from the hotel onto the A647 towards Canal Street. Then it turns off onto the M621, exits at Junction 3 onto the A61.'

'Where abouts on the A61?'

'Hunslet, back of Costco, if my memory serves me correctly.'

'And nothing since?'

'No, sir, no further cameras were pinged.'

Ziggy felt a rush of excitement. 'Right, let's get any cars in the area to check it out, and the surrounding industrial estates.' He looked at Sadie. 'Shall we head over?'

'Absolutely. I'll let Control know we're on our way.'

Ziggy went back to his office and grabbed his car keys, relieved that at last they seemed to be getting somewhere.

RACHEL WAS EXHAUSTED. She'd kept up with Jon's narrative until the early hours. So many times, she felt he was close to letting her go, only for him to change his mind at the very last second. The repeated denial of release had crushed her mentally and emotionally. She'd finally convinced him that she needed her 'beauty sleep' and he had left her alone.

She had no idea when he would return – or who he would be.

Throughout their conversations she'd realised that at times he spoke like his alter ego, Sheila. At those times, he was kind, gentle, understanding. When he was himself, Jon, he was angry, resentful, bitter and cruel.

There was absolutely no rhyme or reason to his sudden change of mood or personality. Rachel knew that if she stood any chance of escape, she had to appeal to Sheila.

She hadn't slept. She'd paced the floor; she'd screamed at the air vent, hoping it led to a street or that it would attract someone's attention. She tore the bedding from the camp bed, then remade it in case it angered him. She'd rinsed the tears from her face so many times her skin was dry and sore.

Her nose had eventually stopped bleeding, but the constant ache and pain lived with her. There was a small mirror above the dressing table, and she'd looked at herself, just once, and it had been enough. The skin around her eyes had started to turn blue-black. She had a bruise across her cheek. Her face had lost its colour, apart from the garish red lipstick he had made her wear. She had used the face cloth to rub the last of it off when he had left, feeling disgusted with herself.

At one point during the evening, he had become obsessed with her hair and had insisted on brushing it over and over with an old-fashioned silver-backed hairbrush, tugging at the knots relentlessly. Her scalp was stinging and tender. She felt raw, exposed. He'd given her a clean night-dress; again frilly, brushed cotton, floor length and buttoned up to the neck. She'd felt physically sick as she realised it had once belonged to his mother. He'd watched her as she changed into it, commenting on her figure, asking where she bought her underwear.

That was when she realised, he'd switched to Sheila.

She had no experience in psychology, but Rachel wasn't stupid, she reasoned with herself. She had a degree in international travel and tourism. She had travelled the world, organising holidays and huge events. She could face a challenge. She was known for being rational and calm when faced with a problem, and right now, she needed to pull on those reserves.

She sat on the edge of the little bed. Until they returned, she couldn't plan her approach, but she had to figure out a way of bringing out Sheila.

41

Tuesday, 18 June

Z iggy and Sadie exited the car and looked around them. It was just gone three in the morning, with a clear sky and a bright full moon. Rachel's car had been found abandoned on the industrial estate close to where it had last been picked up by the cameras. But there was no sign of Rachel. Her mobile phone had been recovered from the passenger footwell, and her bag had been found on the back seat of the car, complete with purse containing her bank cards.

Ziggy had upgraded the investigation to an at-risk missing-persons case. It gave him access to more resources, though he prayed it wasn't connected to the two murdered girls. He'd spoken to Val and explained what was happening. She was, understandably, beside herself with worry. He'd encouraged her to stay strong for Ben's sake and to try and carry on as near to normal as possible, not making any changes to Ben's routine. Ziggy assured Val that he would pull out all the stops, as he would for anyone who was missing a loved one. It was the boot up his arse he had needed to hear himself.

Rachel's car was currently being loaded onto a trailer to be taken for a full forensic examination. SOCO had done a preliminary search and managed to collect fingerprints and fibres, which had been rushed off for processing.

They were now waiting for ANPR and CCTV for the surrounding area to see how she had left the industrial estate. Did she get into another car? Was she being held close by? Local units were trawling the surrounding streets for any signs of Rachel. They also had teams searching the industrial units that they had access to. Sadie had contacted the hotel again to request a list of the wedding-fair attendees. Thankfully, they had been much more helpful and had promised to email it through to Sadie imminently.

After liaising with the team on the ground, Ziggy wandered over to Sadie.

'Anything yet?'

Sadie was scrolling through her phone. 'Yep, here.' She opened the email on her phone, and they scrolled through the names. About three quarters of the way down the list they saw a handwritten name: *Sheila Vincent.*

They looked at each other. 'Bingo.'

'We need to run a Companies House report on the salon. Who's the registered owner?' Said Ziggy.

'I'll get someone onto it.'

They climbed back into Ziggy's car. 'Worth driving past the salon, see if there's anyone there?'

'Don't see why not. Nothing to lose, is there?' Sadie fastened her seatbelt as Ziggy put his foot on the accelerator and sped off. Not long afterwards, they were on the high street outside the salon. A shutter had been pulled down over the window, and the room above the shop looked empty. Not taking any chances, they parked the car and walked around to the back, checking the exits and even poking their noses through the waste bins, but nothing jumped out at them.

A late-night cafe was open, so they headed inside, ordering tea and toast. The sky had started to lighten, with the moon taking a step back as the sun started to push its way through.

'Let's go over where we are, shall we?' said Ziggy as he buttered his toast.

'Sure. Where do you want to start?'

'We have two deceased – murdered – and one missing – Rachel. We don't yet know if they are connected, but let's work on the presumption that they are.'

Sadie took a bite of her toast and nodded. 'I think we should. That way we're covering all bases.'

'So, what's Rachel's connection with the girls? She ran a wedding fair.' Ziggy counted the similarities on his fingers. 'We know Susannah had a stalker, or at the least was being harassed by a man she had met at a wedding fair. Two, Susannah and Rachel were both linked to Scott at some point. Obviously, he's now in custody, so he can't have anything to do with Rachel disappearing.'

'Not directly, but we've bounced the hypothesis around before that two people could be involved.'

'True, but that was based on a woman being the other party, based on the stiletto heel damage to Claire's torso and the synthetic fibre that was found to belong to a wig. I think it's going too far to say three people are involved.'

'I agree. So, what's the common connection with them all, rather than individually?'

They looked at each other, toast halfway to Sadie's mouth. 'Sweet FAs.'

'It has to be connected to that club somehow, I just know it. Jon knew all three girls, in one way or another.'

'But what's the connection between Sheila and Jon? Could they be working together?'

'We need to find the owner of that salon,' said Ziggy.

Sadie picked up her phone and called into HQ. She thanked the person on the other end of the phone and looked at Ziggy. 'You'll never believe this. Jon Mason is the registered owner and majority shareholder.'

Ziggy smacked the table. 'I knew it!'

They stood up in unison and headed for the door with a joint sense of purpose and urgency.

'Sweet FAs?' asked Sadie.

'Hell, yes. And call for back up.'

42

J on was feeling triumphant. He'd woken with a new perspective on the day, and his future with Rachel. He couldn't understand why he hadn't seen it before, but it had crystallised in his mind as he had drifted off to sleep the previous night. Now, all he had to do was convince Rachel, but after their chat last night, he felt certain she would be happy with his decision.

He dressed carefully as Jon, because he was even more convinced that Jon was just the kind of man Rachel and Ben needed in their lives. He smoothed his long hair with hairspray, tied it back with an elastic band and patted aftershave onto his freshly shaven skin.

He headed into the kitchen and prepared a delicious breakfast, complete with mimosas. *It wouldn't be a celebration without it.*

THERE WAS A CRUNCHING sound as various bolts were opened, and the door unlocked above Rachel's head. Who was heading down the stairs? Jon or Sheila? They were carrying a breakfast tray and had a grin plastered on their face.

'Good morning, my dear, how are you?' he called cheerfully.

Rachel was tense and apprehensive. He sounded relaxed, even joyful, but she knew he could turn nasty at the tiniest perceived slight. She knew she would have to continue last night's charade, and the mere thought exhausted her. She rubbed her hands down the dress he had given her and forced a false smile, hoping it would suffice.

'Morning. I'm good, thank you. How are you?' She took the tray off him but noticed that he didn't turn back to the lock door, he just followed her to the camp bed and pulled out the fold-up picnic table he had brought down last night.

'I am very well, thank you. I slept like a baby all night. I think it was our talk that helped.' He turned and smiled at her as he lay out the breakfast things. 'And you, dear, did you sleep well?'

Rachel hadn't slept a wink, but she chose to lie. 'Oh yes, like a log.'

Jon gave her another creepy smile and indicated that she should sit on the edge of the bed to eat. 'That makes me so happy.' He passed her a mimosa.

'Oh, this is a bit much for breakfast.' She looked at him and saw a tiny flicker of anger cross his face, but it vanished as quickly as it had appeared. She must remember to go along with him and have no opinions of her own. 'But it's lovely all the same.'

Jon raised his glass to hers. 'I propose a toast.'

Rachel raised her own glass, hand shaking slightly, which she fought to keep still. 'Great idea. What shall we toast?'

'New-found friendships,' declared Jon.

Not on your life. 'New-found friendships.'

They chinked glasses, but Rachel paused before taking a sip. She wouldn't put it past him to have drugged it.

As if by telepathy, Jon laughed. 'It's safe to drink, dear, here. I'll take a sip of yours so you know you can trust me.' He took her glass and sipped.

Smiling and feeling like she was in some dreadful B-rated horror film, she took the glass back from him and took as tiny a sip as possible. 'Friendship.'

'And something else as well.'

Rachel paused and dread filled her gut. She looked up from the scrambled eggs that were on the plate in front of her. 'Oh, yes?'

'Well, our little family is missing a certain person, isn't it?'

Rachel felt herself physically gasp. 'What... what do you mean?'

Jon had started to cut into his breakfast. 'After our chat last night, I realised that with Scott out of the picture and your ex-husband always busy, you need a proper man in your life. Someone that is willing to take the strain. To help you raise Ben to be the man that both you and I know that he is capable of being. A role model, if you will.' He was waving his knife around as he spoke, and Rachel fought the urge to snatch it out of his hand and stab him in the neck. She knew he would overpower her in an instant.

'Oh, I see.' She had to physically fight the nausea that was building in her. She stood up, walking away from him. She wondered if she could make it to the door. Too far away.

'Please, come and sit down. Let's talk it through. I know you'll understand once I've explained it all.'

Quashing her fears, she retook her place on the edge of

the bed. *Hear him out? He can't mean Ben. Surely, he can't mean Ben.* Clenching her hands in front of her, she prepared herself, all the while looking around for a suitable weapon.

'It came to me last night. We will make such a lovely family – me, you and, of course, Ben.' He took a sip of his drink. 'He finishes school at three thirty today, so I think we should use that opportunity to collect him and set off on our adventures.' He smiled at Rachel. 'Oh, I know we won't have all the right clothes and what have you, but we can make our own way. I have some money put aside that will keep us going until the club has sold, then the world is our oyster, as it were. What do you think?'

Club? Is that where she was being held?

Rachel realised he was waiting for her to speak. Schooling her expression to appear as neutral as possible, she managed to smile faintly at him. She had to buy herself some time. She knew that by now her mum would have raised the alarm, and hopefully Ziggy was on the case. She had never needed his skills more. Thinking rapidly, she turned his plan back on him. 'I couldn't let you pay for everything, Jon. I'm used to being independent. I could pop home and grab some money, and perhaps some clothes too. Ben loves computer games, so I'm sure he'd be happier if we could take some of his familiar things with him.' She held her breath.

Jon remained silent, breakfast long forgotten. When he eventually spoke, his tone was menacing. 'You don't want to come with me, do you?'

'Oh, it's not that I promise,' she managed to splutter. 'I just thought you wanted the best for Ben?'

'We can buy him anything he needs,' he snapped.

'I have money of my own...'

Suddenly, his hands swiped across the table, knocking

everything to the floor. He started shrieking at her. 'You ungrateful *bitch!*' He moved with lightning speed and slapped her hard across the face. 'I am prepared to put everything on the line for *you,* and this is how you repay me?'

Rachel had fallen backwards onto the camp bed with his first blow, and he was now sat astride her, breathing heavily in her face.

'No, no, Jon. That's not it at all. Please.' She was flailing from side to side, trying to avoid the blows as they rained down on her. 'Please, Jon. Stop.'

Jon was past the point of coherent thought. It wasn't Rachel he saw in front of him, it was his mother. She had always thrown scorn on his ideas. She had always pooh-poohed any suggestion he made.

'Let's go to the park, Mummy.'

'Not today, my dear, I'm too tired.' Too busy opening your *whore legs you mean.*

'Let's go swimming, Mummy.

'I'd rather not, I have a lot to do.' A lot of men to do, you mean.

'Can I go to the cinema, Mummy, please?'

'No dear, it's too expensive.'

It all came out in one incoherent monologue, with Rachel cowering beneath him. Blood was splashing the blankets and walls. His hands were dripping with sweat and cut to shreds where his knuckles caught the brickwork as he pulled his fist back to punch her again and again. Her face was a bloody mess, eyes closed, jawline disfigured, loose teeth caught in her throat causing her to gag and spew them out. They landed on him in a mass of spit and mucus, which incensed him further.

He climbed from the top of her and pulled out the ropes from under the bed.

'You've brought this on yourself,' he said. 'Why couldn't you just do as you're told? Why couldn't you behave, just for once? Now I'm going to have to do the thing that I really didn't want to do.'

As he spoke, he lashed each arm and leg to the bed frame, pulling the rope tight to ensure she wouldn't be able to work herself free. Once he'd finished, he stood and went over to the wash basin, rinsing the blood from his hands and face. He pulled out his kit bag from under the bed and found the ball gag that he was looking for. Pulling her head roughly upwards, he strapped it tightly across her face.

Rachel was struggling for breath. With a broken nose, she had relied on using her mouth for oxygen, but that airway had been taken from her. She could manage tiny breaths if she concentrated, but she was in so much pain she kept slipping in and out consciousness. *Must stay awake. Must stay awake. Can't let him win.*

43

Ziggy abandoned his car at the side of the road and marched straight to the front door of the run-down nightclub. He hammered hard against it and had just started yelling when Sadie pulled him back.

'Ziggy, hold up.' She pulled him back by the shoulder. 'We need to do this properly.'

He stood back, hands on top of his head. 'He's got her, Sadie, I know it.'

'That's as maybe but going in all guns blazing will only damage our chances of conviction further down the line. Or worse, push Jon into doing something rash. Just take a step back.'

He walked away, knowing that Sadie was right but wanting to kick the door in at the same time.

Sadie grabbed a hold of him. 'Listen to me. We have back-up on the way. Just hang fire until we have more people and that search warrant authorised.'

As she spoke, three units pulled up. They'd been ordered to approach with caution, and in silence, contrary to Ziggy's actions.

One of the Armed Units came forward. 'How do you want to approach this, sir?' he addressed Ziggy, but it was Sadie who answered.

'There are two entrances that we know of. The front, which is where we are now, but there's a back entrance down the side. I suggest we approach the back with officers located on the perimeter in case anyone inside decides to do a runner, but happy to follow your advice if you think differently?'

'Rightio, I'll take a recce then decide what to do.' The officer left them and made instructions for the teams to split up. Another car pulled up, and Nick got out.

'Anyone ask for a search warrant?'

Ziggy almost snatched it out of his hand, and Sadie thanked Nick.

Ziggy addressed the team. 'Wait until everyone is in position, then we'll approach the back door. We have no idea what we will find. It could be that Jon Mason is a witness and not a suspect, but we need to thoroughly search every inch of the building. There's a possibility that there is a victim in there right now, so we need to tread carefully.'

Sadie raised her eyebrows at him, having witnessed his earlier actions. He ignored her and carried on. 'I'll take the lead, with Sadie as second in command. Nick, if you could coordinate with the search teams once we've secured any witnesses and/or suspects.'

Everyone acknowledged the role they would play and took up their positions. Ziggy approached the door, knocking loudly and announcing the presence of the police. There was no reply. He tried again, but after a few minutes of receiving no further response, he beckoned for the key holder – a huge red battering ram – to come forward and break the door down. It didn't take much, and pretty soon,

Ziggy was inside along with the other units. They continuously announced their presence, having to shout loudly over the music that seemed to be coming from the bar area. A few of the armed officers had stopped in their tracks. Ziggy pushed his way to the front to see what was causing the hold-up.

The glitter balls were twirling around, picking up the laser show that was playing across the stage and making the dance floor flash with alternating colours. A catwalk had been erected since the last time Ziggy had been there and ran the full length of the room. Multiple speakers hung from the gantry and around the room, filling the space with a rendition of Frankie Valli's 'You're Just Too Good To Be True'.

On the catwalk was a tall, thin woman dressed in what had once been a full-length evening gown but was now in tatters, with ripped seams and slashes across the bodice. It had fallen away at the shoulder to reveal false breasts.

Ziggy was trying to make sense of what was in front of him. It appeared to be Jon Mason in an evening gown, with a full face of make-up and an auburn wig stuck haphazardly on his head. He glanced around for Sadie, who was also watching in disbelief.

'Sheila?' she whispered.

'Jon *as* Sheila,' answered Ziggy. 'They're one and the same.' He cautiously took a step forward so he could get a closer look at Jon's face. He looked as though he was in some kind of trance. Not knowing if Jon had taken any drugs or if he had entered some psychotic state, he approached him slowly, talking in a low voice as he did.

'Hi, Sheila, isn't it?'

No reply.

'Sheila. It's DI Thornes. We met at the salon before, do you remember?'

No reply.

'Sheila. Do you have anyone here with you?'

Jon stopped abruptly and looked at him with glazed eyes. 'Are you here for the show, dear?' He started to walk towards Ziggy, and the units behind him took a step forward. Ziggy held his hand out behind him, signalling that they should stay where they were.

'Show? What show?' asked Ziggy, showing more patience than he felt.

Jon swirled around on the stage, dancing to the music.

Ziggy caught a movement out of the corner of his eye and saw that one of the uniforms was making their way over to the sound desk. The last thing Ziggy wanted was for the music to stop, but he had no way of signalling to him. Jon was clearly having an episode and who knew what any sudden changes could trigger. Knowing he could do very little about it without giving the game away, he continued his slow walk towards Jon.

He changed his tack. 'Jon, how about we sit down and have a chat.'

'About the show?' asked Jon, turning around suddenly.

'Yes. About the show.' Ziggy moved towards one of the booths at the side of the dance floor.

The music dropped, and the room was suddenly filled with deathly silence. Ziggy sensed he wasn't the only one that had stopped breathing. All eyes were on Jon, waiting to see what he would do next.

Jon gathered the folds of his dress and headed towards the sound desk. 'Who turned that off?' he demanded, a complete change in tone to the voice he had been using on stage.

A young PC was standing there, terrified.

Ziggy tried to distract Jon. 'We couldn't talk over the music anyway, Sheila. Here, come and sit down.'

Jon turned back to Ziggy. 'Who the fuck are you?'

Sensing the change in atmosphere, Sadie discreetly waved her arms at a low level, indicating that the units behind her should now move forward, ready to jump into action should Jon strike out.

Ziggy saw what she was doing, but continued to maintain eye contact with Jon. 'It's DI Thornes, Ziggy. We met at the salon.' Ziggy stopped moving and waited to see what Jon would do.

He made his way to the edge of the stage and held his hand out. 'Would you help me down, dear?'

Ziggy stepped forward, noticing the change in timbre to Jon's voice. Who was he now? He decided to hold off speaking until it became clear.

'Would you like a drink, dear?' Jon headed for the steps that led to the bar, seemingly oblivious to the mob of police officers that filled the place.

Ziggy followed and carefully placed his hand on Jon's elbow. 'Not just yet, why don't we sit down first?'

Ziggy's plan was to get Jon into a position where he could be placed in a confined space so that he could find out if Rachel was being held on the premises before they moved in to place him in cuffs. He guided Jon over and made sure he sat in the booth first.

'Tell me, is there anyone else working today?' asked Ziggy.

'No, dear, not until this evening. We have a new girl who I am very excited about. A delicate thing, with luscious dark hair and a tanned complexion. She really is quite the head turner.'

Rachel. Ziggy's palms were sweaty, and his heart was beating out of his chest. 'Does she have a name?'

'Yes. She's called Rachel.'

Bingo. 'And is she here now?'

'She's rehearsing. Says she doesn't want to be disturbed.'

'Upstairs, is she?' Ziggy heard a shuffle of feet as Sadie instructed teams to search upstairs.

'No, dear.'

Everyone stopped in their tracks. Ziggy slowly turned in his seat and nodded his head towards Sadie, indicating that they should continue. 'Where would she rehearse then?' He avoided using names, as Ziggy wasn't sure who he was addressing.

'Oh, she's resting now, dear.'

Ziggy silently swore that his patience would not get the better of him. 'Where would she rest?'

Jon looked at Ziggy. 'Why in bed, of course. You really are silly.'

Jon poked him in the chest, and before he knew what he was doing, he grabbed Jon's hand and twisted his arm up his back. He bellowed for someone to come forward with a pair of cuffs as he pinned Jon face down on the leatherette seating.

'Jon Mason, I am arresting you on the suspicion of murder...'

ONCE JON HAD BEEN PLACED in the back of the police van, Ziggy turned to run back into the club and join the search. A pair of earrings that belonged to Rachel had been found in a bedroom-cum-dressing room, and the jeans she had been wearing when she had disappeared were found in a laundry basket covered in blood. A PC stopped him at the door.

'Sorry, sir, but you can't go in. It's a designated crime scene and officers are conducting a thorough search.'

'I understand, but I am the deputy senior investigating officer. This is my case and my ex-wife is in there, so if you could please let me past.'

The young constable raised his hand and placed it on Ziggy's chest. Ziggy looked down in disbelief. 'I'm sorry, sir, but I'm under strict instructions not to let you past.'

'Ridiculous. Who by?'

'Me.' Sadie exited the building in a full forensics suit. She removed her hood and face mask as she walked up to Ziggy. 'We haven't found her yet, Ziggy, and I'm not letting you in due to your personal involvement. You would do the same if it were any one of us.'

Ziggy was furious. 'Don't you dare, DS Bates. That's the mother of my son in there.'

'And that's exactly why you're not going in. Whitmore agrees, so if you have any more to say, speak to him.'

Ziggy felt close to tears. Frustration, anger and helplessness washed over him. He knew Sadie was right, but it didn't stop him from wanting to be in there. He turned around so she wouldn't see his face.

'Ziggy. I know this is hard but trust me, if she's in there or been in there, then we will find her.'

He tried to force his face into a neutral expression before facing Sadie. 'I know. I'm—'

'Sir!' shouted a voice.

They both turned around.

'We've found someone.'

Ziggy and Sadie shot forward. They stood at the back door as two officers exited with a woman who had her arms draped around either of their shoulders for support. 'We wanted her to wait until the paramedics arrived, but she insisted.'

Rachel! Ziggy had never felt anything like it in his life. He darted forward and scooped her up in his arms, cradling her. 'Rachel?'

Her face was a bloody mess, and she had teeth missing top and bottom. She was dressed in an old-fashioned night-gown that was caked with blood. She was slipping in and out of consciousness. She tried to open her eyes, but they were so swollen they appeared as little lines between two black eyelids. 'Andrew?'

'Shh, don't talk. The ambulance is here.'

The doors of the ambulance opened, and a stretcher was wheeled over. Ziggy let the ambulance crew do their job and stepped back. As the stretcher was wheeled back in, Sadie stepped forward.

'Go with her, boss. We've got everything covered here.'

Dazed, Ziggy climbed in beside Rachel and took a hold of her hand. 'It's going to be all right, Rachel. I'm here now.'

Rachel smiled weakly before closing her eyes fully and slipping back into a place where everything didn't quite hurt so much.

44

Ziggy had re-joined Sadie back at the club after leaving Rachel sleeping at the hospital. Her injuries were severe, but thankfully not life threatening. She would need to give a statement, but for now, she needed to rest.

SOCOs were processing every inch of the scene, from the basement where Rachel had been held through to the loft space where a bag of clothes belonging to Scott Ball had been recovered. A search team were currently going through the salon and a registered address had been traced to a Jon Vincent. Unsurprisingly, he had changed his name over the years, which is why there had been no criminal record of him as Jon Mason.

'How is she?' asked Sadie as Ziggy walked over.

'Not too bad. They've cleaned her up and dressed her broken nose. She's battered and bruised but no permanent damage, thankfully. They've given her pain meds and something to help her sleep.'

'That's good. And, how are you?'

'Yeah, I'm good, thanks. Bit shaken if I'm honest, but just glad we found her before he could do any more damage.'

'SOCOs have uncovered all kinds of interesting evidence that links Jon to the murders of Susannah and Claire. There was a hamper of clothes stashed in the basement where we found Rachel, and a massive collection of vintage scarves which seems to have been a bit of an obsession. Still, at least we know we've got the right man and can give the families some closure.'

'I'm just amazed he was able to live such an alternative life like that for so long and not get caught.'

'I know. I've looked at his record. Feel a bit sorry for him, to be honest. Would seem the system let him down time and again.'

'Really? I haven't even had a moment to glance at it. What did it say?'

'He's been sectioned on numerous occasions and seemed to live a kind of Walter Mitty life. Psychological reports from over the years state that he had multiple personality disorder amongst other things. He flitted between one persona and not just one but several others, though Sheila had seemed to be a favourite. He never displayed violent tendencies though. I guess it all became too much for him?'

Ziggy nodded. 'Yeah, maybe. I'm sure the psychiatric assessment he's currently undergoing will tell us more.' It was difficult to feel anything for the man that had ripped Rachel's life apart, but he knew Sadie was right. Maybe forgiveness would come to him in time. For now, he had a case to build against him, and ensure that all the loose ends were tied up.

. . .

THEY HEADED BACK to the station and made their way to the office. They were congratulated on their way in, but Ziggy made sure to point out that it was a team effort and without the diligence and perseverance of the whole team it wouldn't have been possible.

Just after four in the afternoon, everyone had gathered, and Ziggy ran them through the final stages. He thanked everyone for their time and efforts, but he knew the hard work started now with the pulling together of all the evidence to present to CPS.

At five, they all headed over the road for a well-deserved drink. Ziggy bought the first round and took it over to the corner table where Sadie, Nick and Angela were waiting. He updated them on how Rachel was doing and explained that he couldn't stay long as he was going to see Ben.

Nick raised his glass. 'To a successful conclusion.'

The rest joined in and they chinked glasses.

'It seems obvious now that Jon was Sheila, don't you think?' said Sadie.

'Do you think so? I think he was very clever,' commented Angela. 'I wouldn't have seen it, in all honesty.'

Sadie took a sip of her wine. 'I must admit, it definitely had us thrown. But you were right, Nick. The link came unexpectedly. It took me a while to process what I was seeing when we walked into the club.'

'Hate to say I told you so. But yeah, bit weird. Clearly the man has serious issues.'

'I know his defence team will try the diminished responsibility angle, but you have to be in your right mind to be that manipulative and cunning,' Sadie said.

General banter ensued, the team relaxing for the first time in weeks ahead of dotting the I's and crossing T's that would occupy them in coming days.

Ziggy finished his drink and stood up to leave. 'Right, I'm heading off. Stay and enjoy your success, but back in at nine tomorrow.'

They said their goodbyes and Ziggy headed for his car. Just as he fastened his seatbelt, his mobile phone rang.

'Hello, stranger.' It was Lolly.

'Hey, sorry, it's been a manic one.'

'I know, I've heard. Don't worry about it. Just wondered if you had time for a quick drink with your oldest friend?'

'Ah, Lolly, I'm just on my way to see Ben.'

'Oh right, well no worries. Just thought you might want to offload.'

She sounded disappointed, and he would have loved nothing more than a catch-up. If ever he needed to offload it was now. It was how their friendship worked, and probably why it had lasted so long. 'How about you pick up a take-away and meet me at mine in a couple of hours?' he suggested as a compromise.

Her voice immediately sounded brighter when she replied, 'Perfect. Indian?'

'Sounds good to me. See you soon, just let yourself in.' Lolly had had a key to every house that Ziggy had ever owned.

Shortly afterwards, he pulled up outside his mother-in-law's. Ben was in the window waving. He came to the front door and Ziggy scooped him up in his arms.

'Hey, champ, how are you?'

'Fine. Come and see what level I'm on,' he insisted, drag-ging Ziggy by the hand.

Val stood on the doorstep and laughed. 'He's so pleased to see you. He's missed you.'

'I know. I've missed him. Have you spoken to Rachel?'

'I rang the hospital about an hour ago, but she was

sleeping. The nurse explained that they had given her something, but thank God she's OK. It could have been much worse from the sounds of it.'

'Yeah, we were lucky to get there when we did. She'll recover in time. What have you said to Ben?'

'Just what we agreed. That a bad man had hurt her but that she would be fine. He seems to have taken it well. I'll keep him off school tomorrow, I think.'

'Probably for the best – sometimes these things take time to settle in.'

'Dad!' shouted Ben. 'Come on.'

They both laughed, acknowledging the young boy's resilience. Ziggy walked into the living room where Ben had his games console set up. Ziggy grabbed a controller and started playing, happy that just for a few hours he could focus his attention on his son.

ZIGGY WAS HOME a little later than planned, but he was greeted by the smell of Indian food, which made him realise that he hadn't eaten all day.

'I'm in the kitchen,' called Lolly as he heard plates rattling and the cutlery drawer being opened. 'How's Ben?'

'He's good. Getting better on that blooming game of his. He beat me hands down.'

'How did he take the news about Rachel?' The jungle drums had obviously reached Lolly.

'Quite well but you never know with these things. Val's keeping him off school tomorrow.' He was glad Lolly hadn't berated him for not telling her about Rachel sooner.

'Makes sense. Beer?' she asked, reaching into the fridge. She didn't wait for a reply, knowing that the answer would be yes. 'Isn't it about time you did something with this place?'

Ziggy laughed and took his beer from her. 'I guess so, but where do I find the time?'

'Get someone in then, Ziggy. It can't be good for you coming back to the house being upside down every day.'

'It can be a bit disheartening, to be honest. Maybe I will. Now where's that food? I'm starving.'

They sat at the counter and tucked into the feast that Lolly had brought. With bellies full and a fresh beer in hand, they headed into the living room.

'So, how are you?' asked Ziggy, adjusting himself on the sofa so that he was facing Lolly. He was surprised to see her hair was as close to a normal colour as he'd ever seen it. She had a habit of dying it all colours of the rainbow.

'Yeah, I'm not too bad. Been busy myself to be honest. Thinking about moving in with Frankie.'

Ziggy nearly spat out his beer. For as long as he'd known Lolly, she'd been a free spirit, moving and living wherever she liked, or wherever the job took her. 'I'm sorry, what?'

Lolly laughed. 'I knew you'd react like that. It's not like I've just met her, is it?'

Frankie and Lolly had been dating for over two years. 'Besides, means I'll be closer to you and Ben as well.'

'Move to Leeds, you mean?'

'Yeah, Frankie's been looking at moving to a new place for a while and it makes sense.'

'Dr Turner, is this you growing up?'

'Cheeky sod, but yeah, maybe it is.'

'Wow, must be love,' he teased. 'Seriously though, I'm happy for you. And Frankie certainly seems to make you happy so go for it, I'd say.' He raised his bottle of beer. 'To happier days.'

They laughed, took a swig and Ziggy put some music on. The rest of the evening was spent catching up and chatting about potential areas that Lolly and Frankie could move to. By the time she left, it was gone eleven, and Ziggy was dead on his feet. He locked the front door behind her and headed upstairs to bed, figuring the washing up would wait for another day.

THREE MONTHS LATER

Ziggy stood on the court steps, allowing the cool air of late summer to revive his tired eyes. The jury had taken six hours to reach the verdict of guilty in the case of Jon Mason. For the first time in months, Ziggy allowed himself to breathe and felt the tension leave his shoulders. As he stretched to ease the knots in his back, Sadie joined him outside.

'Great result, and definitely the right one,' she said as she adjusted the bag on her shoulder.

'Absolutely though it was never really in any doubt.' Ziggy started down the steps, heading for the car park.

'For a second, when the defence was detailing the abuse Mason was subjected to as a child, I thought we'd lost a few members of the jury.'

Ziggy agreed. It had made for hard listening as the abuse was listed out for the benefit of the jury. Throughout his childhood, Jon had been systemically broken down by his mother until he was so unsure of himself or his place in the world that he had taken matters into his own hands. Though it could never be proven, doubts now circled around the sudden and unexpected death of his mother. Not that any of his past excused his future sickening behaviour.

'What now boss?' asked Sadie as she climbed into Ziggy's car.

'Back to HQ then I'm out of here,' Ziggy fastened his seatbelt and started the engine.

'Meeting with Whitmore first?'

'Yeah, there is that,' Ziggy sighed as he changed gear and headed towards the inner ring road.

DCS Whitmore had eased up on the pressure now that it been drawn to a successful conclusion, but Ziggy wouldn't forget that he had threatened to take him off the case. Not that he was one to hold grudges, but it had pissed him off. Still, Ziggy had his packed suitcase in the boot of the car and was more than ready for a break with Ben and Lolly.

As they entered the building it was clear that the verdict had been heard by what seemed to be the entire station and they were greeted with platitudes and calls of congratulations. The compliments continued as they walked into the office. Ziggy smiled, accepting the praise for once. He walked to the front of the room.

'It would seem that the jungle drums have beaten me to it, but I have a few things I would like to say. Firstly, this has been a team effort and I applaud you all for your hard work, commitment and dedication,' he broke off to add his own applause. 'Secondly, Jon Mason will be sentenced next week, but having been found guilty of two counts of murder, one of attempted murder and various other related charges it's safe to say he won't ever be a free man again, so we have delivered justice to the victims and their families.' Ziggy stayed silent as murmurs went around the room. 'Finally,

I'm taking annual leave from today.' With that he pushed himself away from the desk he had been leaning on, raised his hands to the ceiling, cheering headed for the door with the team's laughter ringing in his ears.

He knocked gently on Whitmore's door, keen to get it over with so he could leave. 'Sir?'

'Ah Andrew, great result. Well done, knew you'd catch the bastard in the end,' smiled Whitmore from behind his desk.

Really? Ziggy ignored him, deciding to let the comment fall on deaf ears. It wasn't worth getting riled up about. 'About to go an annual leave sir, so if there's nothing else?'

'There is just one thing Andrew,' Whitmore shifted in his seat. Ziggy suddenly noticed the frowned look on his boss's face. 'News just in, I'm afraid a body has been found.'

Ziggy turned on his heel before Whitmore could finish his sentence, 'ask DS Bates to deal with it.' He called over his shoulder, utterly determined to get away.

'Andrew, it's Dr Leila Turner, Lolly.'

Ziggy stopped abruptly in his tracks and felt a bolt of ice run through his entire body. *No, no, it can't be, he'd misheard surely...*

ENJOYED THE WEB THEY WOVE?

Please consider leaving a review on Goodreads, Amazon
or contact the author directly.
cat@catherineyaffe.co.uk

I love to connect with my readers on social media so feel
free to join me on all the usual platforms;
Twitter: @catherineyaffe
Instagram: @cat_yaffe_author
Facebook: /catherineyaffeauthor

You can also join my mailing list & download a
FREE SHORT STORY
'FEEL THE FEAR'
By visiting my website
https://www.catherineyaffe.co.uk

ALSO BY CATHERINE YAFFE

Book 1 – The Lie She Told

Book 2 – The Web They Wove

Book 3 - When We Deceive

Free Novella – Feel The Fear, Ziggy's Story

Free Novella – Little Girl, Lost, Lolly's Story

ACKNOWLEDGMENTS

Writing a police procedural was never on my list of 'books I want to write,' but when I'd completed 'The Lie She Told,' Ziggy stood out as a character that I really wanted to explore. The version you're reading now is approximately the 9th iteration, and I'm quite sure that if I read it back (again) there would still be changes I would make. However, this won't be the last time we hear from Ziggy and his team! This book has been edited to within an inch of its life but I'm sure an errant typo has slipped in somewhere and for this I apologise.

I couldn't, of course, have written this book without the invaluable help of so many people.

Firstly, a special thanks to my wonderful editor Rebecca Millar. Thank you for making the editing process a lot less scary than I imagined, and for encouraging me to push my writing further - this book is all the better for it and I can't wait to work with you again.

To Graham Bartlett (GB Police Advisor) who has provided me with much of the policing procedural information and has been an endless source of knowledge through our one-to-one chats, his workshops and his seemingly endless patience. Any mistakes are my own!

To the advanced readers for spotting inconsistencies that I had become blind to. Where would I be without you?

To the online writing community, we may never have met but your encouragement has kept me going when I considered throwing the towel in. Special thanks to Amanda Campbell (A J Campbell) for being so generous with your time and for sharing your knowledge.

Thank you to all my friends in the true crime community, for keeping me company and entertained as I researched, plotted and planned this book (and giving me ideas for future books!)

To my wonderfully supportive family - Mark, Daniel, Sadie. I can't be easy to live with when I'm writing, and I know it's all I bang on about when I'm in the throes of planning and plotting but I genuinely appreciate all your love and support as I continue my journey. Thank you for being my biggest cheerleaders.

Mum and dad, you continue to inspire me to aim higher every day and I am in awe of you both.

Thank you all so much.

Printed in Great Britain
by Amazon